SWARM

Then I saw something, but what I saw I didn't believe. I nearly dropped the telescope over the side but I caught it and put it to the other eye for a second opinion. I saw the same thing. It was nice to know I wasn't going crazy, but the reality of it gave me a chilly feeling I could have done without.

They came across the water in single file, flying about two feet off the water. They were black and yellow, with huge iridescent eyes and rainbow-blurred cellophane wings. They swarmed over the gunwales of the rowboat and temporarily out of sight. Now I understood what the honey was all about. Then they were climbing into the air again, ten of them carrying a thousand bucks apiece in a sticky wad clutched by their hairy little legs. They were each about the size of a beer can, bigger than I'd ever imagined they could be. I watched them fly across the water to the far end of the lake, until they were out of sight.

We will send you a free catalog on request. Any titles not in your local book store can be purchased by mail. Send the price of the book plus 50¢ shipping charge to Belmont Tower Books, Two Park Avenue, New York, New York 10016.

Titles currently in print are available in quantity for industrial and sales promotion use at reduced rates. Address inquiries to our Promotion Department.

THE ANTENNA SYNDROME

Alan Marks

BELMONT TOWER BOOKS • NEW YORK CITY

A BELMONT TOWER BOOK

Published by

Tower Publications, Inc.
Two Park Avenue
New York, N.Y. 10016

Copyright © 1979 by Tower Publications, Inc.

All rights reserved
Printed in the United States of America

1

I was sitting in my cramped little office one afternoon, blowing smoke at the ceiling and strumming tunes on the guitar, when there was a rap on the door and this smart looking lady walked in. I took my heels off the desk, stood the guitar in the corner and gave her the glad eye. This doll was so sharp she looked like she could cut a hustler before he got within rapping range. She wore a tight-fitting green jumpsuit of shiny material with a gold chain belt snugged around a waist I could have spanned with two hands. The jumpsuit was open to the waist and there was a lot of tanned cleavage lounging around just inside. Her hair was a sunburst tangle of blonde that fell well below her shoulders in the back; she wore a lot of make-up with a lot of style and she looked like she knew it. She was what the kids called a 'space mama'.

"Have a seat," I said, "and tell me what's on your mind. My name's Keith Savage."

She nodded to me in a vacant sort of way and looked around my office as if she were trying to fix it in her mind. I'll admit there wasn't much to fix. I had a grey filing cabinet in the corner with a few sorry case histories in the top drawer and fifty pounds of old *Rolling Stone* magazines in the bottom two. I had an old birchwood desk the size of a large shoebox, whose border was scarred with the burn marks of a thousand and one cigarettes. There was a phone on the desk with an answering machine, and a fan on the windowsill that kept the hot air circulating.

"I'm Natalie Ferris," she said, still standing.

"As in 'Ferris wheel'?"

"As in 'Jordan Ferris'."

"Who is running for mayor?"

"Who is my father."

"Well, that's nice. If you're not going to make a speech, you might as well sit down. What can I do for you, Miss Ferris?"

She sat down in the only other chair in the room, rummaged in a brown leather handbag and snapped open a cigarette case disguised as an oyster shell. She held it across the desk in offering. It was chockful of fat little joints neatly rolled in baby blue papers.

"Not for me, but you go ahead." I slid the ashtray across the desk and began cleaning my fingernails with a guitar pick. She lighted her joint and took a smoky lungful. I held my breath along with her and waited for it to come back out. Twin contrails jetted out her nostrils and convulsed in the turbulence from the fan before drifting upwards to sprawl across the ceiling in a blue haze.

"I want you to find my sister."

"What's her name, how old is she and how long's she been gone?"

"Muriel's twenty and she left home yesterday."

"Happens all the time with twenty-year-olds. What makes you think she's not coming back?"

"Muriel was a thalidomide baby. She's got no arms or legs. She's never been out of the house before. I think she's been abducted."

"Have you notified the police?"

"No way. My father doesn't need that kind of publicity. He doesn't even know she's gone yet. I want you to find her before he returns next weekend."

"The police are usually pretty discreet on a kidnapping case. I don't see why..."

"Muriel's been a dark family secret for years. If the scandal sheets got wind of this story, they could ruin my father's chances for the election. I don't think he'd take it very well."

"Guilt trips thrive in secrecy. Maybe the exposure would cleanse him."

"Spare me your dishwater philosophy. I can get

better than that for less money from the palmist parlors on Eighth Avenue. Besides, I don't think it's a kidnapping. She's been writing regularly to an astrologer in the Village. He might have helped her get away. In any case, I suspect he might know where she is. Do you want the job or don't you? A thousand bucks if you find her before the weekend."

I didn't waste too much time thinking about that one. A thousand clams could buy my way out of this closet and into an uptown office where the big money strolled around on its lazy afternoons. "Alright, I'll see what I can do. Have you got a name and address to go with this astrologer?"

"Joel Uranium." She pulled an index card from her purse and skimmed it across the desk to me. The guy had an address on Hoople Street. "I went there this morning but I didn't find him. There's a comic book store at that address but it was closed. I don't have the time to go looking for him myself because I have to catch a plane to the West Coast in a couple of hours. I'll be back in a few days. If you find her before that, can you keep her someplace until I return?"

"I suppose so. But why not take her back home?"

"She might disappear again. All I need is some time to talk to her and I think I'll be able to straighten her out." She pulled out a checkbook and used a gold fountain pen to fill in the details. She ripped the check out and wafted it across the desk. "Five hundred should get you started and I'll give you the rest when you deliver."

I looked at the check. The amount was five hundred alright but the name at the bottom wasn't Natalie Ferris. "Who's Stanfield Coughlan?"

"Let's just say he's a friend of my father."

That didn't really satisfy my curiosity, but if the check didn't bounce, Stanfield Coughlan could be my friend too. I folded the check and tucked it in my shirt pocket. "Okay. I'll get on it right away. Have you got a picture of Muriel?"

She fished around in her purse and gave me a passport-sized photo of a girl with dark hair cut in

Chinese-style bangs. She had dimpled cheeks, a cute little nose and very sad eyes. She looked as normal as anyone you might see on the street, but then the photo didn't reveal anything of her appearance below neck level.

"Good luck." Natalie Ferris stubbed the roach in the ashtray and stood up. "I'll see you towards the end of the week."

"Is there someplace I can reach you before then, in the event that I find her or any problems turn up?"

She gave me a phone number with a California area code.

"And a local number?"

"When I return, I'll get in touch with you. Good day, Mr. Savage." She went out the door in a hurry.

I tilted my chair back until my head touched the wall, and stared at the ceiling where the blue haze hung. The air dripped with the honeyed reek of marijuana. From the vacant lot outside my window came the thwok-pok-thwok of a tennis buff volleying shots off the building opposite. Upstairs in the Ace Insurance office, an electric typewriter rattled with machinegun intensity. I put the index card and the photo in my shirt pocket with the check, turned off the fan and turned on the Memory-phone. I locked the office and hit the street. It was eighty degrees plus outside and I worked up a sweat getting to the bank before it closed for the day.

With five hundred in my pocket I strolled back to my block and got my beatup Astromobile out of the parking lot. I drove over to Hoople Street and snuggled up to the curb between a grey Caddie and a Coke truck. Hoople Street was half residential and half smalltime business. There was an Italian restaurant on the corner with a couple of old guys sitting outside dozing over a game of checkers. Further down the street was a T-shirt shop with incense and mellow jazz leaking out the doorway. In the window hung a shirt that said, *Hustle Hustle Hustle*. I moved on down the narrow sidewalk past whitewashed stoops where sallow-faced dudes sat eating pizza and drinking from cans in paper bags.

Outside the Cosmo Comix Center, a man with a green duffle bag and a bloody forehead was lying on the sidewalk. He had white hair and a couple of days' growth of silvery chinwhisker; he was snoring and snorting in his sleep and fidgeting at his crotch like a kid in a wet dream. I stepped around him and went in the door.

There were no lights in the Cosmo. From the rear wall, down the aisles of *Eerie* and *Vampirella*, day-glo posters shimmered like heat lightning. A barricade of old pop crates was built up in the corner beside the front window: behind it sat a young man with balding head, granny glasses and a nose buried in a paperback, *Spiders of Mars*.

"Looking for something?"

"Dr. Strangelove, I presume?" I fished a card out of my pocket and gave it to him. I could tell by the way he dropped his book that he liked my act. He grinned and said,

"Can I keep this?"

"Trade you for some information."

"If you like pussy, smile." He twiddled the card in his nicotine-stained fingers. "I like that. What do you want to know?"

"Who had this place before you?"

"A health food store. But they got busted selling imported herbs. I'm okay as long as I keep the mutant nudie mags out of the front window."

"Know a guy called Joel Uranium? He used to get mail sent here." I glanced at a slim silver bracelet on his wrist and read the name upsidedown. *Davey*.

"Never heard of him. Must have been before my time. I've only been here a couple of months."

"Who's your landlord?"

"You wouldn't want to know. He's a Jewish slumlord; he reads Nietzsche. I've got rats in the basement and they're eating all my secondhand *Bugs Bunnys*. I tell him he's got to get an exterminator. He tells me, 'Once you had wild dogs in your cellar, but in the end they burned into birds and lovely singers.' He's as twisted as a pretzel."

"What's the name and where do I find him?"

"Sid Wiseman. Step outside, take the door on your left, go up three flights and knock loudly, he's got a bad ear. You ever read *Spiders of Mars*?"

"Can't say as I've had the pleasure. I tend more towards Venusian company."

"Your card told me that already." He took a plastic-sealed paperback from one of the boxes at his feet and gave it to me. *Spiders of Mars,* the same one he was reading. On the cover, four huge red spiders were attempting to defoliate a leafy green lady. A heroic type with a low forehead, a sword and a codpiece, was chopping away at them with primal abandon. "Take it for your space-ship library. You can read it while you go into deepsleep."

"What's the catch?"

"No catch," he said. "I got it in the mail yesterday from a friend. Just a coincidence that I already had a copy. Keep it. No charge."

I'm not a guy to ignore the classics of sci-fi. I stuck the paperback in my pocket and took a run upstairs. A naked bulb hung over the stairwell and the walls were covered with anti-Semitic slogans of no literary value.

Sid Wiseman yanked the door open on me before I had time to bang twenty times on it. He was a round little man with a shiny black suit and a nose you could have built a synagogue on. He looked at my hands to see that I wasn't carrying a gun, then at my feet to make sure I didn't have cloven hooves. I appeared to have passed inspection. He hooked his hand towards me like a bear snatching a salmon and said,

"Don't stand in the hall. I wouldn't want the ceiling should fall on you. What are you looking for?" He looked over his shoulder at me as he walked to his desk, an elephantine construction of teakwood that couldn't have weighed less than a ton. It was an excellent advertisement for the structural solidity of the third floor. Heavy wire mesh covered a dirty window behind his desk; a wooden bookcase of musty old tomes leaned against one wall.

"I'm looking for a man."

"Somebody who owes you money?"

"Nothing like that. An astrologer named Joel Uranium who might have rented the Cosmo space downstairs."

"Aha!" Sid banged his fist on the teakwood desk. I could hear gorillas and rhinos fleeing through the jungle timber. "Somebody who owes me money."

"It's a weird name. Did you ever see any proper identification?"

"I think his Social Security card was forged. The plastic was brown."

"Maybe it was the radiation. Where does he live?"

"If I knew that, would he still owe me money?"

"Ever get a collection agency after him?"

"Forty dollars he owes me. They won't talk to you for less than a hundred dollar debt. They take twenty percent."

"Got any ideas where I might look for him? When I catch up with him, I'll mention that you're hurting for forty."

"I'll give you ten percent if you collect."

"Where's he hang out?"

"I have seen him twice on Beatnickel. You know where that is?"

"Lower East, downwind of Nuke Flats. What's he look like these days?"

"Yellow sunglasses, blue sports jacket. Older than you but in good shape. Both times I saw him standing outside Universal Games. I would have stopped but the transport traffic on Beatnickel was too heavy. Those drivers'll run over a cop car if it gets in their way."

"You don't believe in living dangerously?"

Sid looked at me in a thoughtful sort of way. He took a walk around his desk, ran a hand over the dusty mantle of the bookcase and directed a few choice words to a cluster of cobwebs in the corner of the ceiling. *"I love those who do not know how to live, except by going under, for they are those who cross over."*

"Troubled times for the superman, huh?" I wished I had the time to sit and talk with Sid. There was a certain holy quietude about his office. But I had an appointment with an elusive astrologer and I couldn't tarry. "Supposing I find Uranium but he can't cough up forty bills, would you like me to give him a few lumps on your account?"

Sid smiled, showing one gold canine. "Yes," he said. *"A little revenge is more human than no revenge."*

Buzz could have killed both of them. They were old people. Their arms and heads would come off easily. The meat wouldn't be very good but the blood would be okay. He might have done it if the dogs hadn't been there.

He showed the paper. They opened the door and let him in the house. The dogs didn't like it. The man took them away and the woman showed him upstairs. Buzz locked the door and took Crabby out of the box. He opened the door to the chimney and Crabby climbed up inside.

Buzz smelled glue. He sniffed along the bookcase and took out three books. They had leather bindings. He ripped the bindings off and nibbled on the glue where the stitching held the pages together. He wrapped the binding around the books again and put them back on the shelves. He could have eaten the other nine volumes in the set but he didn't bother. He'd eaten better glue.

Crabby came down the chimney with the girl. His black hairy legs were wrapped around her. She wore a blue ballerina body shirt with a snap-flap crotch. She had big boobs. Buzz guessed her at sixty pounds. She looked good enough to eat. He could have eaten her in one sitting. He'd eaten bigger girls than her.

Crabby climbed in the box with the girl. Buzz put the lid on the box and started the air conditioner. He opened the door to the hall and carried the box to the head of the stairs. He smelled wax. A chandelier hung above his head. He reached up and took a handful of candles from the holders. They'd never been used. They'd never be missed.

Buzz walked out of the house and put the box with Crabby and the girl in the back of the van. He got on the expressway and set the van on max cruise back to town. He took the candles out of his pockets and chewed on them as the suburban landscape flickered past in a thousand splintered windows.

It was good wax. He'd go back there some night and get the rest of it if it weren't for the dogs.

Beatnickel was a dirty stretch of blocks on the Lower East side where interstate transports rumbled by with Mafia types riding shotgun on the way to secret warehouses. I went around and around on the industrial traffic merrygoround until a parking slot opened up on a oneway street a block from Beatnickel. I left the Astromobile in front of a Korean laundry with a prayer that the local car thieves would consider the scarred wagon beneath their dignity to steal or vandalize. I walked up with the traffic flow, wishing I'd brought my Viper with me or left my money at the office. Punks of all size and description stood around on the corner of Beatnickel and Fourth. There was puke on the sidewalk and rock music pounding from speakers at the door to Universal Games. Kids in denim, with chains for belts and knives in their boots, sat slumped along the sidewalk in dopey stupors while others panhandled the passersby.

"Spare change, man? I got a sure mark for a five buck game on Stellar Combat. All I need is a quarter ante." The kid who propositioned me was maybe twelve years old, with long brown hair, an alky's nose and a square silver belt buckle as big as a TV screen. A naked woman in relief rode upon the back of a chimera. She was twisting hell out of the lion's mane and he looked like he loved it.

I gave the kid fifty cents and said, "Do you know a guy called Joel Uranium? Wears yellow sunglasses and draws horoscopes."

The kid turned his head and whistled. "Hey, Janis." A small blonde girl twenty feet away tossed a tangle of buzzed-out hair over her shoulder and wiggled up to close range. She had green eyes, a plastic see-through blouse and a big safety pin holding the fly of her jeans shut. "This guy's looking for Sunshine. Do you know where he lives?"

"Sure. Spare change, ace?" The little blonde winked a crusty blue eyelid at me and fingered a pack of smokes out of the boy's denim vest. They had a little wrestling match over that while I fished in my pocket for another two quarters.

"Would I find him at home this time of day?"

"Maybe. He was here just an hour ago. Do you know where Export International is?" She pointed down Beatnickel. "There's a half-street just around the corner from it: Holmes Street. Sunshine lives in Number Forty of Belvedere Towers. I went up there one day to let him do my chart."

"And feel your ass." The boy in the vest laughed and punched her in the shoulder. She hit him back. I left them trading punches before they started to play pass-it-on. I bruise easily.

Just to make sure Joel Uranium hadn't eluded their attention on a return run, I stuck my head into Universal Games to see if he wasn't there. The air was full of smoke and sound. There were three corridors of game machines: pinball and electronic hockey, sharpshooting galleries and Grand Prix racing, tic-tac-toe and Stellar Combat. Competing with the rock cacophony was the shuffle and bing of mechanical games, the buzz and wail of wild sound effects from the electronic games.

"Anybody seen Sunshine?" I hollered to no one in particular. I doubted that anyone heard me anyway.

"He ain't here."

I turned and saw an old guy with grey hair and a cigarette clinging to his lip. He was sitting behind a high counter next to the door with piles of change stacked before him. There was a gold ring in his ear and a Band-aid over one eye.

"If he comes in, would you ask him to call and leave a message where I can find him? I've got some rich customers lined up." I gave the changemaker one of my legit cards, just the name and phone number, along with a dollar. He put the card in his shirt pocket without looking at it and pushed four quarters across the counter at me. That wasn't what I'd intended, but I put the change in my pocket, nodded my thanks and took a fast walk east on Beatnickel.

Belvedere Towers was at the dead end of Holmes Street, a five-story structure of old brick that was chipping away at the edges and coming apart at the seams. Laundry hung on the rails of the fire escape balconies and in many windows there was cardboard where glass should have been. From the penthouse came the *chukka-chukka* rhythms of reggae music and the shrill laughter of a woman who was high on booze, dope or life itself. The pigeons had left their mark on the front steps, but I went up the stoop in two jumps without defiling myself. There was no lobby door to wheedle my way through, so after I'd checked mailbox number forty and found *Sunshine* on a piece of masking tape stuck over the metal bracket designed to hold a card, I climbed the gritty stairs to the fourth floor and knocked on the door of my quarry.

"Who's there?" queried a man's voice from within.

"That's for me to know and you to find out. Is that you, Sunshine?" I sensed an eyeball giving me the scrutiny through the peephole.

"What do you want?"

"I want a horoscope."

"Sunshine went away. Won't be back until next week."

"That's too bad. I've got some money for him." I took five tens from my pocket and fanned them out in front of the peephole like a poker hand after the betting's over.

"Who sent you?"

"Davey."

"Davey who?"

"Davey at the Cosmo Comix Center."

Thoughtful silence. Then the clatter of a bolt withdrawn and a lock turned. The door opened to a man in his late thirties who might have passed for a high school gym instructor. He wore red sneakers, a close-fitting pair of jeans, a black T-shirt that showed his muscles, and a pair of yellow sunglasses. He had fleshy lips and short black hair.

"What do you want?"

"I understand you draw charts." I looked over his shoulder into a shady room with an Indian print over the window, a mattress with sleeping bag on the floor and a doorless refrigerator full of books leaning against the far wall.

"No law against that," he said.

"I never said there was."

"Not much money in it either."

"I can believe it, if you treat all your prospective clients like me. May I come in?"

He closed and locked the door behind me. While I glanced around in search of a chair, he danced across the room, lighted a stick of lavender incense and put a record on a stereo outfit that might have retailed for $39.95 brand new. The flutey sounds of *Memphis Underground* burbled from a pair of midget speakers. Sunshine flexed his biceps and strutted around the room with Herbie Mann backing his every move. Any minute now I figured he'd ask me if I wanted to dance.

"Nice guy, Davey. Did you get it on with him?" Off came the T-shirt. He had lots of body hair, a heavy line of it from throat to navel, another crossing it from nipple to nipple. He moved towards me, weaving and snapping his fingers.

"Keep your pants on," I said. "I'm not looking for wrestling lessons."

"Play hard to make and see where it gets you." He came in fast, one hand scooping low for my crotch. I gave him a quick jab in the face that broke his sunglasses in two and stopped him cold. He stood flat-footed, looking kind of surprised at me as if I'd just hatched out of the ether. He snapped his fingers a couple of times but his heart wasn't in it anymore. I crossed to the door and snapped on the overhead light. He squinted at me. Tears started out of his eyes.

"I'm looking for a girl named Muriel Ferris," I told him. "I understand you might know of her whereabouts."

"I thought you wanted to get it on," he whined, groping his way to a flimsy wooden table in the corner. He rummaged around in a cardboard box and came up with a pair of sunglasses identical to the ones I'd broken. He put them on and threw the broken pair in a waste basket. "Davey shouldn't have sent you if you didn't want to swing."

"Davey didn't have anything to do with it. Have you seen Muriel Ferris?"

"You a cop?"

I gave him ten bucks. "Just tell me what you know. She's left home and her family are worried about her. I just want to find her and make sure she's alright."

He took the ten, rolled it up in a cylinder the size of a cigarette and tucked it behind one ear. "I don't know any Muriel Ferris. Only Muriel I know is a Muriel Riordon."

"How long have you known her?"

"Last year I put an ad in *The Speaker*, looking for business. She wrote me a letter and I did her chart. We exchanged letters for a few months but now I haven't heard from her for quite a while."

"You corresponded during the time you had the place on Hoople Street, but not since then?"

"Right. I asked the guy who took the place after me, a health food dealer, and later, Davey, to forward any mail but I guess she just stopped writing. People drift apart."

"She ever mention to you that she was in...uh...kind of weird physical shape? No arms or legs?"

He glanced towards the stereo as the record ended and the tone arm creaked back to its resting place. Then he looked at me and said, "What goes on between an astrologer and his client is a confidential matter. Whatever troubles anybody has, that's their business and nobody else's."

"Are all astrologers so scrupulous?" I peeled off another twenty and held it out to him.

"They ought to be, but I can only speak for myself." He took the bills, rolled them and put them behind the other ear.

"Now that I'm one of your clients too, have you any idea of where she might have gone? Have you still got her letters?"

"I don't save old letters."

"Do you know any of her friends?"

"I don't think she had any."

"You don't count yourself?"

"Sure."

"Then for chrissake why don't you open up and help me find her?"

"I don't even know who you are. You haven't offered any ID. For all I know, maybe you're a nuke pimp looking for recruits. Is that your line, stocking the games rooms for the pervs in Upper East?"

I reached into my back pocket to get my snooper license and some more money. I was convinced Sunshine knew something of Muriel's whereabouts and it was only a matter of time and money before I got it out of him. *Spiders of Mars* fell out of my pocket as I was groping for my wallet. Sunshine stooped and picked it up.

"Another epic in the Fallik series," he whistled, looking at the cover. "I haven't read this one."

"You can have it," I said. "Sword and spacery's not one of my main interests anyway." Finding Muriel was my one goal and if I could win Sunshine's favor through handouts like that, he was welcome to it. Easy come, easy go.

He tore off the plastic wrapper. "You know, I just remembered something Muriel said in one of her last letters. She'd heard about some new clinic on the Lower West side that specialized in work on nuke mutants and she wanted to know if I knew anything about it and whether I thought it would be a good idea to get in touch with them."

"Do you recall the name of the clinic?" I crackled the fresh bills between my fingers to spark his memory.

"Let me think a minute. I know it'll come to me." He riffled the pages of the paperback novel and then opened it at random. What he saw there shocked him so badly that he dropped the book. But not soon enough.

A red spider as fat as a golfball catapulted out of the book and landed on Sunshine's bare chest. He screamed and jumped back, swatting at it with his hand. It sprang clear of him in a jump that took it halfway across the room and then Sunshine was thrashing on the floor and gargling in a frenzied way as pink froth spilled out of his mouth.

I whipped off my jacket and swung it at the spider as it jumped for me. I'd never seen a spider that could move so fast: it scared the shit out of me. I knocked it to the floor but before I could stomp on it, the damn thing jumped again and landed atop the fridge bookcase. I grabbed a heavy magazine off Sunshine's table and tried to swat it. We chased each other around the room. Finally it hopped into the tiny bathroom adjacent to the kitchen and disappeared down the bathtub drain.

I grabbed a bottle of rubbing alcohol from the medicine cabinet, spun the cap off and poured the works down the drain. I fumbled a matchbook out of my pocket, set it afire and threw it in the tub. A bolt of flame shot up out of the drain and blistered the paint on the ceiling. A few wisps of scorched hair drifted down to settle on the white porcelain bottom of the tub and the air was suddenly foul with the smell of *spider flambé*. I turned on the bathtub faucet and left it running while I puked my lunch into the toilet bowl.

My shaky legs got me back out to the living room where I knelt beside Sunshine and took off his sunglasses. There was an ugly swollen gash above his heart but it hadn't bled much. I peeled back his lids and looked at his eyes. They looked like a pair of smoky marbles.

I listened for a few moments to see if anyone was going to appear in response to Sunshine's screams. From across the hall came the heavy backbeat of a rock number loosening the plaster. I took a pair of thin plastic lab gloves from my wallet, slipped them on and made as thorough a search of Joel Uranium's possessions as time allowed. I poked around the junk on his work table and saw nothing worthy of note. There were some astrological texts, a lot of loose charts lying about, some stationery, a few small bills in a tobacco tin. Under the table was a cardboard box full of file folders alphabetically arranged. I pulled the 'F' folder and didn't find what I wanted, then pulled 'R' and got Muriel Riordon. I slipped it into a 10x13-inch manilla envelope, scribbled a name and address on it and added lots of postage. I picked up the crumpled plastic cover the paperback had come in, wedged it inside the hollow section of the book where the spider had lain, then shoved the book into the envelope. I got the money from behind Uranium's ears, added most of what I'd been given as retainer and put that in the envelope too. I tried to think of what I was forgetting. I slipped Muriel's photo and the index card with Uranium's address in too. I spilled a random heap of his books on the floor and went through them looking for letters. Zilch. I threw them back where I'd found them, put the plastic gloves in the envelope and sealed it. I flipped Herbie Mann over, turned the stereo on again, left the door ajar and went downstairs. As luck would have it, there was a mailbox on the corner of Holmes Street. I dumped the envelope, went back to Belvedere Towers and used the payphone in the lobby to call the police.

The two detectives who answered the call were both in their early thirties. Sergeant Mundt was a big blond with a pair of shoulders Atlas would have traded the world for. He had a big flat face like a fresh clay bust someone had hit with a shovel. His partner, Sergeant York, was a skinny little guy with bags under his eyes and black hair tucked wetly behind his ears. After the ambulance crew had taken Uranium away and the forensic boys had done their thing, Mundt and York poked around and came up with six ounces of marijuana stashed in a fifty-pound bag of brown rice. They weren't satisfied with that and went on looking until they turned up half a liter of amyl nitrite in a bottle of refrigerated soda water. Then Mundt took three cans of Miller's beer from the fridge and we got cosy in the living room while York rolled a few joints.

"Here's to the High Life," said Mundt, distributing the cans and snapping his own open.

"And here's to the low life," said York, lighting up.

When your nerves are jangled after a close encounter with a killer spider, there's nothing like a beer and a joint to get mellowed out. I had a drink and a toke and a drink and a toke and after another drink Mundt asked me why I did it.

"I told you what happened already. Uranium and I were talking. This spider crawled out from under his mattress and jumped him. Uranium fell down dead. I chased the spider down the drain and put the torch to it. Then I phoned in."

"I've heard some fruity stories in my time but that takes the cake," Mundt said. "You can do better than that." He looked at the shiny Rolex on his wrist as if he intended to time me for how long it took to think up a better story.

"Take the drain apart and you'll find one burned spider." Even as I said it, I doubted they would, considering the amount of water I'd run down the drain after it.

"If you don't come straight with us, I'll take you apart," Mundt said. "What was your business with Uranium?" He smirked and added, "Besides kissing in the clinches."

"I wanted him to do my chart."

"You're a goddamned snooper. What's the angle?"

"No angle. Lots of people get their charts done. It's just as legit as psychoanalysis."

"It's a crock of shit."

"Believe what you want to believe. I was intrigued by an account I read in *The Speaker* a couple of months back. An astrologer had been approached by a certain person to help locate a missing pedigree dog. The astrologer drew a chart and interpreted from it that the dog would be found confined in the company of friends near flowing water. The bitch turned up a day later at the Riverside Animal Shelter."

"So what?"

"If it's a reliable method, I'd be interested to learn more about it. Some of my work entails the finding of missing persons. I wanted to sound out Uranium on the feasibility of collaboration."

"On what case?" Mundt growled.

"No case," I said. "Just thinking about the future."

"Yeah? Well, I see you doing ten to twenty on the Island if you don't shake loose."

"Keep talking," I said. "I'll tell you when I get scared."

Mundt screwed up his face, blew smoke out his nose and ground the roach under his heel. He took a walk around the room while York sat motionless on the windowsill, a finger in his nose and a look of exquisite boredom on his face. Mundt stopped in front of me and said, "It's been too long since I punched a faggot. I forget how mushy it feels when you hit one."

I looked up at him from where I sat in the chair they'd brought from the kitchen to put me at my ease. I was still trying to think of something smart to say when he hit me with a cast-iron fist on the left side of the neck. I fell off the chair like a stunned bunny and hit my head on the radiator by the window. I lay there awhile, wondering if he'd hit me again if I got up too fast. Not that I had the option: I felt as capable of swift and decisive action as a deep-frozen catatonic.

"Freud could have written a book about you," York was saying. I didn't know whether he meant me or Mundt.

"You want to stand in for a couple of punches?"

"I want to go home to bed. I haven't seen my wife in two days. When I do get home, I'm so tired I don't have the energy to feel her up."

"She probably thinks you're a swish."

"If so, she must wonder about my partner too."

"Slip your yap out of gear and roll another number. We'll get high and work the truth out of this motherfucker."

"Take it easy on the guy. He looks like the type that bruises easily. You don't want to drag him back to the station looking like a ripe peach that's been used as a hockey puck. You know what they did to Gustafson for getting heavy with the hands."

"Sure I do. He got sent down to the waterfront where the punks punch back."

"You'd look great on a tag team with Guffy."

"Do I look worried? Favreau will back me up blow by blow. He's an old fag-hater from way back."

"He's sitting up," York observed me. "You can probably hit him again."

"Take a break," I told Mundt as he squared off in front of me for another round.

"Sure," Mundt said. "We'll pop open a few more beers and have a party. We've got nothing on our minds but small talk. We've got a car outside with a trunkful of stiffs. You think we're sweating Uranium?"

I tasted blood in my mouth. I felt in my shirt pocket for a handkerchief and found a bent cigarette I hadn't known was there. I straightened it out and stuck it in my mouth. I was always finding things in my clothes I couldn't account for. So when I put my hand in my jacket pocket in search of a match, I wasn't that surprised to pull out a plastic bag full of scag.

"Throw a little light on the subject?" Mundt's hand dollied in so fast I jerked my head back thinking he was having another go at knocking it off. But all he wanted to do was flick open a silver Zippo and help me get my tobacco ignited. Nice guy, Mundt. I blew some smoke at the ceiling and looked at York. He shrugged as if to say it was an old movie but it had a sound plot.

"What's the story?" I said. "You plant shit on me and call it robbery with violence? After I've put in the call for you? What moron's going to buy that?"

"You'd be surprised," Mundt said. "Now you can talk turkey or we can take you back to the station and introduce you to Guffy's stand-in. He's a husky lad from the Chicago stockyards. One punch from him and you'll wish I was still around to tickle you."

"What are you doing for motive and weapon?"

"Money's the old standby. We'll give you a fistful so it'll look like you cleaned out Uranium's dope receipts. After we talk to the forensic boys and find out what killed the fairy, we'll find something that fits. Back at the station, we've got a garbage can full of knives, scissors and ice picks."

"No poison arrows?"

"I should hit you again. As soon as York and I finish this joint, I think I will."

"Do you play this game with all your witnesses? No wonder nobody wants to get involved."

"Just with the murder cases, pal, just the murders." Mundt hit me again, on the other side of the neck this time. His left hook was every bit as good as his right. When I picked myself up off the floor they took me back to the station. I saw now where I'd made my mistake. I shouldn't have called the cops. I should have gone home and taken an aspirin.

2

Around six in the morning my cell door banged open and an old guy with a face like a tired bloodhound came in with a cup of coffee and a wad of paper towels. He asked me if I was awake and I grunted. He left the stuff on the floor and went away. I had trouble getting my head off the dirty mattress; when I sat up the pains in my neck moved upstairs and started banging around in the tin can hollow I called my brain.

I drank the coffee, which tasted like something drained from the oil pan of a farm tractor, and cleaned myself up as best I could with the paper towels and some rusty water from the sink. I sat on the edge of the bunk and counted my bruises as I made my tentative way back to the land of the living. My neck was plenty sore from where Mundt had socked me last night, but that was nothing compared to the way my solar plexus ached. I opened my shirt and was surprised to see no marks. The muscle was painfully tender to my probing fingers so I gave it up and considered myself lucky that I wasn't puking blood.

I'd been quizzed again when they booked me, in front of a tape recorder this time, but I hadn't changed my story any. Not that they didn't try to persuade a full confession out of me. I never did see the Chicago slugger—maybe it was his night off. Anyway, they seemed perfectly content to work me over with the stungun in lieu of personal contact.

The stungun was something which only cardiac patients and interrogees were very familiar with, at least from the reception point of view. Basically it was just a handheld electroplate jacked into a generator capable of delivering shocks up to four hundred volts. It was like taking a grenade in the stomach and surviving to relish the sensations. The first jolt cleaned out my bladder and the second, my large intestine. The third one made me ejaculate, but if thrills of that order ever become the norm for sex, I'll swear off without a backward look. After nine jolts I stopped counting, and not too many after that I passed out.

That was history now. Life goes on. I looked out the window and saw a bit of sun spreading across the sky. It looked like it might be a nice day. I hoped they didn't plan on spoiling it by rubbing my belly with the stungun again.

A splashing in the toilet interrupted my reverie. A small black rat, soaking wet, climbed over the porcelain rim of the bowl and dropped to the floor with a smack. He took a stroll around the room with his nose along the base of the wall, pausing every now and again to fix me with a pair of beady eyes. He found something the size of a pea and stopped to eat it. Then he wandered under the cot and I watched him as he scratched tentatively at the mattress stuffing that hung down between the cot's metal slats.

He wasn't feeling nervy enough to take a bite out of my ankle so he ambled on over to look behind the toilet just in case some puking inmate had missed the target. I searched my pockets to see if I had some little morsel he might be interested in: a bag of peanuts or a roll of Tums. I felt sorry for the little guy; I could almost see daylight between his ribs. The best I could come up with was a tinfoil packet of ketchup from a takeout counter. I ripped it open and tossed it on the floor. He pounced on it like Big Simba onto a white hunter. Ketchup shot across the floor in a crimson squirt. He lapped it off the floor and leaned his weight on one paw to squeeze the last drops out of the packet. I never knew rats were so fond of ketchup, but then maybe he thought it was blood. When he was finished he licked his whiskers off and gave me a look as if to say, Where's the hot dog that goes with it?

Just then a pair of steel-plated boots came clattering

down the hall like a runaway army tank. The rat clambered up onto the rim of the toilet bowl and executed a swan dive into the murky waters. I hobbled over to the toilet and worked the flush to speed him on his way. I only wished I could have gone with him.

"Let's go, Savage." A young turnkey banged the cell door open and hooked a finger at me. He was a big faceless jerk with a pair of hands powerful enough to rip in two the entire Encyclopedia Britannica set, all twenty-eight volumes, in one go. He snapped a cuff on my left wrist tight enough to render it numb in two seconds and towed me at top speed down a long well-lighted hallway past unshaven faces and black eyes peering from behind a hundred and one cell doors.

"What's up?" I ventured when I caught my breath on the elevator that took us laboriously upward.

"Shut up." Said very nicely, in a well-modulated voice with a sound like chicken bones going through a meat grinder.

I got shut up before I got started. I kept my eyes on the blinking numbered indicator above the door, trying to ignore the red smear at head level along one wall and the little bits of enamel on the floor that crunched beneath the turnkey's boots. We get off on the fifth floor and walked down a short hall towards a large translucent window at the end. From the other end of the hall I heard a low-pitched wail broken by a *whap-whap-whap* like a police siren getting thumped with a riot stick. Business as usual? I casually broke out in a cold sweat. The turnkey snapped hard left and dragged me into a windowless room with matte green walls and two desks, joined at waist level like Siamese twins, behind one of which sat my old pal, Mundt, he of the kind word and the gentle hand.

"Morning, Savage." It was a statement, not a greeting. Mundt didn't look happy and it didn't make me feel happy to see him that way. The turnkey was gone before the pins and needles started invading my hand. I rubbed it with the other and tried to stand erect and confident like a man with nothing bad on his conscience. Mundt said nothing, just looked at me with a pair of eyes that could have given Dracula lessons in intensity.

"I want to call my lawyer," I said.

"No lawyer," Mundt said.

York came into the room with three cups of coffee, kicked the door shut behind him and held out the first offering to Mundt, who took it with a grunt and slurped swiftly. York gave me a cup. He still had bags under his eyes but his pupils were as big as dimes and there was a nervous little twitch of a smile at the corners of his mouth. I guessed that he'd been keeping late hours, but dexies were backing him up minute by minute. With one hand freed, he jerked his chair out from behind his desk and skidded it across the floor to me. I sat on it and York sat on the edge of his desk and swung one leg back and forth like a metronome. We all drank our coffee and looked soulfully at each other. I wondered what was in store. Neither one of them seemed ready to talk and the silence was getting on my nerves. Then I heard it.

A high-pitched buzz, like a handful of excited wasps in an empty beer can. I'd heard that sound before, and hearing it again gave me a pain in the guts. Beyond York's desk was a narrow door left partly open so that I could see the padded table with the harness straps hanging loose and the chromium piece of equipment that lay there on the table, attached by a heavy electrical cable to the generator, out of sight, but not out of sound.

"How're you feeling?" Mundt shook a couple of cigarettes out of a pack of Exports, lit one of them and offered me the other. I held the butt up to his Zippo flame and it didn't shake much.

"Lucky," I said and tried to look like I thought I'd stay that way.

"How's your imagination this morning?"

"About the same."

"Have any bad dreams?" Mundt was grinning. York's leg was going like a piston but he was staring off into the great void of nothingness as if this didn't concern him at all. Mundt crumpled his empty cup and pitched it ten feet into the waste basket by the door. He took a big breath and smiled like he'd just run a three minute mile.

"Yeah, I had dreams. Giant red spiders with a Rolex on every leg kept chasing me around the dance floor of the Policeman's Ball, waving joints as big as baseball bats and screaming, 'Have another hit'."

Mundt's big open hand smacked the desktop with a report like a gunshot. His shoulders jerked up and down and his breath chugged in and out like a two-cycle lawnmower engine with ignition problems. There was an amused crinkle on his face, so I guess he was laughing or trying not to. York turned and looked at him, then at me, then off into the ozone again.

"Any last words before we strap you down on the table and let York give you another belly massage?"

It took me a minute to get out a "No."

"Then sign this and get the fuck out of here." Mundt shoved a thin sheaf of stapled typewritten sheets across the desk at me. I read it through. It was the statement I'd given to the tape recorder last night. I signed it with my own pen which Mundt had dumped on his desk along with the rest of my personal effects.

"I'm free to go?"

"You're free to take a flying fucking into the East River," Mundt said. "Scram before I change my mind."

"What happened?" I appealed to York.

"The Forensic boys identified the poison. It came from a Mexican jumping spider which, it turns out, are fairly common illegal immigrants via the banana wholesalers and tequila importers. Holmes Street is smack in the middle of the warehouse zone where such Mexican products are stored. A kid was bitten to death by one of these spiders last summer on Beatnickel. Guess it happens all the time down old Mexico way. What didn't happen is that Uranium didn't die. He's in a coma." His spiel finished, York drifted back out into space.

"Now fade, snooper," said Mundt, "and fade fast. I don't want to see you again."

I could have told him the feeling was mutual but I

thought I'd just about used up my share of luck for the day. I faded faster than a pair of cheap denims in a bucket of bleach.

Doctor was very happy. Crabby and the girl were happy too but they didn't count. Doctor was happy and so he gave Buzz a big injection of sugar in the thorax. Buzz hurried off to his room to play.

The light switch at the door made the walls glow ultraviolet. The floor was blue tile. Buzz locked the door and took off his clothes. He turned on the TVs. There was one in each corner. He watched a baseball game, a tennis match, a football game and a blue movie all at the same time. The football game got him excited. All those bodies running into each other.

The blue movie was good too. It gave Buzz a hardon. He had a cock thirteen inches long. It was as tough and flexible as plastic can be and it glowed in the dark.

He danced around the room, kicking a soccer ball off the fluorescent walls. He was everywhere at once. He was fast and hungry and ready for dinner.

"Bird," he squawked in his metallic voice.

A chicken popped out of the food chute on a blast of compressed air. It was a line drive into right field. Buzz snagged it one-handed, snipped the head off with the other pincer and tossed it in his mouth like a walnut. He upended the chicken and squeezed it. Blood streamed from the pulsing gourd of the bird's body. He thrust his pincers through the chicken's breast and broke it in two. He took his time and finished it in four bites. He picked the loose feathers off the floor and ate them too. Waste not, want not.

Now Crabby was mad. Somebody'd been writing his girlfriend love letters. She'd been giving her money away. Crabby wanted it back and the letters too. He gave Buzz an address and told him to fix the other guy.

Buzz was bored. Sure he'd fix him.

I took a subway downtown. It was hot and noisy and I wished I'd picked up something for my headache.

Across the aisle from me was a girl, maybe seventeen, maybe pretty once, but now the left side of her face was a twitching mass of half-baked flesh, the eyelids puckered in over a hollow where an eye should have been. Her left arm and leg were withered and covered with the same scabby skin, like she'd fallen asleep under a sunlamp. Just another reminder of 1980: the nuclear generating plant explosion, the race riots and the looting. I looked at that girl and forgot all about my headache. Things could be worse.

I climbed back up to daylight at the Beatnickel stop. I walked down Fourth and, miracle supreme, found my Astromobile just where I'd left it yesterday. This had to be some kind of record. The hubcaps were gone but who needs them, and the plates were too, but I had spares at home. I climbed behind the wheel and drove away. A quick cruise past Holmes Street, wondering if there was any percentage in checking out Uranium's place again for something I might have missed, but the thought of Mundt and York kept me moving.

First on the agenda was Davey at the Cosmo Comix Center. I found a parking slot on Hoople and walked half a block. The place was closed. It was nine in the morning. Could be that he was the type to sleep late and open up only in the afternoon when the rest of the comic book crowd crawled out of the sack. I peered into the dark little store. From the back wall, a green fluorescent Hulk peered back at me. The door didn't look too solid and I was seriously considering kicking it in and browsing around at will when I saw in the window reflection a car parked across the street with a dark ugly type in it watching me like a hawk. I smelled dick. Could it be the cops had put a tail on me, thinking there was more to the Sunshine caper than I'd put on tape? There was one way to find out. I walked across the street and leaned on the door of his wagon, a black Ramada with air scoops on the hood and the ass end jacked up waist high.

"Looking for somebody?" I said, giving him the inventory eye. This dude was a few years younger than my twenty-five, but he had the battle scars to show that he'd been around. Two parallel lines showed whitely across the cheek nearest me and another two lines were notched into his chin. He had a tanned and hairless face and a nose like a flint tomahawk that spelled Indian. Glossy black hair, thin lips, dark eyes, small ears. He was wearing a brown cord shirt with the sleeves rolled up to his biceps.

"A star freak, name of Uranium," the big buck said. "Know where I can find him?"

"Try the hospital."

His eyes narrowed to slits. A well-muscled arm snaked out the window and his hand flicked my jacket open on either side, politely, but insistently. I stood still for it. He pulled a pack of smokes off the dash and shook one out for me. "You put him there?"

"What's your interest in the man?" I accepted his cigarette and used my matches for ignition.

"He's the friend of a friend I'm looking for."

"This friend, is she a bit on the short side?"

"Yeah, really short."

"Like, no legs?"

"Maybe you'd better come in out of the hot sun and tell me how come you know so much about it."

"Maybe I will." I went around to the other side of the Ramada and got into the front seat. The buck's name was Nick Bowman and he'd been hired by a Mrs. Riordon of Cloverlea to find her daughter, a twenty-year-old girl named Muriel who had no arms or legs. Bowman was holding a hundred dollar retainer and a promise of two hundred to join it if he could find the girl. Mrs. Riordon didn't want the police poking about in her family affairs.

"It looks like a kidnapping," Bowman said, "but there's been no ransom demand. I was out to the house where she was snatched. It's one of those old mansions that have a fireplace in every room. The girl had the top floor to herself. Two days ago, an air conditioner repairman came to the house to replace a unit in a study on the second floor. Seems he pulled the panel off the unused fireplace in the study and climbed up the chimney to get into the girl's room. No signs of a struggle but it looks like he took her back down the chimney and smuggled her out of the house in a fake air conditioner."

"Two days ago? When were you put on the job?"

"Just yesterday evening. I thought about that too. She took her time looking for help."

I told Bowman about Natalie Ferris and the very sketchy details she'd given me of her sister's disappearance. I told him how I traced Uranium, what happened there, and my run-in with the law.

"Serves you right," Bowman said. "You shouldn't have called attention to yourself."

"If I'd left Uranium without calling the cops, he'd be dead now."

"He's no help to us in a coma."

We decided to pool our resources. It was clear we were looking for the same girl, Muriel; whether her last name was Ferris or Riordon was immaterial. We'd worry about the finer details after we found her.

"Sit tight," I said, "while I run across the street and see if the landlord can give us Davey's home address."

"Ask him for a key and we'll take a quick riffle through the store and see if anything turns up."

I went up the three flights of stairs and banged on Sid Wiseman's door. He had a pair of reading glasses propped on his big nose and a little black skullcap on the back of his noggin. I said I hoped I wasn't disturbing him.

"Come in, come in." He was hospitality personified. He gestured to a straightbacked wooden chair that stood at one end of the faded carpet in front of his desk. "You found Uranium?"

"Yep. He's in the hospital now."

"Ah, revenge." He rubbed his hands together. "But no money?"

"He's going to need everything he's got to pay the doctors."

"Not so good." Sid shook his head sadly and wearily lowered himself into his chair. He looked at me over the rims of his glasses. "What do you want now?"

"Have you got a last name and a home address for

Davey, the guy in the Comix store?"

Sid pulled open a desk drawer and riffled through a small index card file. "David Watroboski. No address but I've a phone number." He started to read it off to me. "No, wait, that's the number downstairs. This other must be his home number."

"May I use your phone?"

"There's a payphone on the corner."

"Thanks, I'll use yours." While the phone rang at the other end of the line, I breezed through the directory in search of Watroboski. Thank god for weird names. If I'd been looking for Smith, there'd have been a thousand addresses. As it was, only one D Watroboski and an address only a dozen blocks away. Finally a girl answered the phone and I asked for Davey.

"He's sleeping right now. Is it important? I could wake him."

"Don't bother. I just called to say goodbye. I'm leaving for Canada this afternoon. I'll send him a postcard. What was the apartment number there? I've forgotten."

"Eight-B. I'm going out in a few minutes. If you want to call back again in an hour, he'll get up to answer it."

"No, that's alright. I'm leaving for Penn Station in ten minutes."

"Have a nice trip." We hung up.

"What's Canada got that we haven't?" Sid said.

"Newfoundland," I said. "Have you ever eaten seal flipper pie?"

"Is it kosher?"

"I'll send you one airmail and let you decide." I pulled ten bucks out of my pocket and laid it on his desk. "Have you got a key to the Comix Store? I must have dropped my passport in there yesterday afternoon and I have to recover it immediately."

"What's this?" He caressed the ten with a finger while his other hand pulled a ring of keys from a desk drawer.

"Uranium managed to cough up a down payment, sort of a goodwill gesture towards clearing the debt."

He opened the ring and slid a brass key across the desk. He put the ten in his pocket and nodded. "Don't forget to bring it back."

I went downstairs and unlocked the door to the Cosmo Comix Center. Bowman crossed the street and came in behind me. Between the two of us, we ransacked the place in an organized sort of way and turned up one clue in the bottom of a waste basket. It was an envelope with the address, Joel Uranium, 134 Hoople Street, written in a thin spidery hand. Postmarked a week ago in Cloverlea, but no return address and no letter inside the envelope.

"Could have been from Muriel," Bowman said. "If she writes with her mouth, the shaky scrawl would fit."

"But Uranium told me he hadn't heard from her in a long while."

"Either he was lying or this Davey cat's been opening his mail. What now?"

I locked the door behind us and took the key back to Sid.

"Find your passport?"

"Yep." I patted my jacket pocket where the envelope was. "Davey must have spotted it right away and set it aside. I'm all set to travel now."

"You don't need a passport to go to Canada."

"You're quite right," I said. "I'm allergic to snow anyway. Maybe I'd better go to Mexico instead."

"Just so long as you go." Sid waved a tired hand at me and bent his head to the book he was reading backwards.

I went back across the street and sat with Bowman in his car while we decided what to do. He was keen on having a pow-wow with Watroboski. I felt more like returning to my office and pressing a cold beer can against my aching head, so I gave him the address and told him to watch out for Mexican jumping spiders.

"What are you going to do?"

"Sit down with a phone directory and look for a medical clinic on the Lower West side that specializes in handling nuke mutants."

"Where'll I find you later?"

I gave Bowman one of my business cards. We agreed to get together shortly after noon and see if our separate enquiries added up to anything like a signpost towards the missing Muriel. I climbed out of the car; he gunned it to life and the Ramada went down the street like a dragster, leaving ten feet of rubber printed on the paving and half a dozen dogs barking in its wake. I went back to my car and drove to the parking lot around the corner from my office. The kid in the control booth had an earphone radio on and was singing off-key to a pop song. I took the time card and paid a visit to the deli on the corner where I bought a *Speaker* and breakfast.

Back in my office, with the fan rippling the pages of the *Speaker*, I ate a pickled egg and sipped from a large can of beer. Uranium's accident rated three column inches on a back page and my name wasn't mentioned. That was fine by me. After I read the funnies I yanked out the Yellow Pages directory and went through the Medical Clinics section. There were only about forty of them on the Lower West side. How wonderful.

Now I had to start getting cagey. Chances were, Muriel Ferris-Riordon might be going under an assumed name to avoid publicity or to elude the attention of snoopers like myself who might be trying to find her. Asking receptionists over the phone whether they had any thalidomide brunettes in residence was going to get me nowhere fast. What I needed was some inside information, somebody who had a handle on the whole clinic scene, like a public health official, but I didn't need to wrack my brains for long to realize that I didn't have any such contacts. Things looked grim. It also occurred to me that the clinic I was looking for might not even be listed in the directory. What then? I broke out in a sweat, thinking of forfeited fees. If only Uranium had coughed up the name of the clinic before he opened the spider book. If only he'd saved his old letters. If only I was clairvoyant. If if if...

Now there was a thought. Flashing back to the line I'd given Mundt about the astrologer finding the lost dog, I saw a glimmer of hope in what was otherwise a gloomy case of search and rescue. Was there a chance that some other astrologer, equipped with the chart I'd taken from Uranium's files, might tell me where Muriel had gone to? If all else failed, I intended to give it a try. I pulled the phone off its cradle and dialled a number. A familiar girl's voice answered.

"Hi, Wendy, it's Keith. I was afraid you might have left for classes already."

"Keith, where've you been? Did you forget the movie date we had for last night? Or did somebody else pop up?"

"A little trouble with a claim, honey. I had to drive upstate and spend the night getting the facts from the police." I'd never told Wendy what my real line of work was. We'd only known each other a couple of months. She believed I was an insurance investigator, which made it only a white lie in any case. "Listen, Wen, you're going to get a manilla envelope in the mail today. You haven't got it already have you?"

"Our mail doesn't come until the afternoon. What is it, dirty pictures?"

"Dirty pictures is right. They're the official police photographs from the suicide I was investigating. I don't think you'd better open the envelope at all. They're pretty gruesome. He used a shotgun on himself."

"Yecchhh. Why'd you send them to me, you perv?"

I'd risen from my chair in this time and opened the door silently. Now I slammed it. "Listen, Wen, somebody just came in. I'll tell you all about it later. Put that envelope in a safe place when it comes, will you, and I'll see you tonight."

"Okay. Make it six and we'll go to an early movie and then go home to bed early."

"Uh, I'm not sure about the movie date. I might still be busy with this job. Now I've got another favor to ask of you. Is that psych prof, whatsisname, the one who's into astrology, still around the university?"

"Dr. Aquarius. I see him nearly every day at the cafeteria. Why do you ask?"

"I'm interested to find out if he can predict a suicide from a client's chart. It would be a big factor in certain policies. Would you make an effort to see him today and get his phone numbers, both at home and at the university?"

"No problem. I'm not sure he'd think that an ethical

thing to do, but..."

"You'll get his numbers. Good girl. Love and kisses. See you later."

"You'd better show. There's a hunk of a rugby player I could be going out with tonight."

"You'd be wasting your time. Ruptures are an occupational hazard in that game."

"Don't be catty, Keith. Bye bye."

I lighted a cigarette and stared at the clinic listings. There had to be some faster way of finding out to which one she'd gone. Uranium hadn't kept his old letters but maybe Muriel had. I wondered if Bowman had thought to follow that line of investigation. Probably not, or we wouldn't still be farting around in the dark. I made a mental note to myself that I should get the Cloverlea address from him and pay a visit to the scene of the crime. No telling what might turn up; something that means nothing to one man might be a vital clue for another. Besides that, I wanted to find out if Muriel had a sister. If so, why had she and this Mrs. Riordon hired independent investigators? And if not, who was the lady who said she was Natalie Ferris?

I looked at my watch. Eleven o'clock here made it seven in California. Maybe around noon, if nothing had developed from Bowman's visit to Watroboski, I'd give the mysterious Natalie Ferris a ring. In the meantime, there was one other phone call I might profitably make. I dialled Franklin General Hospital where, according to *The Speaker,* Joel Uranium was lying in a coma. The switchboard op put me through to the ward nurse and I asked her if there was any improvement in the spider's victim. She wasn't going to tell me anything until I told her my name was Walter Uranium, Joel's brother, and I had a legal right to her information.

"He's still in a coma," she said. "Your mother flew in from Texas this morning. She's with him now."

"Fine, but don't tell her I called. It's impossible for me to get away from work right now. I'll see her later."

"Very well, Mr. Uranium. Good bye."

I hung up the phone and paced a few quick circuits of the room. I picked up my guitar and banged a few chords on it like I do when I'm uptight and don't know what to do with my hands. It was a safe assumption that the cops weren't going to get the story of the booby-trapped paperback out of Uranium. That meant my story and I were safe from the likes of York and Mundt. Now if only I could get a line on Muriel.

The phone rang. I grabbed it and said hello. It was Bowman. "Where are you? Did you see Watroboski?"

"Yep. I got him out of bed and twisted his arm a little. Well, maybe I twisted it a lot. I got quite a little story out of him. Seems he's been intercepting Uranium's mail all along. The first one he opened had some money in it, apparently to pay off Uranium for having done a friend's chart. Then Watroboski got the bright idea of wooing her by letter and asking for more money. He figured out after the second letter that there was something wrong with her and that she'd never show up at the door to confront him. Meanwhile he made up some excuses why he couldn't come see her: he was sick and he needed money for a doctor. Actually, he's got loan sharks on his back for a couple of grand. Anyway, she had access to money and she bought his story. He managed to wheedle close to a thousand bucks from her in a month of love letters."

"Any reference to the clinic she was considering?"

"Yeah, there's something here about a Limbo Clinic. I might be misreading it. Her writing is hell to make out. I've got a whole fistful of letters here. Maybe you'll be able to sort some of it out. She mentions another guy called Crabner. Somebody who had an operation at the clinic."

"What about the spider in the book?"

"He swears he doesn't know anything about that. He says she sent it to him in the mail but he never opened it because he already had a copy."

"She sent it to him? And they were trading love letters? Something fishy there? Did you think to check at her place for correspondence?"

"Sure did. Mrs. Riordon said she'd been getting mail, but when we looked where she thought it was kept, nothing. Looks like whoever snatched her also cleaned out the correspondence to make it hard finding her."

"Have you got a phone number for her home? I might want to take a run out there if we don't get anywhere with this so-called Limbo Clinic."

Bowman recited the number. In the meantime I cast my eye through the clinic listings and saw no Limbo. I told Bowman he'd better come on down to the office and we'd pore over the letters together.

"Hold on, chief, something's happening here."

"What? Are you calling from Watroboski's?"

"I'm in a phone booth just down the street from his building. A dark blue van, can't make out the license plates, just pulled up in front of his place. A tall skinny guy's going into the apartment building."

"So what's the connection?"

"Mrs. Riordon said the air conditioner repairman was tall and skinny and came to the house in a dark blue van. I've got to check this guy out."

"Wait for me. I can be there in five minutes."

"He might be gone by then. I'm going back up to Watroboski's now. You can meet me here."

"Put those letters in your car and lock it. I'll be with you as soon as I can. And be careful."

"There's nothing to worry about. I've got a gun. You just hustle on over here as fast as you can. I'll bet you we sew this thing up by the end of the day. Meet you at Watroboski's."

I dropped the phone and got my Viper out of the top desk drawer. It was a ten-shot Czech 6mm automatic that just covered the palm of my hand. It was small calibre but it had enough punch for my purposes, designed with a cutaway muzzle into which a silencer snapped. I slipped it into my pocket with an extra clip. I hadn't practised much with it lately but there was a time when I could put four out of five shots through a matchbox at ten paces. I almost hoped I might see another Mexican jumping spider to see I hadn't lost my touch.

I was parked outside Watroboski's apartment building in less than five minutes. Bowman's black Ramada was there and so was the dark blue van. It had a pair of vanity plates that read *BUZZ*. I checked the Ramada but the door was locked. In the lobby I found *Watroboski* on Box Eight-B. I hesitated to ring the buzzer to have the lobby door opened. If the van man was in there with Watroboski, I didn't want to be the one that scared him off. On the other hand, Bowman might be there with the pair of them, waiting for me to show. I was saved the decision when an old guy in a Panama hat and a gasmask toddled around the corner with a weary dachshund that had to walk on its tiptoes to keep its belly from dragging. I fumbled in my pockets as if I couldn't separate my keys from a fistful of change. The old guy doddered up behind me, pushed a scaly finger on 4-A and said into the speaker, "It's me, Gertie. Put the kettle on."

The lock buzzed. I jerked the door open and took the elevator to the eighth floor. 8-B had a heavy door with a brass peephole at neck level. I rang the bell. No answer. I rang and rang and rang. Inside the apartment I could hear a radio going, the announcer saying '...your respirators at home because the Contam reading's up to four point five...' I shook the doorknob and used my shoulder on the door. I was going nowhere fast by that method.

I went to the apartment next door and rang the bell. Someone inside said 'Who is it?' and I said I was here to fix the kitchen sink. She opened the door, a stout lady of fifty in a blue housecoat who said, "You mean, the toilet." I didn't argue with her. I walked into the bathroom, saw that it had a good-sized window, and locked the door behind me. While she stood outside the door and insisted, "There's a trick to it," I climbed through the window and, hanging by the sill, got my feet onto the rickety railing of the fire escape balcony next door. With a heave away from the window, I tottered for a moment trying to get my balance before I fell eight stories down the airshaft. I dropped down on all fours on the balcony of 8-B, noticing as I did that someone at the bottom of the airshaft was just disappearing into the building via a door. For all I knew it could have been the janitor. I hammered the wing

41

nuts off the screen window and climbed in over a kitchen sideboard littered with the interrupted makings of a lettuce-and-tomato sandwich. All was quiet but for the radio, from which now came the soothing and insipid lyrics of a commercial for Plasid, the swift agent for correction of stomach upset. One look in the living room and I could have used a little bottle of Plasid myself.

I recognized Bowman by the tan cord shirt, the well-muscled mahogany arms and the cowboy boots on his big feet. He was lying flat on his back close to the hall door. The little silver bracelet with *Davey* on the name plate verified the identity of the other body. He was lying on his stomach in the doorway to the bedroom. I had to rely on body description for identification. There was a lot of blood around but their heads were nowhere in sight.

I unhooked the chain latch, slipped the bolt and ran down to the end of the hall where a window overlooked the street corner. I got there just in time to see the dark blue van pull out of the side street and accelerate swiftly down the avenue. So much for a chase sequence. By the time I got to my car, the mystery butcher would be long gone. I went back to 8-B, locked the door and surveyed the carnage.

Both men had their necks truncated in what appeared to have been one massive chop. No ragged edges from sawing with a bread knife, no multiple lacerations from hacking away with a hatchet. It looked as though they'd been decapitated by one stroke of a sharp sword. I looked at the position of the bodies and tried to reconstruct what might have happened. Bowman's position so close to the door suggested that he'd been jumped as soon as he came in. If that were the case, the butcher was already in the apartment with Davey, either by consent or unfriendly persuasion. Davey'd opened the door for Bowman and the butcher'd done his thing. Maybe that was a surprise for Davey and he'd tried to make a run for it but the butcher got him too. The question now was, who was the butcher? The same person who'd mailed the spider book, or a loan shark?

I looked at the mess on the living room floor. That wasn't the work of a shark's muscleman. Broken bones, acid in the face, partial dismemberment: that was more their style, something that would leave the victim walking around for advertisement purposes. Furthermore, the violence would have been confined to Watroboski. No need to ice Bowman too. So it was the party or parties unknown who'd sent the boobytrapped book, and it had been Bowman's bad luck to bumble into the proceedings. Or was it that simple? Watroboski wheedled money out of Muriel; Muriel was kidnapped; Bowman tried to find her; he and Watroboski got greased. Where was the connection?

The letters from Muriel. Where were they?

I checked Bowman's pockets. No letters but I lifted his carkeys and slipped them into my pocket. Nothing on Davey. I went into the bedroom and cast about for letters. There was a big double waterbed on the floor, flanked on either side by lamps made from 120-ounce bottles of Canadian Club. On the walls were posters of Spiderman, Wonderwoman and a whole crew of weird comic-book types that I couldn't put names to. A small TV hung from the ceiling by a pair of chrome chains; atop it was a handful of opened letters but when I checked them I saw they were all addressed to a girl named Janis Murphy at this address. There were girl's clothes in the closet and a cloth handbag with the name *Janis* stencilled on the flap, so I surmised that Janis was the girl I'd talked to on the phone.

Next door the lady in the housecoat was pounding on the bathroom door and asking me if I'd flushed myself down the toilet.

There was no writing desk in the bedroom, no stashes of letters in the clothes drawers, no address books lying around on the kitchen table. I was fresh out of nooks and crannies to stick my prying nose into. There was nothing for me here but the smell of fresh-spilled blood and a growing sense of uneasiness. I had to make tracks.

No phone calls to the cops this time. I'd learned my lesson at Uranium's. If Mundt and York found me hanging around the scene of a multiple murder, they'd really put me through the wringer this time. It was going to be hell on Janis to come home from work and find that kind of mess in the front room but there was nothing I could do about that. I considered myself lucky that I wasn't lying there in the living room with the other two.

3

I checked Bowman's car and found what I'd feared: zilch. The guy'd been too confident of his abilities to think that someone might take the letters away from him. Now someone had done just that, and more, and I was left out in the cold with two thin leads: the so-called Limbo clinic and the Riordons' phone number in Cloverlea. I climbed into the Astromobile and scooted out of the neighborhood. I knew I'd have to back-track over the ground Bowman'd already covered, just in case he'd missed something. I stopped at a phone booth a few blocks away and phoned Cloverlea.

"Hello, Ferris residence," said a lady with schoolteacher enunciation.

"Is there a Mrs. Riordon at this number?"

"Speaking. Who's calling please?"

"My name's Savage. I've been working with Mr. Bowman to find your daughter."

"And have you?"

"I'm afraid not. I'd like to come out there and look over the situation, maybe ask you a few questions."

"Mr. Bowman already made a thorough enquiry. Couldn't he tell you...?"

"It's a bit too complicated to discuss over the phone. Mr. Bowman is busy now working on another angle. He thought it would be useful to crosscheck the information he already has. Could I see you this afternoon?"

"Well, if Mr. Bowman thinks..."

"He does. One o'clock okay with you?"

"Come as soon as you like. I can give you lunch. Do you have the address?"

"Yes," I lied, "but give it to me again just to make sure

I've got it right." She gave me the address and we said our goodbyes and see-you-shortly's. I climbed behind the wheel of my wagon and tooled on out of town just before the traffic started getting heavy during the noon rush-hour.

I smoked a couple of cigarettes on the ride out and listened to the radio as I worked my way through an obstacle course of family wagons that were determined to stay within the speed limits and block anybody else who might not be similarly inclined. I took the Cloverlea exit at twice the suggested speed, leaving a bit of the Astro's rubber on the snug turns, and raced up a two-lane highway into Cloverlea, a suburb that seemed to require nothing more than a hundred-thousand-dollar home for a residency fee. Through the trees on either side of the road I caught glimpses of large white pillared houses with Caddies and Rolls' lounging around the doorsteps, and pedigreed dogs sporting upon lawns as immaculate as the putting greens of pro golf courses. After a mile or two of this, the road ended in a hairpin turn with a large flowered traffic island in the center. Following the directions I'd received over the phone, I drifted around the island and went through a stone wall portal with the number 800 in raised bronze letters above the entrance, and up a birch-shaded lane to a house seldom seen outside of rich men's dreams.

I parked the Astro between a Suburban station wagon and a yellow Mussolini Sport with tail fins sharp enough to slice the arms off unwary pedestrians. The house was big, with the requisite pillars flanking the front door, and of a whiteness so intense that it hurt my eyes to look at it. As I stood there with my eyes smarting, two full-grown Doberman Pinschers came over a four-foot hedge like jumpers in a horse show.

I was backed up against the car saying "Nice doggie, nice doggie," while they barked and showed their teeth, when an older man came through a slot in the hedge and whistled them down. The Dobermans sat and hung their tongues out and looked at me as if to say, Had you worried there for a minute, eh sport?

"These are Hansel and Gretel. They keep strangers out of the flowerbeds. My name's Bud Riordon." He held out his hand and gave me a dry hard squeeze. He was in his fifties or very fit sixties, a wiry grey-haired gent just under six feet tall. He was a little dark under the eyes and the eyes themselves were a watery grey. He wore a light red nylon jacket, a snug pair of denim jeans and a pair of canvas shoes with wet grass trimmings on the toes. He had a natty little grey moustache that I'd missed at first sight because it was cut right to the contour of his lip. It was about as thin as a razor blade and might have looked smart on a World War Two airforce ace, but on him it looked like something left over from breakfast.

"I'm Keith Savage. Perhaps your wife mentioned I'd be coming to talk about the disappearance of your daughter."

"Daughter?" He looked at me in a blank sort of way, as if he'd forgotten he had a daughter. "Oh yes, you mean Muriel. Let's go in the house."

He led the way and I followed, flanked by the Doberman escorts and meanwhile wondering how many daughters this guy had and how many of them were missing. We went through a central foyer as big as a barn, with enough paintings on the walls to open a small art gallery, past a drawing room, billiard room and library, all with fourteen-foot ceilings and carpets as thick as the hair on a wintering bear.

Mrs. Riordon was in the kitchen flinging salad around in a wooden bowl the size of a dugout canoe. She was a nice big woman with greying blonde hair and red cheeks, a good-sized bust in the right place and legs no man would scorn. She wore a blue print dress with little white teapots all over it, and a pair of comfortable nurse-type shoes on her big feet. She gave me her hand but I didn't have it for long, just long enough to feel it was as cold as a North Atlantic herring, but maybe that was because of the chilly vegetables she'd been handling.

"Have a seat, Mr. Savage. We're just about to have lunch. I hope you like crêpes."

"I've been intimate with a few in my time."

Bud took an opened bottle of white wine from the fridge and poured two glasses, one for me and one for him. We sat at a cozy little table in one corner of the large kitchen. Behind me was a door through which I saw a dining room with chandelier, polished wood cabinets and a table as big as the deck of an aircraft carrier. Mrs. Riordon set the salad bowl on the table and followed up with hot plates bearing crêpes blanketed in a creamy cheese sauce. Whatever anguish the Riordons were suffering over their daughter's disappearance, it hadn't spoiled their appetites any.

"Has Mr. Bowman had any success in his enquiries?" Mrs. Riordon asked as she seated herself at the table.

I thought of Bowman's headless body lying sprawled in Watroboski's apartment. I chewed thoughtfully on a mouthful of seafood crêpe while I searched for an evasive answer. "He's a bit stumped for the moment. He wondered if he hadn't overlooked anything out here, so he asked me to see if I could turn up any clues."

"Does this mean it's going to cost us twice as much to find her?" Mr. Riordon said.

"Now shush, Bud. You know the money doesn't matter. What is it you need to know, Mr. Savage?"

"First off, who owns the house?"

"Jordan Ferris."

"And what's the arrangement here?"

"We take care of the place. He lives here some of the time. He's got an apartment in town too."

"And does he have a daughter as well?"

"Uh, no." A bit hesitant, Mrs. Riordon.

"Where is Mr. Ferris now?"

"He's got a secret place up in the mountains," Mr. Riordon said. "He's up there working on his campaign strategy."

"So he doesn't know about your difficulties?"

"No," Mrs. Riordon said.

"Don't you think he's got the kind of contacts that could help you?"

"Even if I did want his help," Mrs. Riordon said, "I don't know how to get in touch with him. He's deliberately made himself incommunicado. Besides, we don't want to bring Mr. Ferris into this. It wouldn't be good publicity."

"Publicity be damned. Your daughter's missing. You don't seem too worried about it."

"Now listen here, mister..."

"It's alright, Bud. Mr. Savage is only looking for an explanation. After all, he's working for us, aren't you, Mr. Savage?"

"In an advisory capacity to Mr. Bowman."

"I'll write a check," said Mrs. Riordon. "Will a hundred suffice to begin?"

"Right." I sighed inwardly. This was turning into a bit of a fruitcake case, but there had to be something behind it all to warrant the murder of two men. I'd have to take it from the beginning. "Why don't you tell me when and how your daughter disappeared."

"It was shortly after lunch two days ago," Mr. Riordon began, "when a van came up the driveway; this man knocked on the door and said he was here to replace an air conditioner. I said it was news to me, but he had a work order in hand for installation of a unit in Mr. Ferris' study. I didn't think too much of it at the time. Mr. Ferris usually left that sort of thing for me to attend to, but sometimes he took it upon himself to get after the repairmen. He's a sonofabitch when it comes to perfection. He'll junk a TV if it's got just a hint of a ghost image and he's a regular terror when it comes to his cars. He sent that Mussolini back to the garage four times before he got the exact shade of yellow he wanted."

"Okay, I get the idea. This repairman, would you recognize him again?"

"Sure. He was driving a Buzzell's van—that's the outfit that originally installed all our units—but he wasn't one of the regulars. He was really tall, almost seven feet, and as skinny as a rail. Blond hair and a long straight nose that was pressed close against his face. Couldn't tell you what color eyes because he wore wraparound sunglasses. He talked without moving his lips, like a ventriloquist. Now that I think of it, I wonder if he had any lips at all. He had a long jaw and there was something funny about his face, bulges in his cheeks, as if he had a hockey puck in the mouth. And just a sort of slit where the words came out. Couldn't see his teeth."

"Did he seem to know his way around or did he have to be shown where the study was?"

"Uh, I don't know," Bud said. "You see, when I opened the door, the dogs went crazy on me. I mean, they always act up for a stranger—you saw how they went for you—but usually all it takes is a holler from me and they shut right up. They're very well trained. But with this guy at the door, they wouldn't settle down. They would have torn him apart if I hadn't collared them in time. I think he got quite a scare from them. Anyway, I kicked them back in the hall and closed the door until I found out what this guy wanted. Then I went inside, put the leash on them and took them out the back door. I told Viv they were acting up and asked her to show the guy at the door where the study was. Then I took the dogs out for a run in the woods and by the time I got back the guy had finished his business and pulled out."

I turned to Mrs. Riordon. "What were your impressions of the man?"

"He looked the same as Bud described. He didn't say much to me, except that he'd want to keep the study door closed because when he started up the new machine, it was going to make a smell and there was no point in spreading it through the whole house. It made sense."

"What did he bring into the house?"

"A new air conditioner, a really big one." Mrs. Riordon held her arms out, measuring roughly a 3x2x2-foot volume. "But as it turned out, he didn't install it. He took it away with him again. Said all the old one needed was a new thermostat."

"How long was he alone in the study?"

"Long enough to take the panel off the fireplace," Bud said, "and get up the chimney into Muriel's room through her fireplace. You can come upstairs and see the markings in the chimneys, but how the hell a guy that size ever got up and around the switchbacks is beyond me."

"Okay, I'll see that in good time." I prompted Mrs. Riordon for more information. "Did you notice anything else about the man that might identify him?"

Mrs. Riordon clucked her tongue. "Now that you mention it, there was a name above the pocket on his coveralls. I thought at the time that his wife had done a pretty little job of stitching but that she hadn't finished the job. I thought it was intended to be the company name, Buzzell's, but all she'd done was *Buzz*."

"Nothing else?"

"He did make a peculiar noise when he walked."

"Explain."

"Well, as he followed me upstairs to the study, I heard this *clickety-clackety-click*. I thought he was snapping his fingers but when I turned to look I saw that was impossible because he had his hands full with the air conditioner. I was curious then, so when I opened the door to the study I let him go in first, to see if he hadn't some tools at his belt that struck together. But there were none. The sound was coming from his leg joints as he moved. A clicking sound like a cricket makes."

I chewed on that one for awhile. Tall skinny guy with wraparound sunglasses and a slit mouth. Makes cricket noises and drives the dogs wild. Goes by name of Buzz. It wasn't much of a personality profile but I got the general idea: a weirdo.

"How about a look upstairs?" I suggested.

"Second floor or third floor?" Bud said.

"Both of them if that's alright."

"Sure. Only reason I ask is that in this house you don't get to the third floor by climbing the stairs from the second."

"Oh? How do you get there?"

"You take the stairs to the second floor but the old staircase from second to third is sealed off. If you want to go up to the third, you take the elevator from this floor." Bud pointed down the short hallway to the rear of the house. "That's where our quarters are. The elevator's down there."

"Kind of a peculiar arrangement."

"Mr. Ferris fixed it up that way," Mrs. Riordon said. "The place out back is comfortable but it's really not big enough to accommodate Muriel too, what with the special equipment she needed and the space for her workroom. So Mr. Ferris kindly gave her the run of the third floor and fixed it up for her. There just didn't seem to be any need for a connecting passage between her floor and his floor; besides, it could have been dangerous if Muriel had run over the edge in her wheelchair."

"Okay, let's have a look at the study."

Both of the Riordons came up to the second floor to show me around. Jordan Ferris had extensive apartments at the front of the house: huge bedroom with shag carpet, king-size circular bed with room to spare for half a dozen queens; private lounge with bar and pinball machine—the room smelled nicely of aged whisky and imported cigars; kitchenette with all the accessories; lavish bathroom with sunken tub and gold enamelled fixtures. To the rear of the house: another library, a radio room with ham operator's outfit, an exercise room with gym equipment, and the study.

It had wall-to-wall books, a nice solid desk big enough to park a car on, four husky leather chairs standing around like bodyguards, an air conditioner on the windowsill and a fireplace with an engraved copper panel across the hearth.

"The house is a hundred and fifty years old," Bud said. "Maybe you noticed there's a fireplace in every room, although only the one in the central living room is functional. The chimneys are still intact but they're really not fit to burn a fire in, so the rest of the fireplaces are panelled off. Here's where the bastard went upstairs."

He took the copper panel off the fireplace. We put our heads together inside the chimney and he shone a flashlight up the flue. I could see where the old carbon-

and-dust layer had been scuffed off the brick wall all the way up to a switchback twelve feet above.

We went back downstairs and into an elevator not much bigger than a phone booth that took us up to the third floor. There were a couple of big rooms at the rear of the house that were used for storage, and up front, two more, Muriel's.

They were both big airy rooms with windows that admitted a lot of midday sun. A bathroom with some complicated toilet fixtures was built in between the two main rooms, with doors into both. The bedroom was the smaller of the two, with a bed in the corner and a push-button console beside it. There was a lot of sound equipment: a reel-to-reel tape recorder, miniature cassette deck, turntable with a complex record changer, quad speakers, wallrack of LP's, mikes on stands. A small arborite table stood against one wall, accompanied by a lone chair.

"And here's where he came out." Bud pulled the panel off the fireplace in the bedroom. Here the flue went up only four feet before taking a right angle turn to meet the chimney that rose from the study below. "Now I know that guy was skinny," Bud said, "but it beats me how he could have shimmied up the chimney and around two sharp turns without getting stuck."

It had me beat too, but it seemed that's how it'd be done. "Anything else been disturbed here?"

"Except for my having moved the panel to see what'd happened, nothing's been rearranged."

I walked into the other room. There was a low counter along one wall, covered with palettes and tubes of paint, rags and cans of thinner, bottles of brushes and pencils. And then there were about forty canvases in oils and acrylics, in various stages of completion, some of them lacquered and hung upon the walls, others of them standing on easels with outlines and basic tones blocked in. But without exception the subject matter was the same: insects.

A red and black ladybug nestled upon a broad green leaf, from whose tip hung a pendulous dewdrop. Body hair fuzzy with pollen, a monstrous honeybee rolled around on an incomplete sunflower. A man-sized praying mantis, forelegs locked about the headless body of its late lover, gazed pensively at a green inchworm suspended from a filament of spittle.

"This is Muriel's work?"

"Yes," Mrs. Riordon said. "She was fascinated by bugs. They're very good, aren't they, especially considering she painted with her mouth. This is the chair she worked in."

I had mistaken it for a laundry trolley. It was a hammock-slung leather seat with a complicated-looking headrest mounted on an aluminum frame. A battery-powered motor was connected by gearbox to four rubber tires.

"She controlled its movements with her head." Mrs. Riordon tilted the headrest to one side and the electric motor whirred as the vehicle pivoted smoothly upon one wheel. "It was built to specification by one of Mr. Ferris' engineers."

I snooped around the two rooms. No signs of a struggle. But then I supposed a limbless girl could hardly offer much in the way of resistance. I wondered if she had bothered. Despite the conveniences, this part of the house had a distinct air of enforced solitude. Between these front rooms and those at the rear, there was a landing half a flight lower than the floor, where once the stairs from below had met it but was now blocked off. That meant there was no way for Muriel in her wheeled apparatus to get to the elevator at the back of the house. She was trapped.

"Was she happy here?" I asked Mrs. Riordon.

"I should think so. She had her work: her paintings and her music."

"There's more to life than work. Didn't she ever leave these rooms?"

"She was extremely self-conscious of her handicap. All she wanted was to be left alone to her paintings."

"No friends, no visitors?"

"None."

"No communications with the outside world? Letters or telephone conversations?"

Mrs. Riordon paused. I could practically hear the cogs turning as she grappled with some dilemma. Her hesitation attracted Bud's attention.

"There was nobody..." he started but she cut him off with a wave of her hand.

"There were a few letters," she said.

"I never saw any letters for her," he said.

"They were enclosed in envelopes addressed to me," she said.

"You never told me that before," he said.

"Why the secrecy?" I said.

"That was Muriel's idea," Mrs. Riordon said. "She nurtured her secret existence. She was crazy about spy stories. She saw herself as a secret agent living completely underground, a great and anonymous artist. But as she became more successful as an artist in the last year, she must have felt a greater need for communication, so she picked up a couple of penpals."

"Any of those letters still around?"

"Mr. Bowman and I looked. They're all gone."

"Do you remember the names?"

"Really, Mr. Savage, do you think...?"

"Dammit, Viv, the girl's been kidnapped," Bud growled. "Give him the names."

"One was Joel Uranium, 134 Hoople Street. He's an astrologer whose ad she answered in *The Speaker*. He drew her horoscope. The other was Billy Crabner, #602, 1113 Scranton. She answered his ad in the Personals column and they got to be steady penpals. The only other is her agent, Len Moskovitz, but I relay all messages between them when I deliver her paintings to his gallery on Greenwich Avenue."

I finished jotting this info into my notebook. "I take it her paintings provide some income."

"Quite a good one. In two years she's put almost thirty thousand into her bank accounts."

I whistled. At that rate, there was probably a couple grand's worth of finished work in this room. "You must be very proud of her."

"Oh yes. And it's given me the opportunity to deal with Mr. Moskovitz and through him, a few of the gallery people who buy her work. Mind you, the money is all Muriel's."

Was it my imagination or did I detect a grimace from Bud? My first impression of him had been that of a womanizer. I wondered how well he managed his affairs on the caretaker's income he received from Ferris. Whatever it was, I bet it wasn't enough. Guys like Bud always want more.

"What's the arrangement with Moskovitz?"

"We have a contract. Muriel delivers a minimum of twelve paintings a year and Mr. Moskovitz is sole agent for the retail of her work."

"Does she have a will?"

"Yes. Twenty percent of her estate goes to me and the rest to various medical charities."

I was tempted to say that an arrangement like that hardly seemed generous towards the father of the artist, but I could see he probably felt the same way and there was no need to provoke a heated discussion on that point. What their interfamily financial affairs were was hardly my business.

"And do you have access to her bank account? I'm thinking now of what might happen if there was a ransom demand. There hasn't been one already, has there?"

"No," she said. "And that's odd, isn't it?"

"They might only be giving you time enough to get worried before making their demands. Maybe too they needed time to get her to someplace where she couldn't be found by the police or anyone else who might be looking for her."

"Muriel's money is split up. There's about ten thousand in bank bonds and ten thousand in a checking account. And then, you'll probably wonder about this but it's another of Muriel's crazy ideas, along the lines of some spy thriller, that she's got ten thousand cash in a safe deposit box."

"And where's the key?"

"Hidden."

I could see Bud was taking this in with a certain undivided interest. He was hanging on every word like a mountain climber with his fingernails in a groove of rock and his feet dangling over a thousand foot precipice. I could hear the cogs in his brain turning too. I'd bet dollars to doughnuts he had money on his mind. Or was I just projecting my own brand of wolfishness on the man?

I looked at my watch. I'd been here more than an hour. I'd had some lunch and a look around and asked a few questions and now I was getting tired of the Riordons. I didn't doubt they were getting tired of me too. Give us a break and fade, Savage.

Buzz lay on his belly watching blue movies. He humped the carpet. He held a chicken in his pincers, squeezing it softly. The chicken was scared stiff.

Crabby was bitching about money. He was pissed off at Buzz because he hadn't found any at Watroboski's. Buzz didn't care. He'd had fun anyway. The heads were buried in the back yard. He'd dig them up in a month and eat the worms.

"Muriel's going to get the key. But that's not enough. I wonder if Mrs. Riordon's worried by now. If I sent her a note after Muriel phones... I'll bet she'd shit."

Two men were fucking one woman. A big man was fucking a little boy. Buzz wished Crabby would shut up. He couldn't hear the moans and groans. That was the best part.

"You think those bees are smart enough to follow a map?"

"They'll do anything I tell them," Buzz said.

"Okay, you get them ready. I'm going to find a typewriter." Crabby came down out of the net in the upper corner of the room. "You hear me, Buzz?"

"I heard. Fuck off."

Crabby went away and Buzz could hear the boy yelling as a baboon fucked his ass. That was more like it. Buzz fooled around a bit with the chicken. It only squawked once but it was a loud one. Buzz got rough with it and split the bird open from stem to stern.

The heart was still beating. It made a tasty appetizer.

When I got back to town, I pulled off the expressway into Lothario's, a drive-in burger joint. As soon as I drove into an empty parking slot, a TV unit dollied up in front of the windshield and the screen began to flicker with fornicating couples. This was Lothario's gimmick: blue movies with your burger. The first fifteen minutes were free but if you wanted to watch more after that, you had to start feeding the machine quarters.

I ordered a coffee and a young brunette in a ponytail and red cheerleader's outfit brought it out to me. The other waitress was wearing shorts and a halter top. There was no uniform at Lothario's but the girls had to show their legs. I paid my girl for the coffee and asked her, "Does that number mean what I think it means?"

She tugged the waist of her red sweater with the big white numerals 38 on the front. She had a quick smile for me. "It's not my age, if that's what you're wondering."

"You've got a few nice wrinkles in that sweater."

She snugged in the waist with her hands on her hips. "There's a couple that are pretty hard to iron out."

"I'll bet they're like knotted muscles: they ought to be carefully kneaded out."

"I don't know. You look like a guy with cold hands."

"Cold hands, warm heart." I slipped my hand out the window and put my arm around her waist. "What's your name?"

"Tracey."

"I like it." I gave her bum a friendly squeeze. She was as hot and wholesome as fresh-baked bread.

"And yours?" She stroked a finger under my chin and tilted my head a few degrees up until our eyes met and locked. Hers were baby blue.

"Keith."

"You want another coffee, Keith? I've got some other customers to take care of."

I let the coffee pass but I got her phone number from her before she went away to take care of business. With a casual eye on the TV screen, I reviewed my afternoon with the Riordons. There was something about them that bothered me. Grief was absent with their daughter. Maybe they were just as happy to be rid of her. A lot of people don't like mutants.

And there were a lot of them around. Ever since the nuclear generating plant explosion, the so-called Nuke Fluke, which never should have happened, if you could believe the experts, mutants had been springing up like mushrooms. For most of us who lived in and around Nova York at the time of the Fluke, we had only the occasional blackout and hot flashes to contend with. For those people, and their descendants, who had lived downwind of Nuke Flats at that time, physical abnormality and mental derangement were their lot in life. At one time there'd been some active lobbying to undergo 'selective termination' of the worst of the mutants, but nobody knew just where the lines would be drawn and eventually the liberals raised a hue and cry against the projected genocide and there the issue had lain for the past couple of years, still hotly debated in bars and backroom conventions of the American Nazi Party, but for the most part, accepted by the general public as a sort of 'mark of Cain' on the face of modern man.

But then Muriel wasn't that kind of mutant anyway. She was a handicapped but talented young lady with a handsome bank balance and a couple of penpals that I'd better get after if I was going to make any headway in this case. I chucked my empty coffee cup into a garbage can, waved goodbye to that cute little cheerleader and headed crosstown to Scranton.

When I climbed out of the car on the 1100 block my nostrils were assaulted by the ripe stench of garbage gone long uncollected. Scranton was a concrete canyon of what had once been business buildings in Central West, but after the Fluke and the race riots, most of the occupants pulled out of town. Slumlords bought properties for a song, hacked the buildings into loft-style apartments and began renting to the Upper West refugees that had been burned out of their homes in '80. I walked up the street. I would have walked up the sidewalk but I couldn't see it for piles of funky garbage. I put my hand in my pocket and closed my fingers reassuringly around the Viper. In a tumble of chicken bones and eggshells I saw a pair of rats the size of alley cats. One of them hissed at me as I passed. I yanked the Viper out of my pocket and blew his head off. His pal moved right in and skinned him on the spot. It was that kind of neighborhood.

Up ahead, a twenty-foot Nazi banner hung from a third floor window. I heard martial music and a chorus of beer-laden voices singing the Horst Wessel song. I'd driven past this place before. It was the Goering Hotel, a flophouse of sorts for fascist druggies who ran away from their homes in the midwest and came to Nova York where the movement was at its rawest. That meant they didn't go in for boycotting Jewish merchants; they stalked bignosed girls on the night streets and mailed parts of them to their fathers with advice to leave town.

I crossed the street to 1113 Scranton. It was a big grey anonymous building of eight stories. I checked the occupant board and found two names, Crabner and LeVeen, listed for #602. I thumbed the buzzer.

The door buzzed back. I pushed my way through and walked straight into the elevator. Trusting soul: didn't care who was calling on him. I shook a butt out of my pack and had a couple of drags as the elevator pulled its way hand-over-hand up to the sixth floor. I walked down a tiled hallway and used my knuckles on #602. The door opened as far as a pair of chains would let it and a tall guy with grey eyes peering out of a tanned bearded face gave me the once-over.

"Shit," he said.

"Sorry I don't come up to expectations."

"What are you selling?"

"I'm looking for Billy Crabner."

"He doesn't live here any more."

"Where can I find him?"

"What's it to you?"

"I owe him some money."

"How much?"

"What's it to you?"

He started unlatching the chains. "You by yourself? You want to come in?"

I looked up and down the hall. I seemed to be alone. "Yeah, if you've got a couple of minutes to spare." I stepped inside as he pulled the door back. I looked into a big sunny living room with flowerpots on the windowsills and bamboo prints hanging on the walls. There was a bookcase along one wall with a TV and some wooden sculpted birds atop it. A low couch flanked another wall and there were pillows and a beanbag chair sprawled in between. I headed for the beanbag chair but before I got halfway across the room, a pigeon, which had been perched on the windowsill amid the foliage, took to the wing with a cry and darted out the open window. I watched it loop upwards to the roof on the other side of the airshaft.

LeVeen went to the window and stuck his head outside. "Hermie. Come on back, man. Hermie, Hermie." After a bit more of that he gave it up and pulled his head back inside. "It's no use. I can't get him used to strangers. He freaks out immediately anyone comes in. He wouldn't even stay in the same room with Crabner, and he was here for six months."

"How long's he been gone?"

"Three weeks. The prick owes me a hundred clams for the rent. How much money you owe him? Maybe you could just pass it on to me and we'd cancel the debts. Want a cold beer? Toke? Snort?"

"A beer's fine." I followed him into the kitchen as he went for it. I looked into the other two rooms. I could see where once it had been one big office room and since been subdivided by pre-fab partitioning. There was a bedroom with a lot of clothes thrown helter-skelter and a 4x6-foot mirror dominating one wall. The other room had a big plywood sheet propped up on sawhorse legs, a draftsman's lamp clamped on the edge, a typewriter and boxes of paper placed in orderly array, a bulletin board on the wall with a handful of newspaper clippings. "You work here?"

LeVeen handed me a bottle of Heineken. "Sorry I

don't have any glasses. Yeah, I'm writing a TV script." He leaned in the doorway of the workroom. "This used to be Billy's room. Before he left I used to work on the kitchen table. This is better but the rent is fucking killing me. I'm trying to find a little woman to move in and pay half the rent. Somebody to do a little cooking and cleaning up too. I'll fuck her silly, lick her asshole, do anything she wants, so long as she gets out of the house at nine every morning and leaves me alone for eight hours a day so I can get some work done."

"You're not hard to please."

"That's what I used to tell Billy. But the little fucker was always getting on my nerves. He'd play his banjo while I was trying to work. At night when I'd bring home a piece of tail, he'd sit around in his wheelchair with a dirty old robe on, farting the air blue and trying to gross out my chicks. He used to be into Yoga before he fell out of a tree and smashed his spine, paralyzed him from the waist down. But he was still as flexible as Rubberman and could put both ankles behind his head. He'd sit there watching TV and gnaw on his toenails. Ask me if that wouldn't turn a girl's stomach. We fought all the time. Finally he just buggered off."

"Has he been getting any mail here?"

"Not since he left." LeVeen went into the living-room, picked up a small wooden box from the bookcase and pulled out a joint as fat as a weiner. "Want to help me with this? I was just going to have one to relax after a hard day at the typewriter. I'm expecting a young lady to come up here in a few minutes."

"Didn't Crabner leave any forwarding address?"

"He was too cagey for that. He knew I'd track him down and squeeze the hundred out of him." LeVeen took a long hit off the joint and passed it over.

"Do you know anything about a chick named Muriel? She was a penpal of Crabner's." I took a drag off the joint. It was Columbian. I could taste the grit from under the nails of the peons that had picked it.

"I never knew Billy to have any chicks. Why don't you just leave the money with me and if there's any left over after my hundred I'll see that he gets it. He might turn up sometime to pick up some stuff he left."

"What kind of stuff?"

"Cardboard box full of junk. Music books mostly."

"Mind if I take a look at it?"

LeVeen uncoiled himself from his squat position on a pillow and brought the cardboard box out from his workroom. I overturned it and went through the stuff as I put it back in the box. There was a lot of music books: *Bluegrass Picking* and *101 Banjo Chords* and more of the same. There was a folder of pencil sketches: longlegged women being humped by giant spiders. Pretty meaty stuff. The closest thing to a letter was a bill for $36.85 from Luna Deli. I asked LeVeen what that was about.

"Crabner had a weird stomach. He was a sort of veggie, lived mostly on yogurt and bean sprouts, brown rice and seaweed. But every night, without fail, he'd send out an order to Luna Deli for this weird sandwich. Oyster paste with Swiss cheese and Spanish onion on pumpernickel. His Gonad Burger is what he called it. Had one for midnight snack every night he lived here."

"If he was a veggie, what was he doing eating oysters?"

"He didn't count them. He ate eggs too. Along with the Gonad Burger he used to get a side order of dill pickles, but he wouldn't eat them. He'd just spread them out on the paper and sniff them. Weird, huh? And you wonder why I'm glad he's gone. Anyway, he was such a regular with Luna Deli, seeing as how they're one of the few that deliver these days, that they let him run up a monthly tab and he paid it when his Disability Check came in. He never missed a bill. But then he fucks off and lets his roomie take it in the ear for a hundred bucks rent money. I'd like to meet him on the street—I'd push his wheelchair in front of a fast transport."

"You say he hasn't received any mail here nor left a forwarding address? What about his Disability Checks?"

"Beats me," LeVeen said. "Hey, there's the buzzer,

man. Here comes skin on the hoof. It's been nice talking to you. Sure you won't leave me that money? No? Well, I don't blame you. Leave your name and I'll pass it on to Billy if he ever comes back."

I gave him my card, along with ten bucks. "Let me know if he gets any mail. I'd like to get a line on the man."

"So would I. Hate to give you the bum's rush but you know how it is."

I went out the door and down the hall. Just as I got to the elevator, a leggy redhead in a slinky dress and high heels sauntered out of the car and headed in the direction of #602. As the elevator door closed me in I heard a "Baby, you're lookin' swell" and then a squealed "Ronneeeeeee!" As the elevator descended, I took out my notebook, jotted down LeVeen's phone number and, on the Things To Do page, wrote 'Check Department Health—Disability Checks.'

4

Back out on the street again, a fine mist was drizzling out of the sky and making life miserable for a couple of alkies who were sitting on the curb, propped back-to-back as though they planned on spending the night there. As usual, the lights had been shot out on this street and it was dark enough that I didn't see the punks around my car until I got within ten feet of the wagon. They were wreathed in clouds of reefer smoke and the misty smell of stale beer on sweaty clothes. Three of them sat on the hood while a fourth tried to get a bent coat hanger through a slot in the window. They were white boys but they were dressed head to toe in black leather and there was charcoal on their faces. Night fighters.

"Scram." I pulled the Viper from one pocket and a penlight from the other. I angled the light across my hand so they could see the gun.

"Essen mein arse," said the one with the coat hanger.

I shot him in the leg. His knee banged against the car door as he took the bullet somewhere in the calf. He tried to get a grip on the door handle but his fingers missed and he fell on his ass. I kicked him away from the door. He screamed. The other three birds sat woodenly on the left fender. I unlocked the door and slid behind the wheel. They climbed off the fender and I drove away.

I turned onto Seventh and went downtown. The street lights were good here and there were people on the beat; people looking for sex, dope, money, excitement; people looking for lost dogs, lost children and lost dreams. I wished them better luck than I was having in my search for Muriel.

I drove through Timeless Square. Lots of people here, going in and out of movie-houses and drama-dromes, restaurants and sex clubs. All white folks. No spooks in sight. No spooks south of Central Park. NNoot since the race riots. Too bad. I missed the spooks. The streets used to be funky. Now they were just gritty. There was no place a white man could hear a decent jazz combo this side of South Park. Go uptown if you dare, white boy, but you'd better go blackface and take your chances. What was left to us was the mechanized backbeat of Hitler rock or the diddleybop syrup of CBX balladeers. There was some of that on the radio right now, a sick ballad about some jerk who'd castrated himself in an anti-war protest and now decides that he misses his tool but all he's got is four inches of rubber hose to play with. I switched channels to WNAZ: a hard-driving song called "Wastage" by a group called Krieghof, and they were celebrating the rape of schoolboys. At least they had the positive approach.

I was hungry. It seemed the last good thing I'd had to eat was the pussy of a blonde chick I'd picked up a few nights ago. I could still taste her under my tongue. She'd been sweet but not very nourishing, like cotton candy. I needed a steak or, failing that, some black cooze, but like I said, spooks were out of fashion in 1981.

The music was fading in and out. So were the street lights. After I went through a red light without stopping, I realized it was me. A sudden hot flash left me with sweaty palms trying to keep my grip on the steering wheel. The next one gave me a couple of seconds' blackout and a moist feeling in my crotch like I'd just pissed myself. I was having one of my little attacks of Fluke blackouts. I had to get off the street before I had an accident. Luckily, home was just around the corner. I pulled the car off Seventh, went four blocks and idled the car into a backyard garage where twenty other wagons crouched beneath a couple of fluorescent lights and an old tough named Grumpy kept the stable in order with a sawed-off Ithaca pump shotgun. I left the car with Grumpy and got inside the building before the next flash took me on the stairs and left me wondering where I was. I sat there a couple of minutes and smoked a cigarette. A homely girl in a red sweater came up the stairs with a paper bag squashed between her tits. She had a face that looked like an open can of worms. Another Fluke victim. They were everywhere. This one's name was Marsha and I knew now where I was. Marsha was my neighbour down the hall.

"What's the matter, ace? You're looking all in." She stopped a few feet below me, hiked up her skirt and put a high-heeled foot a few steps above the other. "Need some help?"

"Know where I can find a chick named Muriel Riordon-Ferris?" I dropped my cigarette and couldn't find it again. I was almost totally blacked out. I could see this ugly broad with the forty-pound knockers just an arm's length away but I couldn't find my cigarette or a little lost girl with no limbs. And I called myself a snooper.

"You don't need no Muriel when you've got a Marsha just down the hall. C'mon." She hooked one arm under my armpit and hoisted me to my feet. I just tagged along. Marsha worked in a canning factory and had muscles a stevedore might envy. Every week she brought home a dozen complimentary cans of mercurized tuna and fed them to the stray cats that wandered from the roofs down to her place via the fire escape.

Now the neighborhood was full of cats running around with their ass ends out of control, falling off fences and landing on their heads like cats do when they've OD-ed on mercury. And if you thought that was tragic, you could look around and see the people who ate the same stuff. They made Minimata disease victims look like ballerinas on amphetamines. Limited responsibility and no public liability was the name of the game for food manufacturers these days. They knew the product was screwed up but they didn't have anything else to offer the public. So they printed a proper evaluation of contents and let the public take their chances. *Caveat Emptor* was just another way of saying, 'Let them eat mercury.'

By this time we were in front of what I supposed was my door and Marsha had her hand in my pocket on the pretense of finding my keys but for a girl who's adroit enough to run the tin cutter at the factory, she's not very swift at coming up with the keys. Instead, she's got a grip on my cock through the lining of my pocket and she's making like a farmer's daughter with a cow's teat. If I hadn't the presence of mind to interrupt, I'd have had a pantleg full of milk in a minute.

I gave her an elbow under the chin. She sat on the floor. I opened the door. She got halfway through. I was trying to get it closed but she had one of her tits in the way. I couldn't get the chain fastened. I felt like crying. Tell me it's not going to be one of those nights.

I woke up and looked at my digital clock. It was shortly before midnight, the same day. I got out of bed. There were a couple of empty beer bottles on the floor. I didn't remember leaving them there. I went to the bathroom and had a leak. There was hair in my mouth. I didn't know anything about that either and I didn't want to think about it. I had a long hard look at myself in the mirror. I didn't like what I saw and I didn't like the way I felt. I stepped into the shower and got clean again. I gave myself a blast of cold towards the end, then climbed out and towelled the goose bumps off my body.

I phoned Wendy. Nobody home. She was probably out with that rugby player. It'd serve her right if she got crotch rot from him. Maybe if I took a run over there now I could get into her place and pick up the mail I'd sent there. Fuck it. That could wait until tomorrow. I wanted to get in touch with that astrologer too for whatever info I might get out of him but it was too late for that too. It was too late for just about everything. Everything but a midnight snack. I still hadn't had anything to eat. I checked the fridge. There was some hamburger that had turned black and some cheese that had turned green. The fridge was full of visual delights but nothing that was fit to put inside me.

I decided I'd go out for something to eat. I put some clothes on, locked up and went down the back stairs to the garage. It was a shame I couldn't walk the ten blocks to Sammy's, my favourite all-night hash stand down in the Village, but it just wasn't a safe thing to do this time of night. Besides, after a bite or two, I might feel horny enough to scoot over to Swingles and pick up a hot little actress type to play the lead role in one of my porn fantasies.

"Evening, Mr. Savage." Grumpy sat in the doorway of his little office with the Ithaca across his knees. He was wearing a red felt hunting cap and a pair of beat-up denim overalls with rolled-up cuffs held in place by large safety pins. Grumpy was fifty years old although he looked closer to a hundred and fifty. He had the dessicated skin of a pharaoh but his eyes were as bright as freshly volcanized obsidian.

"Hi Grumpy, what's new?" Through the door I could see *These Violent Times* on the TV, with lots of screams and gunfire rolling off the soundtrack.

"You still owe me for last month."

"I'm sure I paid you." The old bastard knew I had blackouts. And he had a dexie habit that needed every extra dollar he could wangle out of me.

"I wouldn't forget a thing like that. You don't have a receipt do you?"

I looked in my wallet. I didn't have a receipt. I gave Grumpy twenty bucks.

"Thanks, Mr. Savage."

"What about my receipt?"

"Oh yeah, I almost forgot." He ducked into his office and wrote me one.

"Where's Werewolf tonight?"

"Out killing cats, I imagine." Grumpy shook a pair of dexies out of a matchbox and popped them in his mouth. He offered me one and I took it.

"I hope he's not eating them. He'll get mercury poisoning."

"He knows better than that. He don't kill them for

food anyway. It's just for sport." Grumpy grinned, showing me a mouthful of stainless steel teeth. No sooner had he spoken than we heard a terrific yowl, high-pitched and spitting, that ended just as suddenly in a guttural rip. Then a long and low-pitched howl that sent the hackles scurrying up the back of my neck. "Sounds like he got another one."

In a minute Werewolf strolled into the garage with a tattered grey cat in his mouth. He dropped it on the floor and then placed one forepaw atop its head like a white hunter posing with his dead lion. Werewolf was Grumpy's dog, part collie and part mastiff, a big yellow bastard with a hunchback like a hyena. He was kind of a sly old bugger, but fairly goodnatured for those few people who'd troubled to make friends with him. I put a hand out slowly and rubbed my knuckles atop Werewolf's bony skull. He half-closed his eyes and growled softly like a worn-out chainsaw.

"He likes you, Mr. Savage." Grumpy took the cat away from under Werewolf's paw and threw it in a garbage can. "He won't let anybody else lay a hand on him. Course, not many people want to, what with the mange."

"Yeah." I put my hand back in my pocket and went to the car. I wheeled out onto the street and drove to Sammy's. But it was closed. Broken glass littered the sidewalk and the windows were boarded over. Punks had gone to work with spray cans and covered the plywood sheets with swastikas and hate slogans.

I cursed the sonsabitches that were turning this city into a fascist cesspool. They hadn't been satisfied with chasing the spooks uptown. Now they were going after the Yids and the Orientals. I drove east to Eighth and then uptown. Now where was I going to get something to eat? There were lots of places open but I'd grown accustomed to Sammy's, where you could get an extra slice of cheese without being charged another dime, and bagels hot from the oven and a 'Thank you, come again' when you paid. I was leery of strange delis. I bought an egg salad sandwich once from an East Side joint and the fucking sandwich was full of eggshell.

Whoever'd put the egg through the chopper hadn't bothered to shell it. I was crapping eggshell for days afterward and I have the scars to prove it.

I was crossing 20th when I saw a huge neon crescent moon halfway down the block and the name *LUNA DELI* blinking blue letters at the night. I circled the block. It was just a little past midnight. I parked the Astro on the other side of the street and walked across. The place was doing a ripping business. Three old guys in white bibs worked behind a long counter, slapping sandwiches together, scooping sauerkraut and pickled eggs into take-out packs, while another old bird with a pair of wire-rim glasses beat on a cash register and manipulated the gelt from a steady flow of customers. Opposite the counter was a row of two-man booths where young couples sat, holding hands over liverwurst sandwiches and coming alive with canned Pepsi. I walked to the rear of the store, got a can of beer from the cooler, ordered a chicken salad with mozarella on a bun and had it in my hand inside ten seconds. I paid for it and sat in the last booth at the rear. I'd had about two bites of my sandwich and a gurgle of beer so cold it made my eyes water, when a very tall guy in a black raincoat came in and picked up a sixpack from the cooler. His height was enough to grab my attention, but what really clinched it was that he was wearing wraparound shades. And it was pitch dark outside. He went past me without a sideward glance and stopped at the counter.

"Oyster, Spanish and Swiss on pumpernickel, right?" said one of the old guys behind the counter. "Pickles on the side?"

The tall guy nodded, took the bagged sandwich from the server and stepped to the cashier. By then I was out the door. I glanced up and down the street. No dark blue van in sight. I went across the street and wolfed down my sandwich in a dark doorway. The tall guy, whom I presumed to be Buzz, came out of Luna Deli and headed towards Eighth on foot. I tagged along. There were a lot of street punks on Eighth but I still had the Viper to help me out of trouble.

When he got to the Avenue, he turned and walked uptown with the traffic. I was on the same side of the street now and about a hundred feet behind. He glanced back a couple of times and I worried that he'd picked me out as a tail. I crossed the street at the next intersection and walked fast to keep level with him. He was still glancing behind him and then I saw why.

He raised an arm and stepped out from the curb. A dark blue van pulled out of the traffic flow and stopped beside him. Buzz climbed in and the van shot away. I jumped off the curb and tried to flag down a cab. About twenty of them went past me and by then the blue van was long gone. I cursed my luck, walked back to the Astro and drove home.

Wendy was there ahead of me. She was in bed with a bottle of wine and a handful of joints. She had the TV tuned to the blue movie channel and the sound turned off. All I could hear was a low hum coming from under the covers.

"Hi lover." I threw my clothes this way and that and crawled into the sack with her. It was nice coming home to this. I didn't regret having made copies of my keys for her, so long as she knocked before entering.

"I ought to shove this up your ass," she said, pulling a live vibrator from under the sheets. She was a cute strawberry blonde but she had a redhead temper. "Where've you been?"

"Looking for truth," I said. "And don't wave that thing under my nose. You'll make me horny."

"I'll make you more than horny."

"Promises, promises. Did you bring my mail?"

"Yes, and I saw Dr. Aquarius this afternoon. He said he'd talk to you. I've got his phone numbers."

"Good girl."

"You just don't appreciate the extent of it." She lit a joint, put the ember end in her mouth and shotgunned me in the nostrils. When the joint was finished, she dove headfirst under the covers, leaving her pussy within kissing range. Her hot wet mouth enveloped me.

"Mmmm. Bad girl."

I took the vibrator from her and moved it around the

musky folds of her wet puss. Her ass quivered as I moved the throbber in and out. It got too slippery to hold onto. I put it aside and used my tongue. We took a break and lay cheek to cheek, legs entwined, hands nestled in each other's damp crotch.

"I think I'd better go home," she said after a while.

"Not until I've screwed you."

"Not tonight, Keith."

I slapped her across the face. "Mr. Savage to you, bitch."

She sprang out of bed and grabbed her jeans. "Fuck you, Mr. Savage."

I rolled off the bed and grabbed her wrist, gave her a yank that tumbled her sideways across my leg. She took a header into the bed and I gave her ass a smack like a gunshot as she sailed past. I climbed onto her back before she could get up again, jerked one hand forward to the bedpost and snapped an open cuff tight on one wrist, then the other.

"You fucking perv," she yelled. "Let me go or I'll scream the fucking walls down."

"Scream away." I got an orange from the kitchen and jammed it into her mouth. With a pair of neckties I bound her ankles to the brass posts at the foot of the bed. She was crying now but I didn't care. I had a hardon as stiff as a riot stick.

I put a record on the stereo. Metal Machine Music. It was just a lot of noise like metal grating and glass breaking and feedback echoing through a rusty drainpipe. I turned it up loud until it sounded like we were inside a factory run amuck. I pulled the belt off my pants and slapped her ass with it until her buns were red as cherries. I was fascinated by the way her skin turned pale white for an instant after the belt came down, and then blushed a violent red again. She moaned and thrashed about but she wasn't going anywhere.

"You like the belt best of all, you little slut. Wiggle your ass if you want some more."

She wiggled her ass and I hit her some more until my arm was dead. I felt like an over-worked whip man in a ship full of galley slaves. My balls registered an overload. I knelt between her outspread legs, jerked her hips upwards and jammed my cock into her. She sighed around the orange like she'd been waiting all night for it. I rammed her back and forth, licking the sweat from between her shoulder blades, feeling her ass squirm beneath me and then bang bang bang I was going going gone.

Hours later I awoke. There was something in the apartment. I went out to the kitchen and turned on the light. An alley cat, so badly OD-ed on mercurized tuna, couldn't jump from the floor to the waist level sideboard that would get him to the windowsill. I should have done the cat a favor and thrown it down the airshaft; five stories down, it'd surely land on its head. But I didn't. I put it on the windowsill and it climbed down onto the fire escape. Werewolf would take care of it.

I went back to bed, took the cuffs and bonds off Wendy and rubbed some oil on her bum. I pulled the covers over her and kissed her goodnight. Her lips tasted of orange.

Buzz and Crabby drove around town. Buzz put away four beers and used his pincers to crush the cans down to the size of half-dollars. The van stank of vinegar. Crabby had his pickles spread all across the dashboard. They sang along with the loud killer music on WNAZ.

They cruised down to Washington Square Park. Young couples sat around n the benches, talking and smoking, watching frisbee throwers. Crabby rolled down the window and asked a boy and girl if they wanted to smoke some weed. The kids came over to the van to talk about it. Buzz got out and put the pincer grip on their necks so they couldn't move or yell. Crabby sprung the rear door and Buzz dragged them into the back of the van.

They drove down to the waterfront and parked. Buzz fucked the boy and Crabby fucked the girl. Then

Buzz bit their heads off and threw the bodies out the back door and into the bay.

"I wonder if this guy knows anything he shouldn't." Crabby fingered the business card they'd found in the wallet Buzz had taken from Bowman.

They drove around to check out the address. Crabby climbed the wall and jimmied the second story window, then went downstairs and let Buzz in. As soon as Buzz came into the office, he smelled sugar. He went to the bottom drawer in the desk and found the box. He took a handful of sugar cubes and popped them one after the other into his slit mouth.

Crabby jimmied the filing cabinet and looked through the files. He played back the message on the Memoryphone. He picked up the guitar and plucked a few tunes on it.

They tidied up. Crabby wanted Buzz to leave the sugar but Buzz had finished most of it by then and took the rest away with him. When they got back home, Crabby cleaned up the mess in the back of the van and Buzz buried the heads in the back yard.

When I got up in the morning, Wendy had already gone. I read the note she'd lipsticked on the fridge door. 'My bum hurts, you beast. My turn next time. Love and bondage, Wen.'

I went out to buy some milk and eggs for breakfast and picked up a paper while I was at it. Bowman and Watroboski had made half a column on the front page, not because anyone cared about another two dead men, but because headless corpses sold copy. The police were following up on a description given by a woman in the apartment adjacent to the scene of the crime. The heads had not yet been recovered.

Returning to my place, I called Dr. Aquarius at his University office. He was just leaving for a seminar he said, but if I liked I could call him back or meet him at his office at lunchtime. I said I'd meet him.

I made myself an omelet and a pot of coffee. I turned on the TV and watched the morning news while I ate breakfast. No mention of the double decapitation murder.

I spilled out the contents of the envelope I'd mailed to Wendy the day before. I burned the plastic gloves, the card with the Cosmo address and the cellophane wrapper of the paperback. I put fifty bucks in my wallet; I lifted one leg of the bed, pulled off the wheel mount plug and shoved the rest of the money up inside the hollow brass leg. Ever since the run on the banks during the race riots, I've kept my money in my own security caches. I folded Muriel's chart and put it with her photo in my jacket pocket.

I drank my coffee and breezed through the first twenty pages of *Spiders of Mars*. I couldn't read any further because the center of pages 20-180 had been cut out to leave room for the poisonous spider. After twenty pages, I didn't want to read any more anyway. It was pretty gory stuff and my breakfast hadn't settled in yet. I was still troubled by this business of the booby-trapped book. Had Watroboski given it to me to put me out of the way because I was enquiring after Uranium, or had it really been intended for him? If so, who wanted Watroboski dead and for what reason? Because he knew too much about Muriel, through their letters? Was it possible Watroboski had been one of the kidnap plotters but now that his usefulness was over, one of the others had cut him out of the deal?

Questions questions questions. What kind of kidnapping was this anyway? There hadn't even been a ransom demand yet. And who was 'Natalie Ferris' and what was her interest in Muriel?

I phoned the hospital to see if Uranium had come out of his coma yet. The ward nurse told me there was no improvement. I passed on my best wishes without leaving a name and hung up.

I took the Viper from under my pillow, cleaned and oiled it and replaced the two spent cartridges. I brushed my teeth and locked the apartment. Grumpy and Werewolf were dozing by the garage door as I walked in to get the Astro. Werewolf opened one eye and yawned at me. I got the wagon out and drove over to the office. I still had a lot of time to kill before I could see Aquarius.

I bought a coffee from the machine in the lobby and carried it upstairs to my dungeon. The place was stuffy. I opened the window and turned on the fan. I propped my heels on the desk, lit a butt and sipped my coffee. As usual, it was bitter. I pulled open the bottom desk drawer where I kept a box of sugar cubes. It wasn't there. Someone had stolen my sugar.

I inspected the lock on my filing cabinet. I couldn't see any signs of tampering but that didn't mean anything. A good boxman could have opened it in five seconds with the right kind of lockpick, and left no sign. I looked through my files but I couldn't find anything missing. I thumbed on the Replay button of the Memoryphone to see if anyone had called and left any messages. Mrs. Riordon had.

"Mr. Savage, I called your office but you weren't in. Just after you left yesterday, a special delivery letter came in the mail. It's from the people that took Muriel. They want ten thousand dollars delivered to Big Bass Lake tomorrow afternoon at three o'clock. I don't know what to do. Please call me back when you can."

I fired up another cigarette and stared at the ceiling where the fly specks were as thick as the freckles on a redhead's nose. Ten thousand dollars ransom for a kidnapped girl was a bargain basement price. Either this was an amateur who didn't know what price to ask or it was a pro who saw ten grand as an ante to open negotiations for much bigger stakes. I bet on the latter. I dialed the Riordon's number and got the lady on the line.

"Oh, Mr. Savage, it's you." She sounded quite calm and self-possessed. "I'm afraid I was a bit flustered when I called you yesterday but I think I've got things under control now. I went to the bank this morning and got the ten thousand dollars. I think it's a small price to pay for Muriel's return."

"Small price is right. Mrs. Riordon, I think that ten thousand is going to be just a drop in the bucket towards the final ransom demands. This is probably just a test of faith to see that you haven't brought the police into it. You won't get Muriel back that easily."

"You're so suspicious, Mr. Savage."

"In my line of work, you learn to suspect everyone."

"Everyone?"

"Don't misunderstand me. I only wish you'd forestall payment until I've had a chance to come out and look over the situation."

"So long as you come by three o'clock. Regardless of what you think, I intend to go through with the payment. After all, we're not making any progress elsewhere, are we?"

I admitted that solid leads were as scarce as gold coins. I told her I had a lunch appointment concerning the case but that I would come out to Cloverlea as soon as I was finished. She asked me if I had spoken with either of Muriel's correspondents. I said I'd found one but he couldn't tell me anything useful and I hadn't found the other yet but I was still looking. I told her to expect me out there about two o'clock. I'd barely got the phone back on the hook when it rang.

"Savage? Listen, this is LeVeen. You asked me to let you know if Crabner got anything in the mail. Well, something came this morning. I think maybe it's a key. It's in one of those little padded envelopes the film companies give out for mail processing."

"Any return address?"

"No, but it's got a Cloverlea postmark."

"Look, can I come over there now and see it?"

"No way. I'm just about to walk out the door. I've got a meeting with the IRS in half an hour. The bastards are trying to wring my balls for money I haven't even made. Then I've got to go uptown for a story conference with the CBX people. That's good for four hours at least. I won't be back home until after six. Why don't you drop by around seven and you can see what's what. I'll tuck the mail away in a safe place. Crabner won't see it before you."

I said okay, that I would see him at that time, and if Crabner showed up in the meanwhile, LeVeen should try to keep him there until I had a chance to talk to him. I dumped the phone back in its cradle and looked at my watch. It was time to cruise on over to the University and talk to Dr. Aquarius.

The University was built on one huge block of real estate. The separate faculty buildings, eight to twelve stories high, were packed together shoulder-to-shoulder around the block's perimeter like the columns of a huge temple. Within the enclave was the 20-story Centrex building that housed the administration offices, maintenance facilities, a two-story shopping mall, theatre, cafeterias and whatever else a university needed besides classrooms. Around Centrex was a modest little park with hedges, fountains and benches where kids sprawled to neck, smoke dope and sometimes study. By the time I got the Astro safely harboured in one of the parking towers, it was almost eleven-thirty, in-between-class time, and the walkways were full of kids with books. I asked a couple of pretty coeds where the Psych Building was and steered my footsteps in that direction.

Dr. Aquarius' office was on the top floor of the Psych Building. He wasn't back yet from his seminar when I announced myself to the secretary but she told me I could wait in the lounge across the hall. I strolled in and took an easy chair next to the window where I could look across the campus. A few academic types were planted around a coffee table at the other end of the lounge and they were tossing around psychological jive talk like it was music to their ears.

"You know what I told him to do with his orgone generator? I said he ought to hook it up to his manic-depressive wife and give her five hundred volts across the medulla. That'd cure her of the hiccups *and* her Electra complex."

"The poor fellow was anal compulsive. No matter how much I pressed him on the point, he refused to discuss the color of his excrement."

"I told her to lie down on the couch and relax. I left the room to get a fresh tape for my recorder and when I came back, she was naked as a fish."

"Fish? It's interesting you should mention that. I dreamed about fish last night. They were coming up through the toilet and molesting my daughter."

"Don't talk to me about humane research. Look at my poor finger. Those damn lab rats have teeth as sharp as razors and they're not afraid to use them. I swear they can tell which day I'm going to castrate them."

With that sort of patter in the background, I browsed through a couple of psychological journals. I found a fascinating article on Mongoloid idiots. They had faces like wax dummies left out in the sun too long. I looked at my watch. I was tired of listening to the bullshit around me and I was tired of Mongoloids. I decided I'd go find a cup of coffee and take it to the can where I could read the graffiti. But as I headed for the door of the lounge, a tall bird with outstretched hand blocked my way.

"Mr. Savage? I'm Dr. Aquarius."

I shook hands. He had the dry solid grip of a tennis player. He was a few inches over six feet, lean and rangy like a long distance runner who hadn't eaten in some time. A wiry tangle of grey hair exploded from his head in perfect spheroid symmetry, as though he'd just taken a few thousand volts of static electricity in the ear. His eyebrows were long and tufted, swept upwards like a horned owl's in perpetual astonishment. His bright blue eyes were somewhat bulged: I guessed he wore contact lenses. His grey sweater was slashed from shoulder to hip by a zigzag red-and-silver lightning streak. Black slacks and low-heeled boots completed his professorial ensemble. I noticed he wore a watch on each wrist and asked him about that.

"One's just a regular watch." He took me by the elbow and steered me down the hall towards his office. "The other is something that's just come out: an Astro-watch. The only people who'd bother to buy them are astrologers. They're very expensive but well worth it. Press a button and you've got an instant horary chart." He pressed the pin on the side and the face lit up. "See the Zodiac signs around the perimeter: they rotate with the earth in accordance with the rising sign. Each one of these dots is a planet. Here in the center of the dial are the planetary symbols and the sign and degree of their placement in the heavens. It's an amazing piece of technology."

We went into his office. He sat behind a broad desk with an orderly array of binders and books, a telephone and a large porcelain cup with pens inside and a leering ram on the outside. I sank into an easy chair that hissed quietly as it enfolded me. Two matching filing cabinets flanked the narrow window overlooking the downtown area. One wall was all-metal shelving jampacked with books; the other was a painted mural of the Zodiac figures: Ram and Bull and Twins, on through the rest of the cycle, all brilliantly represented in acrylics. I remarked that it must have cost him a pretty penny to have done.

"Just the time," he said with quiet modesty. "I like to fiddle with a brush. The tactile sensations of painting are quite soothing. It's important too that I make a personal impression upon my environment." He leaned back in his chair and put his heels on the desk. "I understand you're in the insurance business."

"Yes. And I understand you can tell a great deal about a person by studying their birth chart."

"One can read certain things," he said cautiously. "But in case you're leading up to it, no conscientious astrologer would predict the death of a person."

"But it can be done?"

"Astrology is a science of probabilities and an art of interpretation. It's possible for an astrologer to discern certain tendencies in a chart, say a likelihood of heart disease or accident-proneness, but it is quite a complex matter to accurately fix the probable time of death."

"Okay, just let me clarify my position. I'm not interested in having a chart analyzed with a view to refusing a client life insurance if there's an indication that he's going to die of lung cancer the next year. We've got medical reports to help evaluate cases like that. What I'm interested in is the location of missing persons."

"Mmmm-hmmm."

"Say a family man goes on a hunting party up in the

wilds. He wanders off into the bush and is never seen again. Search parties can't find the body. Now as far as the law is concerned, the man is missing but not legally dead until seven years have passed. Meanwhile, his family is left without income or compensation and his estate is in limbo. What I want to know is whether you might assist in locating such a person. Maybe the guy banged his head, developed amnesia, walked into a town and started a new life. Maybe his remains are rotting in some bear's cave. Couldn't you determine what might have happened, whether he's alive or dead, or where he might be?"

"This doesn't sound like the concern of an insurance company. Wouldn't it be to your advantage to forestall payment for as long as possible?"

"We're not monsters in the life insurance business. We might get tough with fires that smell of arson, or robberies that work so well we suspect inside palnning, but when it comes to families, it's to our advantage to make things as smooth as possible for the bereaved."

"Very touching, Mr. Savage. You're a humanist and a terrible liar."

"Now listen, professor..."

"I *have* been listening. And I don't believe you work for an insurance company." He fixed me with his steely blue eyes. "I think you're involved in some sort of undercover investigation and you're motivated, not by humanitarian concern, but by considerations of personal gain. You've got subterfuge written all over your face."

"Okay doc, you've got me by the short and curlies. Have you got a couch where I can lie down and make a full confession?"

"Let's skip the psychoanalysis. Just give me the facts."

"What makes you think you don't have them already?"

He pressed the pin on his Astro-watch and turned the illuminated face towards me. "Neptune rising, and squared Mercury. A time of deception, confusion of the issues and outright lies. Forgetfulness and secrecy, the probing of the intellect into occult matters."

"I'm impressed. I'll have to get one of those gadgets." I took a deep breath. "Okay, here's the layout. I was hired by a lady to find her sister, a thalidomide mutant, who disappeared from her home three days ago. She was known to have two correspondents: one of them I can't find and the other was bitten by a poisonous spider before he could make himself useful. Meanwhile, another snooper appeared on the scene. He'd been hired by an elderly Cloverlea couple to find their daughter, same description as my missing girl, but a different last name. They don't know anything about the so-called sister that hired me. This other snooper went off to interview a friend of the poisoned correspondent and the pair of them wound up losing their heads. Now there's a three o'clock deadline to make the first payment on a ransom note. What I want to know is, where do I find the girl?"

Dr. Aquarius pressed the pin on his Astro-watch and jotted down the details on a blank horoscope form. Then he asked me if I could remember when Natalie Ferris approached me with the assignment. I thought back on it and placed the time within a quarter hour of 3 PM. Likewise I made rough guesses for the times of Uranium's accident with the spider and the double murder of Bowman and Watroboski.

"Being only approximations, these times will give only general indications of what was happening on the astral plane," said Dr. Aquarius. "I can make some educated guesses using my limited knowledge of the case in hand, but what would be really useful is the birth data; that is, the time of day, date and location of birth, of the principals involved. If they're locally born, you can get accurate data from City Records and if they're not, you can at least get the date and year from Social Registry. Anything along those lines would really help fill in the picture."

That's when I played my trump card. I took Muriel's birth chart out of my pocket and skimmed it across the desk to him. "That's the girl in question. What can you tell me about her?"

He studied the chart. "Where'd you get this?"

"From the spider's victim. He was an astrologer too. What's it say?"

"Pluto rising makes a loner. She sees life as a drama of drastic endings and new beginnings. Leo ascendant makes her creative and willful and romantically inclined, although I see a Sun-Moon opposition and a Venus-Saturn opposition that could do a lot of harm to her love life. Estrangement from the father is likely. Some kind of sexual blockage results in a high nervous activity that could express itself in artistic or intellectual pursuits. Venus squared Pluto says something about unusual sexual experiences or an attraction towards criminal types. Venus sextile Uranus, easy rapport with unusual people. Sun-Moon opposition indicates strained relations with her mother and a generally unhappy home life. Overall, she's in control of events rather than being at their mercy."

"That's it?"

"Well, there's a lot more, but what do you expect in five minutes?" Dr. Aquarius gave me an exasperated look I'd seen before on the faces of garage mechanics who've been asked, after only hearing an engine fifteen seconds, what was wrong with it and how much was it going to cost to fix? "If you'd leave this with me, I could study it overnight, draw these other charts out in detail and try to correlate the lot. Come back tomorrow and I might be able to tell you something."

"Tomorrow? I've got to deal with a ransom demand this afternoon. Can't you come up with some solid indications before then?"

"If I understand you correctly, Mr. Savage, you've been on the case almost two days and you haven't got anywhere but confused. You only gave me the facts ten minutes ago. If you want help, I'll give you what I can spare. If you want miracles, maybe you'd better appeal to a higher authority. I could refer you to a man who's an absolute wizard with the Tarot cards."

"Jeez, I haven't got time to play card games. Look, I'm sorry I jumped the gun. We haven't even talked about money. If this thing works out, I'll give you twenty percent of my fee."

"That won't be necessary. I'll treat it as an intellectual exercise."

"We'll work something out. How about if I leave this stuff with you and get back to you later today?"

"Tomorrow this time would be better."

"Couldn't we make it tonight? There's a little girl caught in the middle of these machinations. Maybe it's all distant planets and geometry to you, but it's a moral responsibility for me."

"Alright, Mr. Savage. Nine o'clock this evening at my place." He scribbled the address on a notepad and gave it to me. "No need to call ahead. Just come around. I'll see what I can make of your problem."

"Thanks, professor, you're a sweetheart." He gave me a funny look when I said that but I didn't worry about it. I hustled my ass out of the Psych Building, got my wagon out of hock and took the trail to Cloverlea.

5

As I came off the Cloverlea exit and started into rich man's territory, I met a yellow Mussolini Sport coming down the road in a blur. As we passed I thought I saw Bud Riordon behind the wheel but he didn't show any sign of having recognized me. When I pulled into the yard, I saw the little yellow coupe was indeed gone. Hansel and Gretel climbed all over my car as soon as I parked it. I rolled down the window a couple of inches and talked to them until they simmered down. I took my chances and stuck my hand out the window in greeting. Hansel nuzzled it wetly; I was okay in his books. I got out of the car and rang the front door bell.

"Oh, Mr. Savage, I'm sorry I didn't hear you drive in. I had the vacuum cleaner going. Have you eaten?" Mrs. Riordon had a kerchief around her head and a pair of fuzzy-wuzzy slippers on her feet.

"As a matter of fact, no. A sandwich would be fine. Could I see the ransom note?"

The dogs followed us into the kitchen and dumped themselves on the floor. I slipped off one shoe and rubbed Gretel's belly with my sock foot. I tickled her nipples with my big toe. She liked it. Mrs. Riordon didn't. She gave me a dirty look and shooed the dogs out the back door. When she returned she put an envelope on the table. It was addressed to The Occupants, 800 Birchcrest Drive, postmarked yesterday from Nova York. Inside was a single 8½x11-inch white sheet and a typewritten message:

You people,
   I got the girl and she is OK. You want to

see her again? Do what I say and don't talk to the police.

Get ten thousand dollars in twenties. Get a jar of liquid honey. Roll the twenties in packs of fifty and wrap with tape.

Go to the Boat Shop on Big Bass Lake. Get a motor boat and a rowboat. Take them out in the middle of the lake. Put lots of honey on each roll of bills. Put the rolls loose in the bottom of the rowboat. Leave it there in the middle of the lake and take the motorboat back to the Boat Shop.

Go home. I phone you next day and tell you where to find the girl.

I want the money at three o'clock tomorrow on Big Bass Lake. Don't be late or I'll kill the girl.

Frankenstein

"This has got to be a hoax," I said. "Honey and a rowboat. The guy's making it damned easy for someone to observe the pickup."

"What would it matter? They could pick it up with a fast motorboat from the other side of the lake. And maybe the honey's to keep the money from blowing out of the boat."

"Why not leave it in a briefcase?" I smacked the note with my hand. "It's all too ridiculous."

"Ham and cheese on rye, tomato and lettuce on whole wheat." Mrs. Riordon slid a platter of sandwiches and a cup of coffee in front of me. "Ridiculous or not, Mr. Savage, I'm going to follow through. He said he'd kill Muriel."

I shoved a ham and cheese down my throat and burned my mouth on the coffee. "I wonder if he's got her at all. He doesn't mention her by name. Does anyone else besides your husband know about her disappearance? That art agent, maybe?"

"Oh no, I didn't tell Mr. Moskovitz. He'd start doubling the prices on all of Muriel's work. I don't think that'd be right."

"It'd mean a lot of money for you. There's at least twenty finished paintings upstairs."

"I'd rather have Muriel back."

"Where'd you raise ten thousand so fast anyway?"

"I don't think that's any of your business."

"I think it might be."

"As long as I'm employing you, Mr. Savage, it's not. I'd like you to help me this afternoon with the delivery of the money; I don't know how to run a motorboat. But I don't want you to interfere or jeopardize the chances for Muriel's recovery. After she's returned tomorrow, you'll be paid and we can say goodbye to each other."

"You don't like me much, do you, Mrs. Riordon?"

"You haven't been much help."

"Neither have you. You waited a whole day after your daughter was kidnapped before you looked for help. You withheld information about her correspondents. You tried to make me believe Muriel was as happy as a girl could be and yet the evidence points to a prison-like atmosphere that would drive anyone out of their skull. Then you got a ransom note and waited another six hours before you told me about it. You've got money from unknown sources and you're much too calm for a mother whose daughter is in dangerous hands. By the way, where's your husband?"

"He went into town to see someone."

"He's not going to stick around and see what becomes of your hard-earned money? Kind of a callous attitude for a father to take. Why couldn't he handle the motorboat if you object to my interference?"

"He doesn't know about the ransom note."

"Why didn't you tell him?"

"For the same reason that I hesitated to tell you. He wouldn't take it seriously; he wouldn't let me go through with it."

"So who's he gone to see?"

"A friend."

"Lady friend?"

"Yes."

"What's her name and phone number?"

"Why do you want to know?"

"I might like to call and see if that's where he's really gone."

"Leave Bud out of it. He's got nothing to do with Muriel. He has his other amusements."

"How long has this been going on?"

Mrs. Riordon sat at the table and poured herself a cup of tea. She added two spoonsful of sugar and stirred them around and around. "How long have we been married? Thirty years. That's how long."

"Have you got something against divorce?"

"Our religion does. Besides, we've got excellent employment with Mr. Ferris. I'm very happy here."

"So Bud just goes his carefree way?"

"He's a number of years younger than myself. I don't deny him certain distractions. When you get to a certain age, Mr. Savage, you'll find that there's more to life than mindless groping in the dark."

"Is that what Bud's into?" I was sorry I said it as soon as I spoke. I was peeved at her for what I thought were obstructions she'd put in the way of my understanding the case, and I wanted to embarass her. I should have known better. She was long past embarassing. She ignored my remark the way a good hostess looks the other way when her guest drinks water from the fingerbowl.

"It's past two o'clock," she said, sweeping the dishes from the table to the sink, "and it's a half-hour drive to the lake. I think we'd better be on our way."

We left my car at the house and took the station wagon. The dogs wanted to come too but someone had to stay home and watch the house. I drove and Mrs. Riordon sat pressed against the passenger door with a brown paper grocery bag in her lap. I presumed it contained the money and the honey. I had never driven this particular route to Big Bass Lake but the signs were well posted and Mrs. Riordon gave me advance warning on every turnoff. We arrived at the Boat Shop at 2:40.

It looked like something bought second hand from a dude ranch. It was a big cabin of peeled logs that had been lacquered up so that it shone as brightly as a wooden table in a Pledge commercial. A little further down the shore, and joined to it by a wooden boardwalk, was another cabin on a grander scale. Over the main doors of each were large rough boards into which had been burned the names *BOAT SHOP* and *LAKESHORE RESTAURANT*. Mrs. Riordon stayed in the car while I went into the Boat Shop.

It was the end of the summer and the place was as quiet as a funeral parlour on a Saturday midnight. I walked past a lounge where fishnets and buoys hung from the ceiling and a couple of elderly characters were tossing darts at a cork board on one wall. The lobby had a big window looking out onto the lake and, facing it, a cedar-wood counter with nobody behind it. Off in the corner stood a couple of dozen oars and paddles of various sizes. On the floor were a dozen five-gallon gas tanks with the fuel lines neatly coiled around the handles. Through an open door I could see into another room at the back where outboard motors were clamped onto a heavy wooden rail that ran along the walls. I went back the way I'd come in and stuck my head into the lounge.

"Anybody minding the store out here?"

The two old boys didn't pay me any attention. They were too busy clinking big glasses together and drinking each other's health. The chairs were upturned on all of the tables but one, and across it was spread cigarettes, playing cards, a handful of darts, a bottle of booze and a couple of empty Coke bottles. I walked in and said my hellos. One of the men was short and well-rounded like he'd just swallowed a butterball turkey. His sweater was just a little too small to cover his belly and his nose was just a little too big to look comfortable on his face. He had furrows in his brow that went up his forehead and over his bald dome and out of sight. The other fellow had a full head of white hair, close cropped and carefully combed around a pair of ears that stuck out like scoops on a hot rod. He wore loose blue jeans with white paint on them and a pale blue shirt rolled up at the sleeves to show well-muscled arms thick with tattoos of snakes and knives and anchors and naked girls writhing amongst them.

"Drink, sonny?" Muscles held out the bottle.

I read the label. Old Navy Rum. I held the bottle up to the light. It looked old, alright. There was sludge at the bottom as thick as molasses. I tipped it back and took a quick swallow. The booze bit me on the tongue and funneled down my throat like acid through a corroded drainpipe. "*Hisssss,*" I said.

"Scotty's the name, and this," patting Baldy on the head, "is McGee. What can I do you out of, sonny?"

"I want to rent a boat."

"Motorboat, sailboat, rowboat, rubberboat: what do you want? Not much of a day for sailboats. Not enough breeze to blow the stink off a sick dog." He picked up a handful of red darts and threw them in swift succession at the board on the wall, putting all of them in the inner circle. "Let's go see what's still floating." He stepped around me and went out to the rental counter. I followed, wondering if it were the rum or seaman's legs that gave him that swagger.

"I want a small motorboat and a rowboat."

"How long? An hour, a day, a week?"

"An hour."

"Just you?" He went behind the counter, pulled out a dogeared logbook and riffled through the pages to the current entries.

"And my mother."

"Whatcha going to do, have a boat race?" He laughed up a storm, blowing a gale of Old Navy Rum breath at me. When he saw I wasn't having any laughs along with him, he pushed a cigarette in his face and said, "Guess I'll give you Numbers Eight and Twenty-two." He jotted the details into the book, spun it around for me and said, "Sign here and that'll be seventeen bucks, cash on the barrelhead."

I gave him the money and he shoved it in his pocket. He went into the engine room, threw an outboard motor over one shoulder and picked up a can of gas. "Grab a couple of life jackets and whatever you want for oars and paddles," he told me as he went out the door towards the dock. I picked two of the cleanest kapok jackets out of a dirty pile in the corner of the engine room and grabbed two paddles.

Two L-shaped docks jutted out from the lakeshore, the short arms turned in towards each other so that there was a boxed-in corral for the boats. Scotty climbed into Number Eight and clamped the outboard motor into place, then hooked up the fuel line and started the motor with a jerk of the pullcord. The engine burbled away quietly, farting grey gaseous bubbles from underwater. Scotty climbed back up to the dock. "That's Twenty-two right next to it. Have fun."

"I just thought of something. You wouldn't have a pair of binoculars you could lend me?"

"You're right I've got a pair, Zeiss 6x20, and you're right I wouldn't lend them to you. If you knew how many cameras, binoculars and transistor radios I've seen dropped over the side, you'd know how I feel about it. Whatcha want binoculars for? Afraid you'll get lost out there on the lake? Don't worry; if you're not back in a couple of hours, I'll call out the Coast Guard." He laughed some more rum vapor at me and shook his head at my lack of humor.

"My mother's a birdwatcher but she forgot to bring a pair of glasses. I'll buy yours from you."

"Like hell you will. I didn't bring them back from the war just to sell them to some johnny-come-lately tourist and his birdwatching mama. I had to put a clip of .45s into a Kraut that was wearing them and you'll damn near have to do the same to me to get your hands on them." He yanked his cigarette out of his mouth and spat tobacco. "But there's an old telescope in the lounge I'll lend you." We walked back into the boat shop and he pulled an old brass telescope off a rack on the wall. "It's a little corroded around the lens mounts where the water got in. A local diver found it in the lake a couple of years back. You might be able to spot a duck with it if he lands on the bow."

I left him there yukking it up with his buddy and went to get Mrs. Riordon from the car. It was ten minutes to three. We went down to the dock and climbed into the motorboat. I fastened a line to the rowboat and cracked open the throttle. The motor thudded away and we went out into the lake. Water started coming up through the floorboards. I pulled a tin can from under the seat and bailed. When we were halfway between shores, I cut the throttle back to idle and pulled the rowboat up alongside the motorboat. Mrs. Riordon uncapped her jar of honey and dipped the rolls of money, a thousand bucks apiece, until each was covered in the sweet syrup. I scanned the shore as she worked. Summer cottages lined the beach but almost all of them were closed for the season. Here and there a flag flapped atop a pole but there were no other boats on the water, no strollers on the beach. Mrs. Riordon passed each honeyed roll to me and I put it in the dry bottom of the rowboat. We were finished at three.

I cast off the line and cracked open the throttle, heading off towards the far end of the lake. I cruised close to the shore and rounded a wooded point where neat little A-frame cottages stood like wigwams among the birch trees. I swung the boat around and idled back to the point until the bow grounded lightly on the gravel beach. From where I sat I was just able to make out the rowboat sitting in the middle of the lake. I hoped Scotty wouldn't spring into action too quickly if he saw Number Twenty-two abandoned like that.

"Mr. Savage, what's the point of this? We've delivered the money. Now we're supposed to leave."

"If you want to go, you can start swimming. I'm not leaving until I see what's going on here."

"You may consider yourself fired, Mr. Savage! I've had enough of your heavyhandedness."

"You'll get some more of it if you don't shut up. Can't you be still for a few minutes?"

I focused the old telescope on the rowboat. Like Scotty'd said, it'd seen better days. It was like looking through a foggy kaleidoscope. In five minutes I had a nice case of eyestrain and nothing to show for it. No boats in sight. Maybe a diver would swim submerged to the boat and snatch the loot. After another fifteen minutes passed I began to wonder if I hadn't really scared off the pickup by sticking around. Then I saw something, but what I saw I didn't believe. I nearly dropped the telescope over the side but I caught it and put it to the other eye for a second opinion. I saw the same thing. It was nice to know I wasn't going crazy, but the reality of it gave me a chilly feeling I could have done without.

They came across the water in single file, flying about two feet off the water. They were black and yellow, with huge irridescent eyes and rainbow-blurred cellophane wings. They swarmed over the gunwales of the rowboat and temporarily out of sight. Now I understood what the honey was all about. Then they were climbing into the air again, ten of them carrying a thousand bucks apiece in a sticky wad clutched by their hairy little legs. They were each about the size of a beer can, bigger than I'd ever imagined they could be. I watched them fly across the water to the far end of the lake, until they were out of sight. I put the telescope down.

Mrs. Riordon looked at me. She must have been disturbed by what she saw because her own complexion turned as pasty as a lump of pizza dough. "What is it? What did you see?"

I thought of all those paintings in Muriel's room: the ladybugs, the beetles, the dragonflies and moths. It all made a sort of sense and it didn't make any sense at all.

"Giant bumblebees," I told her. "Muriel's been kidnapped by a bug freak."

Buzz and Crabby sat in the van waiting for the bees to come back. They were parked in a wooded clearing a quarter mile from the lake. Crabby was worried the bees might take the honey, ditch the money and hole up in a hollow tree trunk. He didn't trust anybody. Buzz told him not to worry.

"We should have arranged for a pickup in town," Crabby said. "Are you sure they'll be able to find their way back to the van?"

"Sure, it's good practice for them," Buzz said. "And they're more at home out here in the woods than they'd be in town. The smog freaks them out."

"That bitch better have come across with the money." Crabby kept picking at a sore on one of his hairy mid-legs.

"What if she doesn't? You won't kill your girlfriend."

"Huh. Some girlfriend. She was going to have an operation so that she'd look like me. Now she's changed her mind. There's no telling what I might do. If the Doc didn't have plans for her already I'd have done a job on her by now. Dirty little two-timing bitch."

"That joint'll never heal if you keep picking the scab off."

"What makes you the fucking expert? Why don't you just shut your trap?"

Buzz slowly opened and closed his pincers. One of these days Crabby was going to get on his nerves. Open and close. One of these days Buzz might rip him in two and bury his head in the back yard with all the others. Open and close. Crabby saw him flexing his pincers and kept quiet for another ten minutes. Then he started again.

"What's taking those bees so long? For chrissakes, I thought they were supposed to be smart as well as big. Couldn't they find a boat in the middle of the lake?"

Simultaneously in twenty facets of his complex eyes, Buzz saw the bees droning in through the trees. "Here they come."

Crabby jumped out of the van. "Have they got the money?"

Buzz opened the rear door. The bees hovered over the floor, dropped their loads and crawled into the hexagonal compartments on either wall of the van's interior. Buzz switched onto their band and told them they'd done a good job.

"Alright," Crabby chuckled. "Money money money."

Buzz didn't care so much about the money but he insisted that he be the one to lick the honey off each and every bundle of bills.

We returned the boats to the Boat Shop and drove back to Cloverlea. I had to admit the bumblebee pickup had been a smooth one. No one in their right mind would follow them for fear they might turn and attack, and even if a guy was equipped with a stingproof outfit, how could he hope to follow them across the water and through the woods for god knows how many miles?

"How'd Muriel get interested in bugs anyway?" I asked Mrs. Riordon.

"I don't know," she said. "She only started painting bugs last year. She used to paint still lifes and scenics before that but they weren't all that good. Suddenly she began studying bugs and it became obvious that she had a great talent."

"Was this around the same time she started corresponding with Crabner and Uranium?"

"I believe it was. Do you think one of them had something to do with the kidnapping?"

"It looks that way, especially if one of them turns out to have an interest in bugs."

"Well, it doesn't much matter now. The money's been paid and Muriel will be home tomorrow."

"I don't know where you get all this unfounded optimism, Mrs. Riordon, but I hope you're right."

I wheeled the car up the driveway of 800 Birchcrest and parked it. The yellow Mussolini was back in its slot. We went into the house and found Bud in the kitchen rinsing a glass in the sink. He had a nice flush high on the cheekbones and a bright oily look about the eyes that smacked of a couple of stiff drinks.

"Hello. Where've you two been?"

"Checking out the local rental agencies to see if we couldn't find one that'd rented a dark blue van to a tall skinny bird three days ago," I said. "Where've you been?"

"In town." He snapped his fingers. "Dammit. And I forgot to go see the hardware people. Supposed to get new storm windows for this place. Going to be a mean winter, they're saying." He went to the phone and dialed, listened awhile and hung up. "Guess they're closed for the day. Have to call tomorrow."

I looked at Mrs. Riordon. "I guess I'm finished here. I have some unfinished business to take care of back in town."

"Don't go yet." Bud caught my arm. "I'd like a few

words with you, Mr. Savage. What would you say to a drink?"

"Don't you think you've had enough for one afternoon?" Mrs. Riordon said. "I could smell it on you when we walked in the door."

"Don't be a pain in the ass, Viv. Let's have a man-to-man talk, Mr. Savage."

I allowed him to hustle me off to the salon. I was generally opposed to 'man-to-man talks' with rummies because they usually turned into hours-long monologs about how nobody understands them, but I was willing to give Bud a couple of minutes in the off chance that he might have something intelligent to say. Besides, I was still a bit unnerved by what I'd seen on Big Bass Lake. I needed a shot of the *aqua vita* like a three-testicled sailor needed shore leave.

The salon was all polished wood and leather: bookcase across one wall, stocked with leathery old volumes; bar along another wall, stocked with twenty different kinds of glasses and lots of choice booze in cut glass decanters; piano against another wall and some heavy leather chairs sitting around waiting for men big enough to fill them. Bud mixed a pair of rye highballs and we clinked glasses like a couple of old comrades, then planted ourselves in chairs and got down to brass tacks.

"Viv's got some queer notions," he said. "I don't think she wants to get Muriel back."

I had to shove a cigarette in my face to keep my jaw from dropping. After having just helped her fork over ten grand as a down payment on the girl's return, Bud's remark came as a bit of a surprise. "What makes you say that?"

"I heard her on the phone yesterday evening." Bud lowered his voice to a conspiratorial whisper. "I couldn't be sure, but I had the idea that she was talking to Muriel. I heard her say something like, 'You let it happen and now you've got to pay for it. You can stay right where you are until it's all over.' What do you make of that?"

"I don't know. What's your wife got to gain by seeing Muriel disappear?"

"If Muriel dies, Viv gets half of her estate."

"She said the other day, she only gets twenty percent."

"That's a crock of shit. I'm not supposed to know the difference, but I've seen the will. Besides that, I happen to know Viv's got a fifty grand life insurance policy on Muriel."

I whistled through my teeth. This was a whole new can of worms. I could see now why Mrs. Riordon was cucumber cool about the whole thing. She might have engineered the plot from the word go. The gambit today might have been a pre-arranged payoff for the guy who'd done the snatch job. And I was helping her play out the game by suggesting that was just the ante. Maybe tomorrow would come a demand for a quarter million dollars or else. Of course Mrs. Riordon couldn't cough up that kind of money. She'd stall for time. Maybe a day or two later, Muriel would turn up dead in a garbage can and that would be that. To all appearances, Mrs. Riordon would have done her best to recover her child. She'd be grief-stricken and the police would be suitably impressed. Finally, half of Muriel's estate and then the insurance payment would come home to mama. Mrs. Riordon and her multidollars would live happily ever after.

But would a mother sell her child like that?

I was turning this over in my mind, like a red herring on a spit, trying to decide whether to eat it or throw it in the garbage, when the phone rang. Bud was across the room in a flash and answered the antique model that stood atop the piano. He listened no more than a couple of seconds before he clapped his hand over the mouthpiece and hissed at me, "Kitchen extension."

I trotted out to the kitchen and picked the phone off the hook. Mrs. Riordon was nowhere about. For all I knew she was in her room gloating over an insurance policy. I glued my ear to the phone and heard a raspy voice saying.

"... got the girl right here. She's okay right now but

she's not going to stay that way long if you people don't cough up the goods. Here's what you're going to do: rent a white van and pack all of Muriel's paintings into it. At eleven o'clock tonight, drive into town, cruise all the way across Beatnickel, then cut south at First and go down to the Nuke Flats waterfront. Keep going past the Ocean Taxi depot and then park the van in the first empty slot you find at Pier Forty. Leave the keys in the van, walk back to the Taxi depot and clear out. That's a one-man job and there'd better be no tail or you know who's going to get dead dead dead. Say a few words to the folks at home, girlie."

A girl's voice came on the phone. She didn't sound terrified but there was an edge to her voice. "I'm okay. They haven't hurt me yet but don't call the police or they'll kill me. Give them all my paintings. I don't care about them. I just want to come back home."

Mr. Raspy came back on the line. "Okay, folks, got that? Play it straight and everything'll be jake."

"Okay," Bud said. "No cops, no funny stuff. I'll take care of everything."

"You'd better, pal," said the other, "or I will. See you tonight." He hung up.

I put the kitchen phone back on the hook and returned to the salon. Bud had shaky hands but he used them to advantage by rustling up another brace of highballs. He passed one to me and arched an eyebrow for my opinion. "What do you think? Sounded on the level, didn't it?"

"He didn't say anything about when you'd get Muriel back. Funny too that they wouldn't prefer to have money. After all, paintings must be hard to get rid of. It would be an easy matter for the police, after Muriel had been recovered, to check all the art dealers and find out if they'd handled any of her work. Hell, those paintings are worse than marked money. It stinks."

"Maybe they've got a private sale lined up," Bud said. "And it's a sure thing Muriel's work is only going to go up in value. Looking at it that way, the paintings are a better investment than straight cash."

"I agree with that, but why didn't they try for money

as well? Or could they know that Muriel's money's tied up in the bank? If so, how'd they get inside information like that?"

Bud downed his highball and paced a tight little circle on the carpet. "Maybe she told them."

"Who? Muriel or your wife?"

Bud stopped pacing. A brilliant gleam came to his eye. "Viv. She told them. She was here when the tall skinny guy came in and took Muriel. She wouldn't want to give up any money because with a little luck, she might get it all herself. And she's cosy with Muriel's art dealer, that rat Moskovitz. Maybe she's arranged a deal with him. They might have cooked it up together. Consider this: if Muriel dies, Viv gets the money and the insurance payoff and Moskovitz, who's been stockpiling her paintings, can double the prices. Isn't that the way it goes? An artist struggles alone until she makes her reputation and then the dealers move in like sharks to share the profits. If she dies, the stock splits three-for-one because everyone's clamoring for a piece of her work because they know there's no more where that came from."

I had to admit the scene read well. Bud's explanation took care of the inside information, the matter of the paintings' disposal and Mrs. Riordon's detached calm about the whole affair. What it didn't explain, and what I was keeping secret from Bud, was the fact that she'd dished out some money already in a supposed effort to get Muriel back. Two ransom demands in one day, both of them pretty fishy. Both of them handled by one of the Riordons, unknown to the other.

"Maybe we should talk this out with Mrs. Riordon," I suggested. "She might have an explanation."

"Uh-uh," Bud said. "Suppose she blows the whistle for the police. The kidnappers kill Muriel and Viv gets the money *and* the paintings. I say we play it hush-hush and gamble on trading the paintings for Muriel."

"That means Mrs. Riordon's got to be out of the house tonight when you move the paintings."

"That might be arranged. What would you say to

luring her out around nine o'clock? All I'd need would be an hour or so. You could tell her something had come up and you wanted to discuss it privately."

"Something like what?"

"I don't know." He shrugged and reached for the rye, then thought better of it and left the empty glass on the sideboard. "Maybe let on you had something on me and didn't want to tip your hand where I might overhear."

"No thanks. It was your wife who hired me in the first place. I wouldn't deceive her like that. Besides, that would make me an accessory to grand theft. I've already had a little run-in with the cops and I can't afford another. You'll have to handle this one on your own."

"But you heard Muriel on the phone. She said that we should give them the paintings."

"I heard a *girl* on the phone. It could have been anybody."

"It *was* Muriel." Bud grabbed the rye bottle and splashed a double charge into his glass. After he downed it he said, "I can manage it on my own anyway. All I want to know is, are you going to tell Viv about this?"

"Tell me why I shouldn't."

"Maybe you'll be too busy doing something else." Bud took a slip of paper from his wallet, unfolded it and passed it to me. It was a color photograph clipped from a glossy magazine. A well-tanned brunette lay on her belly making fox eyes at the camera. She wasn't wearing anything bigger than a butterfly tattoo on her bum but she had a high broad forehead and a cynical smile on her pretty mouth, as if to say she was above it all.

I guess it was the mouth that intrigued me. It looked capable of something more intelligent than a horse laugh and a 'Whattya say, sport?' Maybe I would take Bud up on his bribe, not so much because of what I might get out of this girl's body, but what I might get out of her mind. Bud was up to something and however slightly this chick knew him, I'd bet diamonds to dogdirt that she could tell me something worth knowing.

"Okay, I'll bite. When do I see her?" I gave him the clipping back and he tucked it in his wallet.

"Why not tonight? I'll call her up and tell her you're coming." Bud was all smiles and chuckles over that one. "Maybe you'd like to go over there right away."

"Uh-uh. I've got a dinner date at seven. Let's make it eleven. Where's she live?"

He scribbled on a book of matches and gave it to me, an uptown address where the monthly rent came in bills of four figures. "Dixie's the name. She'll do you good."

"I hope so," I said, thinking on a different frequency than Bud. "Just out of curiosity, how're you going to get Mrs. Riordon out of the house?"

"Tonight's her bridge night. She goes out at eight and usually doesn't come back until midnight. Lots of time."

"So you didn't need my help anyway."

"Maybe yes, maybe no. She might be too upset over the situation to go out, but I'm betting she'll stick to routine to keep up appearances. Besides, she'll want to see Moskovitz. They're bridge partners, and a little more, but I'm not supposed to know about that either."

"You two are full of secrets, aren't you?"

Bud grinned. "If it weren't for people like us, snoopers like you wouldn't have jobs. Let me show you to the door."

"Thanks. I know the way already." I left there in a bit of a hurry. I suppose I should have said goodbye to Mrs. Riordon. I suppose I should have dropped the case or called the cops or both, but I didn't. Things were getting confused but if I quit now I'd never find out what was going on. It hardly mattered anymore who was the spider and who were the flies. So far I had managed to stay unstuck. Could I stay that way long enough to get an over-view of the web pattern? I had three appointments coming up in the next six hours. By midnight I hoped to have at least half as many answers as I had questions.

6

I had an hour to kill before I went over to LeVeen's to see what had come in the mail for Crabner, so as soon as I got into town, I pulled off into Lothario's to grab a beer and burger. My favorite waitress in the red cheerleader's outfit didn't have much time to spare me because it was the supper rushtime. But she spared it anyway.

"Hi," she said when she brought my order. "I thought you were going to give me a call one of these nights."

"Give me a chance. I only got your phone number the other day. Besides, you told me you had a boyfriend."

"He's gone out of town for a couple of days to play ball."

"At least that's what he told you."

"He can do what he likes. We've got an open arrangement. No vows, threats or promissory notes. And I do what I like."

"And what do you like?"

She struck a pose and sang new words to an old musical melody,

"*Nikons and Porsches and Guccis and Akais
Leathers and boas and cocaine on Fridays
Highrise apartments and big diamond rings
These are a few of my favorite things.*"

"That's great," I said. "I suppose you didn't know I'm a producer in search of new talent."

"Off Broadway, no doubt."

"Way off." I took a big bite of my burger and chased it with the beer that made Milwaukee famous. "Seriously now, what does it take to persuade a girl like yourself to spend an evening of carnal delight with a man like me?"

"I like little presents."

"How little?"

"A little car would be nice. Something like that." She pointed to a sports car that went by on the expressway with a subdued howl. "I like yellow."

"That was a Mussolini, wasn't it?"

"I believe it was," she said. "You wouldn't happen to have a spare at home in the garage?"

"No, but a friend of mine does."

"Maybe you could introduce us. Does he like young girls with a taste for the bizarre?"

"I'm not sure. I'm only meeting his girlfriend this evening."

"Do me a favor and feed her poisoned caviar. I'd love to take her place. Is your friend good looking?"

"He's fifty years old."

"That's nice. I could marry him, screw him to death in a year and inherit all his worldly possessions."

"He's married already."

"Well, let's give his wife poisoned caviar too. Better yet, she and the girlfriend could come here and have fishburgers together. The papers would call it a double suicide. Man, if you saw the fish we get here..."

"I don't want to hear about it."

"Tracey," the cashier screamed. "Get your buns in here and move these burgers. You're paid to serve the customers, not make time with them."

"Duty calls. Catch you later. I get off at 2 AM."

"Don't hold your breath. I've got my own duties." I finished off my beefburger and beer and idly watched the blue flicks.

Somewhere in the back of my mind, suspicions were springing up like mushrooms after a rainfall. Had that been Bud in the yellow Mussolini? Surely he could have found a van to rent in Cloverlea. Or had he come in to town to see Dixie before undertaking the night's rendezvous with the kidnappers? In any case, it was all idle speculation at this point. He was long gone down the road and it was time for me to stooge over to

Scranton Street and see what LeVeen was holding.

There were no parking slots on Scranton so I went around the block and found a place on a side street. After what had happened here the last time I visited, I wasn't keen on leaving the wagon too close to the Goering Hotel anyway. In fact, I got a little leery at the thought of running into those punks I'd crossed the night before. Maybe next time I ran into them, they'd be carrying cannons. I still had the Viper, which was okay for a little short range drilling, but it wasn't the kind of weapon to sustain a running gun battle with a pack of crazies.

I pulled a pair of shades off the dashboard and slipped them on. If I ran into those guys again, maybe they wouldn't recognize me. I opened up my glove compartment and pulled out a plastic bag containing a false moustache and goatee and a tube of glue. I stuck the whiskers on and checked my appearance in the mirror. I added a little black beret, pulled it at a jaunty angle across my head and examined the final effect. Pretty snazzy, Savage. I looked like a beatnik jazz musician twenty years out of joint. All that was missing was a battered saxophone and a dogeared copy of Jack Kerouac.

As I crossed the intersection at Scranton, I had to hustle doubletime to miss getting run over by a highballing van. My head swivelled about as it went by. Was it my imagination or did that driver look like the guy I'd tailed from Luna Deli the night before? When I glanced at the license plates as it went by, I didn't see the BUZZ vanity plates, but a six-digit number that disappeared around the corner before it registered. I chalked it up to coincidence and ambled on down past the Goering Hotel.

Swastika banners were hung like curtains in the upper floor windows. As I glanced up, I saw one of the curtains pulled aside and a gun barrel jutted over the windowsill. I ran like hell. The gun stuttered and I went weaving and ducking down the sidewalk, echoes of the machine-gun fire bouncing off the buildings. I'd run about fifty yards when I realized that the gun was loaded with blanks. I kept running. Loud raucous laughter from the Hotel Goering pursued me down the street. Some neighborhood.

I was winded when I reached the lobby of LeVeen's apartment building. I buzzed his room. No answer. I looked at my watch. Six thirty. He should have been home by then. I picked another apartment and rang the buzzer.

"Yeah?" Man's voice.

"Registered letter for Mr. Heifitz."

"Yeah?" Suspicion in the voice. "Who's it from?"

"State Lottery Awards Office."

"Yeah?" Pleasant astonishment. "Come on up. You'll have to take the stairs. The elevator's kaput."

The door buzzed open and I slipped inside. I huffed and puffed my way up to the sixth floor. I rang LeVeen's doorbell. No answer. Rapped on his door. Same response. I tried the doorknob. It turned, the door opened and I walked into LeVeen's living room.

LeVeen was in the chair by the window, kneeling in the seat and slumped over the back of it with his chin on the windowsill. All he wore was a pair of jeans. I thought maybe he was gawking out the window at his pigeon but when I got closer I saw the black hole in the back of his head. I didn't move him. From where I stood I could see that one side of his face had blown away and most of what had once been brains was lying like a gob of spilled porridge on the window sill. He had one hand stuck out over the ledge but there was nothing in it.

I locked the door, put on a fresh pair of rubber gloves and checked his pockets. I found a few small bills and a check from CBX-TV for three hundred bucks in his wallet. In another pocket, a little black book with a lot of girls' names and telephone numbers. On the floor was an empty envelope addressed to Crabner. I took a quick look around the place, not knowing what I was looking for, but knowing I had to go through the motions. In LeVeen's filing cabinet I found a plastic breadbag full of weed and a manilla envelope full of candid photos. It seemed that LeVeen had a passion for top-heavy blondes.

I looked in the bedroom. The bed was unmade and there were shot spots on the sheets. I smelled perfume. A long black hair lay across the pillow. So he liked brunettes too. Then I saw a pair of pink panties on the floor. Did he like to dress up and swank around in front of the mirror? I opened the closet door. Standing behind it was a tall and naked blonde with a big mouth opened to scream. I clapped my rubber-gloved hand across her face and shook my head no-no-no while she stared at me with eyes as big as portholes.

"Police," I said. "Undercover detective, Sergeant York. Put some clothes on." I took my hand from her mouth.

She took a big breath and stepped out of the closet. As soon as she got her panties on she started to cry. Tears welled out of her eyes and streaked her makeup. I found a soft blue sweater on the floor and gave it to her. She pulled it on and towelled her face dry with the sleeve ends. She picked up a pair of slacks from the floor and put them on too. She ran her fingers through her hair and gave me a watery-eyed smile.

"You won't put my name in the papers, will you?"

"Just tell me what happened."

She took another big breath and then let it go in a fast monolog. "Ron and I were making out. Somebody knocked on the door. Ron put his pants on and closed the bedroom door as he went out to see who it was. A man's voice said, 'Where's the key?' Ron said he didn't know what the guy was talking about and asked him to leave. They started shoving each other around. I heard Ron's pigeon scream and he yelled 'you sonofabitch' and then there was a bang and everything was quiet. That's when I got in the closet. After awhile this bedroom door opened and I heard the guy breathing. Then he went away. After about ten minutes I went out to the living room and saw Ron. I picked up the phone to call the police. Then I thought I'd better get dressed and leave and phone them from a public booth 'cause I didn't want to get my name involved. But as soon as I put the phone down there was another knock on the door and I got back in the closet. Someone came in, closed the door really quiet and just waited. It was creepy. I was scared so badly I could hardly breathe. Next thing I know, the buzzer's ringing and then you walk in. Is the other guy still here?"

I yanked out the Viper and made a thorough search of the place. He was hiding in a cookie jar or there was nobody here but us. I guessed the second visitor had left too silently for her to notice his going. "You sit right there on the bed and don't move," I told her. "Don't touch anything."

"Look," she said, picking a purse off the floor. "I'll give you two hundred bucks if you keep my name out of this."

I thought for a moment. I could take her two hundred. Money always came in handy. I could get her name too and use it as a lever to get even more out of her. It was my guess she might be related to some highlevel CBX exec, but it was also my guess, uneducated as they sometimes are, that her presence here at the time of LeVeen's murder was purely accidental. She was scared and there wasn't much point in keeping her here, especially when I thought of what might happen to her if she fell into the hands of someone like York and Mundt. Knowing their penchant for rough-and-ready solutions, they'd dig up a gun of the right caliber, put her prints on it and arraign her for first degree, then give that to her old man and see how fast he might buy her out of it. Or was I just projecting my own evil plots on a couple of hard-working and honest dicks?

"Keep your money," I told her. "Just sit tight while I make a phone call. Then I'm going to ask you some more questions."

I went out to the living room and picked up the phone. As I dialled Riordon's number, I noticed for the first time a big wire bird cage lying on its side behind the door. There was water and birdseed spilled all over the floor, but no bird. The phone at Riordon's rang and rang and nobody answered it. I hung up and went back to the bedroom but the door was closed and locked.

After I'd jimmied it open with my credit card I found what I'd suspected: an empty room. The window was propped up with a Yago bottle; outside was a fire escape. She was gone and now I had to scram too. I only hoped she'd believed I was a cop and didn't go running to the nearest phone booth to call up reinforcements. I went back to LeVeen and took his address book and the empty envelope. No sense making it easy for the cops to find that blonde, because if they did, they'd get the story of a phony cop in a beatnik outfit. I didn't want any casual observers connecting my description to my car. Besides, that false goatee cost me twenty bucks and I'd hardly got my money's worth from it; I planned to use it again. I took LeVeen's bag of weed; he wasn't going to miss it.

I went the other way around the block and didn't run into any SS street troopers this time. I stepped into an alleyway for a moment and peeled off my goatee, beret and shades and stuffed them in my jacket pockets. I went to the car and got out of the neighborhood. It was still too early to go to Aquarius' place so I headed home.

As I wheeled the car into the home port, I saw Grumpy and Werewolf sitting outside catching the last fading rays of the sun as it came sifting down through the smog. Grumpy was reading a newspaper and Werewolf was gnawing on what looked to be a human thigh bone. I parked and came back outside to talk to Grumpy.

"Evening, Mr. Savage. You've been up to no good again, have you?"

"No more so than usual. Why do you say that?"

"The police were here looking for you this afternoon."

"What did they want?"

"They showed me a picture of a feller. Darkeyed, bignosed, long-jawed mug. Looked like Chief Sitting Bull. Wanted to know if I'd seen him around with you."

Shit, I thought. Sounded like a description of Bowman. I saw the way they'd made the connection. Watroboski to the Comix store, then upstairs to Wiseman, who remembered the snooper asking about Davey and phoning the apartment only hours before two headless corpses were discovered there. It looked like I was in for another question-and-answer period with Mundt and York. It unsettled my stomach just to think along those lines.

"Did they stick around?"

"Nope. They were in a hurry. One of them trotted upstairs to see if you were home and then they blasted out of here like they were late for a date with the Queen of Egypt. I told them I thought you'd left town anyway."

"That was nice of you. Where'd I go?"

"West Coast, I thought." Grumpy tore a sheet out of the newspaper and blew his nose with it. "You know, I was awful disappointed in those dicks. They didn't offer me a measly buck for a little information. If they'd sprung ten on me, I'd have told them you'd be back this evening. Too bad for them fucking cheapskates."

"Yeah, too bad for them," I said, taking LeVeen's bag of weed from under my arm. "Here's something for you, Grumpy. A token of my esteem."

Grumpy weighed it in the palm of his hand, then opened the bag and stuck his nose inside. "Well, well. All the way from South America, huh? That's two hundred bucks easy. Thank you, Mr. Savage. You're a gentleman and a scholar. Anything else I can do for you? My nephew's sitting in a snowdrift right about now. Need anything for your sinus?"

"Not really, but I was wondering if you'd lend Werewolf to me for a couple of hours."

At the sound of his name, Werewolf lifted his head from the bone he was sucking on and gave me the once-over with a bleary eye. He heaved a world-weary sigh. I could tell he wasn't enthused about an outing with me.

"Whatcha got in mind?" Grumpy said. "He's not been feeling his best lately. You know he's getting O-L-D."

"Nothing strenuous," I said. "Maybe a walk down Beatnickel later tonight. You know the rep that street's got. But one look at Werewolf and a mugger would change his mind."

"Sounds alright. How long'd you want him for?"

"A couple of hours at most. And I'd get him a Big Mac after we'd finished the walk."

Werewolf shoved his bone aside and started breathing hard. He jumped to his feet and loped a couple of circuits around me, barking and snorting. Slaver spilled over his lower teeth in a miniature Niagara.

"You said the magic word," Grumpy said. "He's ready when you are."

"That won't be until quite a bit later." I patted Werewolf on the head and got him settled down. "You sure there's nobody waiting for me in the apartment?"

"The coast is clear. But you'd better get going while the going's good. I'm not sure those dicks bought my story."

I went up to my apartment and let myself in. To all appearances, it didn't look disturbed by the heavy hand of the law. I picked up a pack of smokes from the carton in the kitchen cupboard, had a quick crap in the john and washed my face where some of the stickum from the goatee still hung around my mouth. I grabbed an apple to munch on and went back down to the garage.

"Listen, Grumpy," I said, sticking my head into his little office-living room where he'd relocated to watch TV, "you won't say anything about my having returned, or my plans for Werewolf?"

"Not for less than a hundred bucks." Grumpy pulled a carrot-sized joint out of his mug and blew Columbian smoke at me. "This stuff is so good I could step on it with parsley and flog it for three hundred. You're still the highest bidder for Grumpy's favor."

"Good enough." I gave him the high sign. That's what I liked—a man who abided by a strict code of ethics. I wheeled the car out of the garage and headed crosstown to Dr. Aquarius' place.

Buzz was in his room exercising. Doctor had given his muscles another radiation treatment and fitted him with a new fibreglass ball joint for his shoulder. Buzz had a splitting headache and saw spots all morning but he could bench press five hundred pounds without straining himself. Crabby came into the room and watched Buzz work out.

"When you're finished, you can go over to my place and pick up the key."

Buzz lowered the barbell slowly back to the rack. "Why didn't she have it mailed here?"

"Because we don't want anybody tracing her to the clinic, that's why. Now get going. The mail's been there for hours."

"Why don't you go?"

"And have LeVeen see me like this?" Crabby waved his two extra hairy limbs. "No way. Besides, I owe him rent money and I don't want to get into a hassle."

"So pay him off. You've got that ten thousand now."

"Fuck him. Now are you going to get that key or do I tell the Doc that you've been running around chopping heads off and planting them in his back yard?"

Buzz drove over to Scranton. He was prepared to break in if necessary but he found the door unlocked. He was ready to kill LeVeen to get the key but LeVeen was already dead and the key had been taken from the envelope.

Buzz stood in the livingroom listening to the hum of the refrigerator. His headache was a blunt wedge driving itself between his eyes. He didn't feel well at all. Too much radiation in the past week. He went to the bathroom and ate a whole bottle of aspirin. Then he went to the kitchen and drank three beers in quick succession to take the taste of aspirin off his sensitive tongue.

He had the feeling there was someone else in the apartment but he couldn't be sure because his perceptions played weird tricks on him during the radiation hangovers. Then he started to feel boxed in and got the impression that someone was coming after him with a pack of dogs. He left the apartment as silently as he had come and got away from the neighborhood as quickly as possible.

Herschel Domain was on the West Side overlooking the river. It was an apartment tower with a difference. The ground floor plan was in the shape of a five-pointed star. On the roof, forty stories high, was a gardened pavilion with a central fountain that shot up another fifty feet into the night sky. Multi-colored spotlights played up and down the spume of water. From twenty blocks away, Herschel Domain looked like a huge glittering candle with an irridescent flame at its tip.

There was no sneaking into this place. After I'd left my car in the visitor's parking lot, I went into the lobby and presented identification to the uniformed guard before he called Dr. Aquarius to see if he was expecting a man with my name and description. Apparently he was, for the guard triggered the heavy glass doors open and I walked into the central pentagonal foyer where ten elevators waited to whisk me up to whatever level I wished. I walked into one of the 'A' lifts and pressed button 28. Apartment A-28-9 was the door at the end of the hall. I rang the bell.

From inside I heard a dog bark and a man's voice say, "It's alright, Tojo, he's a friend." Then the door opened and Dr. Aquarius was standing there under a dim hall light, looking over my shoulder and saying, "You're early, Mr. Savage, but come in. You can have a glass of wine with us. Or perhaps you haven't eaten?"

"I'm fine, thanks." I stepped inside and closed the door. A big German shepherd with dark coloring slipped forward past Dr. Aquarius and sniffed eagerly at my hand.

"Don't mind Tojo. He's just a sucker for a new smell. Aren't you, boy?" Aquarius ruffled the fur at the big dog's neck, then gestured for me to follow. "Come in, come in."

We walked down a short carpeted hallway: small study and bathroom on one side, large bedroom on the other, and at the end of the hall, a large triangular room with kitchenette separated from the living room by a long wooden counter. Large Japanese lanterns hung from the ceiling and there were Oriental prints of long-necked birds and fishing boats on the walls. Sitting on a stool at the far end of the counter was a beautiful Oriental woman with her hair piled high on her head, fixed in place by what appeared to be a handful of chopsticks. Somehow she didn't look right on a stool. I'd have preferred to see her sitting on a cushion at an ankle-high table, but she was obviously at home and she could sit where she pleased.

"My wife, Yoni, and this is Mr. Savage," said Dr. Aquarius. "Have a stool. Would you like saki, coffee or a beer?"

I pulled out a stool from the end of the counter and climbed onto it. "I'll have coffee when you do. Finish your dinner, please. I'm sorry I came too early."

"No blame." Aquarius seated himself and used his chopsticks expertly to maneuver a clump of steamed green vegetables into his mouth. "You're sure you wouldn't have some sweet and sour pork? We'd be spoiling Tojo to give him all these leftovers."

"I'm sure he can manage better than I." Tojo put his front paws on my legs and rose to sniff at my face. I scratched his ears and casually observed my hosts. Aquarius was wearing a loose-robed orange affair with little stars and moons and nebulae swirling about. His wife was dressed in one of those high-collared Chinese dresses with a slit up the side that revealed a smooth rounded expanse of walnut-colored thigh.

There was no TV visible in the living room but there was a tape recorder, turntable and amplifier. The curtains were drawn back from the two wall-length thermopane windows to disclose the panorama of the city beyond. Looking across to the next wing two floors down, I saw a couple doing a slow and sinuous dance in the nude.

Mrs. Aquarius caught the direction of my stare and remarked to her husband, "I see the Magnussons are opening up to each other a lot more these days."

Aquarius leaned over the counter to catch the view. "Mmmm. It's amazing the progress a couple can make in their relationship simply by changing the environment and moral climate they've been fixed in."

"You know these people?" I said.

"Oh yes. Magnusson's a Math prof at the University. We met in the Faculty Club one day when he was nicely buzzed and got to talking about his sex life. Seems he and his wife were embarrassed to see each other in the nude. Turns out they were living uptown in the same apartment complex as her parents, a stuffy bunch of older business types. I suggested he move into Herschel where they'd be closer to a social life among people their own age and persuasion. Voilà." He gestured across the darkness to where the Magnussons were now wrapped in carnal embrace on their living room carpet. "Mind you, it's not usually that simple, but it certainly helps to live among your own kind. Herschel is probably ninety percent University personnel, so it's like one big commune. Good intellectual rapport and we're all graduates of the free-love generation, so it's a pretty swinging place."

"Lots of business for the part-time astrologer too, I suppose."

"Oh yes, indeed. I could resign my tenure tomorrow and make a very good living just by setting myself up as official astrologer for the residents."

"So why don't you?"

"He'd miss the coeds," Mrs. Aquarius said.

"So I'm a dirty old prof." He stuck his tongue out and waggled it at her. They got a big chuckle out of that. Private joke. Then he turned to me. "But she's right. I need that contact with young people. There's only so much you can learn from your elders and even less from your peers, because you've tended to have pretty much the same attitudes and experiences. But it's the young who are bringing fresh perspectives into our society and it's vital that a man like myself, who pretends a concern for the evolution of consciousness, to stay tuned into what's coming up off the horizon."

"And what is coming?"

"An occult consciousness is on the rise. An awareness of life and sexuality as energy. A realization of the hidden powers and little-exercised powers of the will.

An egolessness, a transpersonal desire to move beyond..."

The phone rang. Aquarius reached behind him and lifted the phone off the wall mount. "Aquarius speaking. Yes she is. Yes you may." He handed the phone across the counter to his wife.

While she was engaged in conversation, he cleared the counter of food and dishes. By the time all the dirties were in the dishwasher, coffee was ready. He put pots and cups and accoutrements on a tray and we moved to sit on a low couch in the living room. He excused himself for a couple of minutes and then returned with a sheaf of papers.

"I spent the rest of the day drawing charts and trying to make out what was happening in light of what information you gave me."

"I really appreciate the time you've put into this."

"My pleasure. A man needs this sort of thing to test his mettle. Here, then, is the first chart, erected for the time when the young lady approached you with an assignment to find her missing sister. You'll see we have Neptune in Sagittarius rising, Gemini descending and its ruler, Mercury, at the midheaven. As I mentioned this morning, Neptune is an indicator of deception and illusion, in the sign of law, religion and the publishing business. Now, to follow this clue as regards publishing, you'll see we have three planets, Mercury among them, in the ninth house of publishing. Furthermore, Neptune is squared Mercury, implying distortion of the facts, while the ruler of the Ascendant, Jupiter, is in the seventh house of dealings with the public, with aspects to Uranus and Pluto, both of them being indicators of political issues. To support the contention of politics, we have as well the Sun and New Moon, unaspected except by conjunction to each other, in the tenth house of public responsibility and power."

"So what does that make of Miss Ferris?"

"I think she's a journalist with an interest in politics."

"I don't think Muriel's politically involved."

"Maybe her father is. Sun and Moon in the tenth house of the father gives credence to that."

I thought of Bud. Somehow he didn't strike me as the political type. "Alright, we'll let that go. I can see I'll have to get in touch with Miss Ferris and talk this out."

"Okay. The next chart we're dealing with is the one set up for the time when Mr. Uranium met with his unfortunate accident. In this case we have Taurus ascending and Scorpio descending, indications of sensuality and materialism versus jealousy and intrigue. We find the Ascendant ruler, Venus, in the fourth house, that of the mother and also the end of the life, conjoined with Saturn, planet of restriction and death. Uranus, planet of bizarre behaviour and accidents, has just descended below the western horizon, in the sign Scorpio. Again, we find our old deceiver, Neptune in the eighth house of sex, death and legacies. The focal point of the issue might be found with the Sun and Moon, conjoined in the fifth house of speculation and love affairs."

"You think Uranium was threatened by a jealous lover?"

"Yes, but the spider wasn't meant for him. That was the bizarre accident indicated by Uranus' placement in the chart. I'm suggesting that Watroboski was supposed to be killed by the spider and that the book in question was sent by another jealous party, someone who resented any intrusion upon his favored position with Muriel."

"But who?"

"Pluto is also in the fifth house. A secret lover. Pluto rules mutants. Maybe somebody who has similar afflictions to Muriel."

"Okay, good enough for now. What else do you have?"

"A chart for the time of the double murder of Bowman and Watroboski. Capricorn rising and Cancer descending. Ascendant ruler, Saturn, in the eighth house of sex and death. Here we have a struggle between the urge to power and the need for security. Mars in the descendant indicates violence and squared Pluto at the midheaven denotes mutilation, particularly of the head, which Mars rules. Uranus in the tenth house gives bizarre publicity. Sun and Moon in the ninth house suggest a religious issue, so maybe this is a cult murder of sorts, but with the Moon approaching conjunction to Pluto at the midheaven, there is again an indication of some political issue buried at the bottom of the whole affair."

"I can't see what relation this kidnapping has to a political issue. The girl's parents are just a pair of glorified housekeepers. Their employer is Jordan Ferris, but there's no reason why he should be politically entangled by his employees' affairs."

"Well, getting back to this chart you gave me, I spent some time doing progressions, which is a method of forecasting future trends on the basis of the natal chart. I can only hope that this chart was based upon accurate and confirmed birth data, because otherwise the prediction time element is going to be distorted. But presuming it was correct, I went ahead with my own calculations. And it looks to me like this girl's mother died when she was only a week old. Her father, meanwhile, is a man in a powerful position and stands to win even greater public favor in the next few months. The girl is currently embroiled in a difficult situation, arising partly from what I gather have been illicit sexual relations. She is estranged from her father and is, metaphorically or literally, a prisoner of underworld forces that threaten to radically change her appearance or personality."

"Brainwashing?" I was having a hard time getting this straight in my mind. Aquarius made it sound as if Muriel was adopted, had fucked-up relations with her father and had been snatched by a political underground unit that intended to use her as a pawn in some power struggle. As far as I was concerned, Aquarius had handed me a bunch of round pegs and I couldn't get one of them into the square pigeon-holes of my mind.

"It's all a matter of degree," Aquarius was saying. "It could be as simple as a face-lifting. On the other hand, it could be radical plastic surgery or lobotomy. You said she was limbless. Maybe she's being outfitted with new limbs."

"Yeah?" I said. "Who's footing the bill for that? The kidnappers?"

Aquarius shrugged. "I suppose some of this doesn't make too much sense. Depending on how much one knows about the people involved, there are different levels of interpretation."

"Changing the subject for a moment, have you ever heard of a place called the Limbo Clinic?"

"I can't place the name right now. Maybe if I let it sink into my mind, the old subconscious will work on it."

"In the meantime, maybe you could draw another chart." Without telling him the circumstances, I gave him the time when I'd arrived at LeVeen's apartment and found him dead. He had the chart plotted in five minutes.

"Pisces ascending and Virgo descending. Ascendant ruler, Neptune, at the midheaven, squaring Mercury at the descendant. Looks like something to do with twins, seeing as how we have the sign of the twin fishes rising, the two-faced Hermes at the descendant ruling Gemini, twins again, at the nadir point, or psychological foundation of the relationship, while the Sun..."

"Hold it. What's this about Hermes?" I'd suddenly remembered that Hermes was the name of LeVeen's pigeon.

"Hermes? The Greek equivalent of Mercury, the messenger of the gods. He's the Trickster of mythology and Jungian psychology. In this case, a go-between for the two agents involved here. As I was saying, we have the Sun in the seventh house of partnerships, while the Moon, indicating environment and perceptions, is midway between Uranus and Pluto in the eighth house..."

"Sex and death again, huh?" I was getting the hang of it now.

"Do you mean...?"

"Another murder."

"Have you informed the police?"

"No, but they're looking for me in connection with Bowman and Watroboski."

"Don't you think you should go to them with what

you know?" He gestured to the charts spread before us on the coffee table. "I mean, we have certain evidence that points to a political conspiracy..."

"Don't kid yourself, professor. The cops would take one look at this stuff and piss themselves laughing. The only person who's willing to take this stuff seriously, and who's got enough of the facts to make use of them, is me. And I'm not going within shouting distance of the boys in blue until I've got the whole mishmash straightened out to my satisfaction."

"That's all very well for you, but now you've implicated me with what? One, two, three murders. And I see in the papers that Uranium is still on the critical list. His death would make it four. What if the police come to me asking about you? I've got a moral responsibility to uphold the laws of our society."

"I'd like to maintain a certain consistency in my alibis. Tell them I've gone to California."

"Seriously now, Mr. Savage."

"Alright, professor. I've got a serious question. Psychologically, what do you make of a girl who paints nothing but insects? Does that mean she's going buggy, or am I being frivolous?"

"You are, but I'll try not to follow your example. It's an interesting phenomenon. Insects have a certain fascination for some people. They're beautiful little creatures of great physiological complexity. They live in a world of great savagery and yet many of them have highly evolved social structures. To answer your question, I'd say the person was an introvert, but one who put society's requirements above those of the individual."

"A commie?"

"I can tell you're groping for that political connection. It's quite possible she is so inclined."

I thought of those giant bumblebees I'd seen on Big Bass Lake. Now there was a social species of insect with a great potential for savagery if they were rubbed the wrong way. And speaking of savagery, I flashed back to the sight of Bowman and Watroboski lying headless on the floor. Whoever did that had nerves of forged steel or a particularly nasty streak of sadism, if not both. Definitely a case for the bughouse.

Mrs. Aquarius finally hung up the phone and joined us in the living room. "The Vortags are showing slides of their trip to Peru. They wanted to know if we'd like to come up and see them. Dr. Eckhardt and his wife are there too. Apparently she's had plastic surgery and looks twenty years younger."

"Sounds fascinating," Aquarius said absently, "but Mr. Savage and I..."

"Have just about had enough of the stars for one night." I moved Tojo's head off my leg where he'd fallen asleep on the sofa between us. "Thanks again for all your help, Dr. Aquarius." We shook hands. "You've given me quite a mass of information in one big lump. I think I need some time to digest it all."

"I'm glad to have helped. Let me know what transpires."

"I think I'll go to City Records tomorrow and see what I can dredge up on the other principals in this case. Would you be free to do a similar analysis tomorrow?"

"That would be agreeable. I have no lectures so you'll probably find me in my office, anytime between nine and four."

I said my good evenings to Mrs. Aquarius and Tojo and took the elevator down. While it was still fresh in my mind, I jotted down the names of the people I'd like to have charts on: the Riordons, Jordan Ferris, Ron LeVeen, Billy Crabner and Natalie Ferris. As I walked out through the lobby, I remembered that I'd forgotten to jog Aquarius' memory on the matter of the Limbo Clinic, but that could always wait until tomorrow. I unlocked the car and drove out of the parking lot. I wondered if I shouldn't have Aquarius do my chart too, but I was reluctant to do so. I guess I believed in the man's techniques and I was leery of anyone having a chart of my psychological propensities. I preferred to remain unpredictable.

7

I was running ahead of schedule on my appointments but I decided to go on to Dixie's place anyway. Better early than late. I might catch her with her panties down. As I recalled the picture Bud had shown me, that would be something worth seeing in the flesh.

Champlain Place was on the Upper East side, a twenty story affair of white granite that spanned half a block. I drove down the ramp of the underground garage to a fluorescent cross bar and a security hut with a TV camera mounted at the window. The rent-a-cop came out of his office, sneered at my Astromobile and asked me what my business was. I gave him five bucks and told him I was delivering a prescription to a lady friend. I thumbed one nostril and sniffed loudly through the other. He tucked the money in his pocket, lifted the crossbar and pointed the way to the visitors' parking slots.

In the lobby above, standing in ankle-deep carpet with classical Muzak whispering from the corners, I found the apartment panel and gave Dixie a buzz. She asked who was there and I replied, a friend of Bud. She let me in and I took the elevator to the top floor. She'd timed my approach perfectly, or there was a hallway TV monitor, because she opened her door just as I got to it.

"Good evening, Mr. Savage. You'll have to excuse my appearance. Bud hadn't told me to expect you this early." Her eyes, expertly made up with a silvery sheen, regarded me cooly from a face framed by a stylish coiffure.

"If you think you need to apologize, I'd like to see

you when you think you deserve flattery." I strolled in through the aura of her perfume and watched her close the door. She wore a pants-and-jacket affair of black diaphanous material that might have originated with Fredericks of Hollywood. The body beneath it was something of which dreams are made, and the transparency of the outfit made it a very lucid dream. The waist of the pants was fastened by a single drawstring, as was the jacket, and it didn't take a Boy Scout to see that the whole thing would come apart with the gentlest of tugs. My fingers got sweaty just thinking about it. There are beautiful girls who exude sexuality from every pore in their lovely bodies, but this kid had something that would have given the Pope a hardon.

Resisting the impulse to jump on her and have it out right now, I dropped down in a heavy leather chair and watched her waltz around the room with some backlighting giving me a silhouette I could cherish well into my old age. I could see myself now, old man Savage nodding off into his nineties, jacking off to a recollection of the cutest little muff this side of the Vegas kickline.

"Like a drink?" She went behind an elaborate bar at one end of the living room.

"I suppose we've got to start somewhere."

"What's your pleasure?"

"Let's have the drink first."

"Not too sure of yourself, are you?"

"Someobdy's got to be sure of himself. It might as well be me." I shook out a cigarette and used the last match in the book to get it going. "Can you mix a Manhattan?"

"No problem."

"If you've got cherry brandy, toss half an ounce of that in too, and another ounce of rye to give it some volume."

"What do you call that?"

"A Manhattan Project."

"Never heard of it."

"Made by the same people who brought you the atomic bomb. Maybe you've heard of *it*?"

"Anybody ever tell you, Mr. Savage, that you're pretty cute?"

"No. Do you want to be first?"

She let that one go by. While she shook my drink she said, "Be a pal and give us a tune. There's some Erik Satie on tape. All you've got to do is turn him on."

Turning guys on was more in her line of work, but I boosted myself out of the chair and crossed the carpet to where an expensive tape outfit was nestled into a walnut shelf alcove. I turned it on and the music came out of a pair of speakers cunningly disguised as National Geographic globes of the world. I didn't know who this Satie was but he sounded like a catnip-stoned feline taking a lazy stroll up and down the ivory boardwalk. There wasn't much melody to speak of but it seemed the right kind of music for a tête-à-tête with some high-class pussy.

I walked across to the other side of the room, parted the heavy cream-colored curtain and looked over a balcony and into the street below. A white Rolls was pulled up in front of Gaylands and a couple of fairy princes in feathers and glitter were helping each other fall into the back seat. I let the curtain drop back and cast an eye about the room, something I'd neglected to do as I came in, having been momentarily blinded by the spectacle of Dixie's nubile bod moving sinuously beneath her translucent garment. There was another leather chair to match the one I'd taken a seat in, and between them was one of those cone-shaped fireplaces built over a base of crushed stone. Three immaculate birch logs lay in a grate that looked as if it had never handled a piece of burning wood before, and close at hand was a vertical brass rack with the polished brass shovel, poker and tongs of the trade, looking equally unused to handling fires. A Swedish style couch with the long-haired bulky look of a woolly mastodon lay with its back towards the bar. Between it and the fake fireplace was a Kodiak bear rug. Sprawled as it was on a red wall-to-wall shag carpet, it looked like the Kodiak had crawled in here and bled all over the place in a last gesture to bad taste.

Dixie came towards me with a drink in each hand. She'd been generous: my Manhattan Project had two cherries, neither one of them much smaller than the nipples I saw just the other side of that micron of black gauze she wore for a jacket. I took the drink from her and sniffed the rim.

"It's a light whisky," she said, "but not so light that you can inhale it out of the glass."

"The thought just occurred to me that it might be doped."

She arched an eyebrow. "Why would I do a thing like that?"

"Because you'd been told to?"

"Nobody tells me what to do." She held out her hand. "Give it back. I'll pour it down the sink."

"I'd rather you drank it."

"I don't like whisky."

"How about a cherry?" I picked one out of the drink and moved as if to pop it in her mouth. She jumped back as if I'd threatened to throw acid in her pretty face. "So it's the cherry, is it?" I walked to the bar and put the drink on the sideboard. "Where's your phone? I think I'd like to call the police."

"There's no need to do that."

"What's in the drink?"

"LSD. I thought you'd like it."

"Couldn't you have asked first?"

"I like surprises."

I went behind the bar. To hell with mixed drinks. I took a big glass, dropped in a pair of ice cubes and set them floating in Canadian Club. She went across to the tape console, brought the bass up a touch and then sat on the couch with her legs crossed and one arm outstretched along the back of the sofa. I went over there and sat beside her.

"So tell me, who's the sugar daddy?"

"That's for me to know and you to wonder about." She smiled and took a sip from her goblet. Her drink, which was green and effervescing so quickly there was a perpetual mist over the surface, looked like the sort of thing that had put Dr. Jekyll into bad straits. She correctly interpreted my enquiring glance and said, "Ether."

"I thought that went out with laudanum."

"It's coming back, in certain circles. It gets you very nicely plastered but without hangovers."

"You don't recognize me, do you?"

"Should I?"

"No, but then I shouldn't recognize you either."

"Care to explain?" She kicked off the high-heeled golden slippers she'd been wearing and pulled her feet up beneath her derrière. There was a pale green mist around her eyes and a warm invigorating scent coming off her. I gave her parfumier full credits. The stuff made me want to rape and plunder but I kept a civilized grip on my pants and regarded her with what I hoped was a glacial eye.

"Ladies first. What's going on between you and Bud?"

"We fuck each other."

"I'm not talking about the obvious. I mean, who are you doing a job on?"

"I don't follow."

"Like hell you don't. What is he, your pimp?" I was pleased to see the crimson flush spring to her cheeks. I hadn't thought she was the blushing type. "Or is it something with a little more style? How do you see yourself, as an entertainer?"

"I know a few men."

"Rich men, married men?" She didn't confirm that but I went on anyway. "You entertain the gentleman here, record some indiscriminate conversation, take a few candid photographs. After a few more visits, you suggest the gentleman give you a present or two, say a few thousand in your account, or you might mail his wife something incriminating."

"You've got it all figured out, huh?"

"I don't hear you denying it. Want to give me a few minutes in the bedroom and see how fast I can find the costumes and whips, the hidden mikes and video cameras?"

"That's not what you came here for."

"Why did I come here? To sip a little acid, trip out and sing, 'I wish I were in Dixie'?"

"Anything can be arranged."

"Including a fall from a twentieth-story balcony."

"You're paranoid, Mr. Savage. Accidents like that don't happen in nice places like this."

"Let's put it on the Keith-and-Dixie level. And I'm not paranoid. You're the one that drinks too much."

"Are you threatening me?"

"I don't know. Am I?"

"I'm beginning to think it was a mistake for Bud to send you here." She swirled the remains of her ether in the goblet. "Perhaps you'd better leave."

"It was a mistake alright, but I'm not leaving until I have a better picture of what's happening behind the scenes with our mutual friend, Bud."

"I've got nothing to tell."

"I do."

"Surprise me."

"You were in Ron LeVeen's apartment when he was killed."

Her jaw dropped so far I could have slipped a brick into her mouth. I'd been waiting to spring that line since I'd walked in here. I hadn't recognized her immediately, because she'd obviously been wearing a blonde wig when I saw her in LeVeen's apartment, but after I heard her speak I knew for sure. I wasn't surprised she hadn't recognized me; considering the goatee-and-shades disguise, and I hadn't said much at the time.

"You're no cop."

"Lucky for you." I shook a cigarette from my pack and felt my pockets for nonexistent matches. "Got a light?"

She reached a hand under the pillow at her end of the sofa and pulled a gun on me. It looked like a Beretta. It wasn't a big gun but it had been known to kill people. Especially at three feet. She set her goblet down on the end table and said, "Take a powder, mister." The Beretta held a steady bead on my heart.

I took the Viper out of my pocket and leveled it at a handful of bare belly that showed between her jacket and pants. "In a Mexican standoff, the lady gets to shoot first."

She pulled the trigger.

Flame erupted from the barrel with a small bang. I leaned forward and dipped the end of my cigarette into the unsteady flame, puffed it to life. I took the Beretta away from her and gave her the cigarette. She looked like she needed it. I pulled out another cigarette and used the lighter gun to get it going. I laid the phony Beretta on the sofa between us and slipped the Viper back into my pocket.

"You bastard."

"Technically, you're right. Morally, you're further down the ladder than I am, so let's not call each other names."

"I didn't kill him."

"I never thought you did. But what were you doing there, besides the obvious?"

"I swear, that's all there was to it." She gulped the last of her drink and pulled hard on the cigarette. "I'm trying to break into one of the TV serials. *These Violent Times*. Maybe you've seen it."

"You're a natural. But not everybody sees it that way?"

"Right. You know how it is. You ball the producer and he says, 'You're hot stuff, baby, but I'm not sure about your acting ability.' So you ball the director and he says, 'I love it, but we don't have a part for you right now.'"

"So you ball the writers, hoping they'll write a new girl into the script."

"Exactly. That's how I happened to come home with LeVeen. As far as writers go, he's a pretty nice guy. He was no great shakes in bed but he was going to write me into the storyline and wing it from there. A girl's got to get a start somehow."

I waved my hand around the room. "Most girls don't get launched from posh pads like this. Who's your benefactor?"

"You don't have to know that."

"Listen, kid, I've got to know everything. You tell me

or the boys in blue. I let you off the hook at LeVeen's because I didn't see the connection. Now there's more substance to it. LeVeen's dead, Bud's playing games with kidnappers and you're stuck in the middle. So who's paying the rent? I can find out another way but I won't be so willing to help you if you don't help me. What's the man's name?"

"Jordan Ferris."

"So you're his private kewpie doll, huh? You rub the knots out of his tired muscles after a hard day of politicking. You play the low-profile geisha girl and he pays the penthouse rent. But get in trouble and he doesn't know you from a piece of dogshit on the street. Is that why you were so anxious to keep your name out of LeVeen's murder?"

"You've got it," she said. "Jordan would cut me off without a backward glance. Right now he's got a name and image that're money in the bank. Nothing and no one is going to besmirch that man's career. He sees himself as Presidential material."

"How do you see it?"

"Just another horny businessman with money to burn."

"You don't see a place for yourself up there with him?"

"Marriage?" She laughed. It had a tinny ring to it, like a couple of thin dimes in an organ grinder's cup. "When Jordan marries, it will be to someone with money or power, preferably both. I'm only playing with him for as long as I have to. If I get a part in the series, I'll be my own woman."

"Does Ferris know about your ambitions?"

"No, and if he did, he'd cut me off before I got on my feet. He thinks the show is disgusting."

"And where does Bud come into all this?"

"Bud? He runs errands for Jordan. He came up here one day to install my sound system. He made a play for me. How could I resist? He's good looking for his age and he's still got the moves. It was just a kick for both of us, a pair of Jordan's employees getting it on behind the boss' back."

"Except it got bigger than that?"

"Give me another cigarette," she said. "Do you want another drink?"

"I'll get the drinks." I gave her another cigarette, went to the bar and got the ether and whisky. I checked my watch: quarter past ten. There was no hurry. I sat beside her and gave her the drink.

"Is it just me or is it hot in here?" she giggled.

I put my hand on her knee. A few degrees higher and her pants would catch on fire. Her heat swam up my arm and pounded in my temples. Another minute of that and I'd have trouble breathing. "You're pretty hot," I said.

"That's what they all say..." She had a vacant look in her eyes now as she sipped the green liquor. I wondered if it were anything like absinthe, whose habitual use caused mental derangement. "The producers, the directors, the writers, the cameramen, the script girls— they all say..."

"Stop it." I took an ice cube out of my whisky, ran it across her forehead and down one cheek, then under her chin and up the other cheek. She took a deep breath and sighed, lifting one hand to grasp my wrist. "You were telling me about Bud," I said. "He's in trouble, isn't he?"

"Pressure, pressure, pressure." She pulled my hand down to her chest and guided it so that the ice cube traced cool wet lines up and down the contours of her breasts.

"Who's applying the pressure?"

"The big fish." She pulled her jacket open and urged my hand to zero in on her nipples with the rapidly shrinking ice cube.

"Loan shark?"

"Can you screw as well as you guess?"

"How much does he owe?"

"It started at five grand, with five hundred bucks a week vigorish. It's probably fifteen grand by now."

"What's he got, a habit?"

"He thinks he's got a system for the horses." She laughed and pushed my hand roughly across her breasts. The ice cube was long gone and so was she. "The poor stupid jerk. I felt sorry for him."

"Lend him money?"

"No way. Jordan paid the bills but he wouldn't give me cash. I live hand to mouth."

"So you helped him make a tape recording. You played the poor little kidnapped girl."

"We disguised my voice. He said no one would ever recognize it."

"What's going to happen to the paintings?"

"Bud's got it worked out between the shark and a crooked art dealer. He'll be off the hook and have something to spare."

"Where's the girl?"

"Bud doesn't know. She had friends snatch her or she was really kidnapped. It didn't matter. After two days and no ransom demand, Bud saw how he could set up a phony demand and clear himself with the shark. So we made the tape and he sprung it when he found a witness to back him up on what came across the phone."

"Where's the tape?"

"I don't know. Bud took it with him."

"Why would Muriel arrange to have someone snatch her from her home?"

"You'll have to ask Bud that one."

"Where can I get in touch with Jordan Ferris?"

"You can't. He's up in the mountains. Incommunicado." She tugged both her drawstrings loose and stood up with a shrug of her shoulders. Her jacket and pants made a silken pile at her feet. "Life's too short for all this chatter. Let's get it on."

"You're not my type."

She put her foot in my crotch and wriggled her toes. "Pull the one with bells on it."

I jerked her ankle up and shoved her. She toppled backwards onto the rug and lay there on her side, one leg drawn up beneath her, the lush globes of her bottom whitely contrasted with the dark silky tangle of hair between her legs. I saw the butterfly tattoo on her ass.

The next thing I knew, I was down there with her, pushing myself in and out of her hot wet center and she was saying 'oh yes baby yes yes yes' with her heels drumming on my back. It was too good to last for ever. We sprinted for the finish line together and she beat me by about two strokes. A soft wet explosion enveloped me, like she'd turned on a fountain inside her, and then I was all atwist with my own agony and ecstasy.

There was something hard pressing against my head. It was the wall. I rolled off her and surveyed the situation. She was pink all over and I felt pretty warm myself. We'd moved about six feet across the carpet from where we'd begun. It was cooler here in the corner by the window. I lay there and looked at my watch. Quarter to eleven. As soon as I caught my breath, I'd hit the road.

She sat up and said "Whoops." She fingered the carpet. "Baby made a drip-drip." She leaned close and kissed me and said, "You're good enough to charge for it."

"I usually do."

She laughed and felt her bottom. "I'd better get a towel and clean this up. Jordan would have a fit if he found a stranger's jism tangling up the shag rug." She wiggled off to the bathroom and ran some water.

I felt like a cigarette. I pulled myself out of the corner and started on hands and knees across the rug to where I saw the pack lying. I shook one out and picked up the phony Beretta to give myself a light. That's when Dixie came out of the bathroom with another gun in her hand. Somehow I didn't think it likely that she intended to light my cigarette with it.

"Why couldn't you have been a good boy and drunk your drink quietly and saved all this bother?" Her voice was very steady and I realized that her earlier drunkeness had been nothing more than an act.

"I don't know why not. I guess I'm just a natural troublemaker."

"It would have been so simple. You'd have gone out like a light and woken up next week with nothing worse than a splitting headache."

"Too bad I don't like headaches."

"Too bad is right. Now I've told you too much. If Bud found out, he'd kill me."

"Just like he killed LeVeen?"

"How'd you know that?"

"I guessed. You just confirmed it. Correct me if I'm wrong. For some reason, Mrs. Riordon mailed the safe deposit key to Crabner's address. Bud found out about it and went to get it. He just happened to show up at the same time you were there balling LeVeen. When Bud killed LeVeen, you were afraid to reveal yourself, partly because you feared his jealousy, partly because you couldn't be sure he wouldn't kill you too to keep his secret."

"Could be."

"Did he get what he came for?"

"I don't think so. He left cursing LeVeen and his pigeon."

"But you're still in his favor."

"Maybe not for long though."

"Your secret's safe with me."

"I couldn't trust you to keep your mouth shut."

"Try me."

"No thanks. I don't need that kind of shit hanging over my head. It'll be a lot simpler to just shoot you, even though that means I'll be busy the rest of the night cleaning the rug."

"Don't shoot me too hard and maybe I won't bleed."

She laughed again, a harsh metallic laugh that sounded like a pair of spent slugs rattling around in a coroner's stainless steel basin. "It's been fun, darling, but enough is enough."

"You'll never get enough. You're too greedy."

She didn't laugh at that and she wasn't smiling anymore either. She'd had enough humor for one night. Her mouth was set hard and her hand was steady as she pointed the gun at me from a distance of six feet. "Say bye-bye, snooper."

"Don't forget to take off the safety."

She angled the gun about ten degrees to the left as her thumb nudged the safety. That was all I needed. I pitched the phony Beretta at her head and dived at her legs. She yelled as the lighter caromed off her cheek. The gun in her hand popped once and I felt something breeze through the hair on my head. By then I'd tackled her and flattened her. I wrenched the gun from her hand before she had time to trigger another shot.

"Fucker, fucker, fucker," she said.

"Thanks anyway, but I've had enough of you for one night." I put my clothes on and finished my drink. She just lay there on the floor with a purple bruise on her cheekbone and a lot of venom in her eyes. It was eleven, too late for her to tip Bud as to what had happened. Or would she? I stood at the door, one hand on the knob, trying to figure her out.

"What do you need, an invitation to leave?"

"I was just thinking..."

"Haven't you strained yourself enough for one night?" Dixie propped herself up on one elbow and fingered her cheekbone.

I went out the door and closed it behind me. We were each on our own again.

Buzz was tripping out. Doctor'd given him some drugs to slow down his motor activity but he'd had a reaction to them, maybe because of residual radiation in his system, and he'd started to hallucinate.

He was trapped inside the lattice-work of a huge brilliant ruby as it floated through a universe of whirling lights and celestial music. Insect creatures with crystalline eyes peered in the ruby windows at him. A moth woman found the door to his jeweled capsule and crawled inside with him.

Her wings, mottled with changing colors and patterns, were heavy as she covered him like a blanket. It was good to be warm out here in the freezing void of space. He stroked her wings, soft and dusty with the ashes of extinct worlds. He stroked her warm pulsing abdomen, found the burning socket of her sex and sank into its whirlpool.

The moth woman took him on a flight through the Milky Way. Her engine pounded in his ears, bruised and sucked his muscles dry, then left him heaving breathless on a barren asteriod. He watched her fly away into the starless sky. Flap flap flap.

"Hey, wake up." Crabby pulled at Buzz's arm.

"You've been out of it all evening."

Buzz raised himself on an elbow and focused his mind on the present. There was dust in his mouth. His headache was gone but he was limp as silly putty.

"All shagged out, huh? I dropped by awhile ago and saw Molly getting her rocks off while you just lay there and took it. She's some beast, huh? One of the other girls told me that last night she took on the whole Raiders basketball team. She likes them big."

Buzz got up on his knees and shook his head. Pins and needles pierced him all over as the numbness left his body.

"Time for my midnight snack. Doc said you should get out for some fresh air anyway. Let's go for a drive."

I wasted no time getting down to the Nuke Flats waterfront. I found the Ocean Taxi terminal easily enough. I cruised on down to Pier Forty but there was nothing to be seen. No white van, no Bud, no nothing. I drove back up to Beatnickel and puttered along amidst a convoy of interstate transports. On the radio, the announcer was just winding up the eleven o'clock news broadcast. I stopped for a red light.

A guy and girl came across the intersection holding hands. Neither of them had legs. Their ass ends were each strapped onto a skateboard and they were using their free gloved hands to propel themselves across the street. When they came to the curb the guy lifted the front end of the girl's skateboard up onto the sidewalk and then gave her a boost the rest of the way. He backed up about two feet, took a roll at the curb and vaulted himself on outstretched arms over the hump. They joined hands again and went on down the sidewalk, pedestrians parting to give them right of way.

I realized suddenly that I'd been stupid. The taped ransom demand I'd heard on the phone was a fabrication, so there was absolutely no reason why Bud should have delivered the paintings to the waterfront at eleven. That was just to mislead me into thinking I could waste the early part of the night elsewhere. Bud had probably moved the paintings as soon as Mrs.

Riordon had quit the house for her weekly bridge game; and the place of delivery was probably far removed from the Nuke Flats waterfront. The only reason Bud had wanted me to overhear the ransom demand was to provide him with a witness to 'Muriel's request.' But if he wanted to steal paintings from his daughter to pay off the loan sharks, that was his business, likewise if he wanted to keep it secret from his wife. But that still left me with the problem of where to find Muriel.

Maybe the payoff Mrs. Riordon had made this afternoon had been on the level. It was too weird to be otherwise. Anyone who used giant bumblebees as couriers must have some real connection to a girl artist with an insect fixation. But where did I look now for leads? Or was it justification I needed? The Riordons obviously didn't want me poking around. I had to get in touch with my original employer, Natalie Ferris, and find out what was happening. I'd been on the job three days and all I'd been able to turn up was a bunch of dead bodies.

It was no longer very clear to me what were the motives behind this search and I wanted to know before I ran into the heavies who were decapitating the people who got too close to Muriel. I was curious about what had become of her alright, but I was damned if I was going to lose my head to a bunch of revolutionary crazies.

I drove to my office. The street was quiet: just a few cruising couples with nothing better to do. I locked the car, opened the lobby door, bought a stale but hot cup of coffee from the friendly machine and went upstairs to my homely headquarters. I got the West Coast number out of my desk and dialled direct. The phone rang for a long time. Out there it would be going on seven-thirty, just about the evening dinner hour. I was thinking maybe I should hang up and call a couple of hours later, when a lady with a Japanese accent came on the line and asked me who I wanted. I told her, Natalie Ferris, and she told me that Natalie had gone to the airport more than an hour ago and would be flying back East late tonight.

I hung up and stared at the wall for all of five minutes. Then I thumbed the replay button on the Memoryphone and found that Miss Ferris had called ten hours earlier to tell me she would be returning tonight and expected a report from me at noon tomorrow. She'd left a local phone number where she could be reached. Well, wasn't that just ducky? I'd barely begun to identify the players in this intrigue and she wanted a report. I'd give her one. I'd show her half a dozen horoscopes, a sci-fi novel with most of the pages chopped out, an address book, an envelope that once contained a key, newspaper clippings of headless corpses and the still-warm gun that I'd taken from Dixie—let her sort it out herself.

I threw my coffee in the waste basket. It was too bitter to drink and I hadn't yet got around to buying some sugar to replace what had been stolen. I locked up and went back down to the car. It was going on midnight. I drove uptown, not knowing just where I was going, only knowing that I didn't want to go home in case Mundt and York were hanging around. Until I had my own questions answered I wasn't interested in answering theirs.

Unconsciously, I guess I must have known all along where I was headed: the Luna Deli. There were lots of parking slots on the street but I slipped the Astromobile into the first one I came to and walked the rest of the block down to the deli. Things weren't nearly as busy as the night I'd been here before. Only one booth was occupied, by a spaced-out individual with a pair of aviator goggles around his neck and a silk scarf tied across his forehead. A full-length khaki coat hung from his shoulders like a cape. A stick of incense burned in the ashtray before him as he chanted Indian mantras over the hardboiled egg he was shelling. I walked down to the beer coolers at the back and scored a Heineken. An old gentleman stood there in the corner humming to himself as he wrote math equations with his finger on the condensation of the cooler doors. His putty colored face had the skin-flaked look of an escapee from a wax museum.

"Give me a shrimp salad sandwich on light rye with

lots of mayo and a taste of tartar sauce," I told the man behind the counter.

"Toasted?"

"Sure." I watched him scoop into the shrimp salad mix. In the tray right next to it was something that looked like oyster paste. It was a fresh batch and hadn't been disturbed. I paid for my beer and sandwich and walked back to the wagon. I listened to the radio and ate my snack with my eyes on the street.

I didn't have to wait long. The midnight news had just come on when a dark blue van went past me and parked in front of Luna Deli. I was waiting for the tall bird to climb out but he didn't. Instead, a bowlegged little guy with hunched shoulders and long arms scrabbled out of the van and into the deli. In about two minutes he scurried back out to the van with a paper bag in one hand.

The light was yellow at the intersection. I eased the Astro out of its slot and cruised past the van with a sideways glance at the occupants. The little guy on the passenger side sat barely high enough to see out the window but the driver was easily a couple of heads higher. I stopped for the red light and watched the van in my rearview. It pulled out of its parking slot and zoomed up into the adjacent lane. The light turned green and we drove west for a dozen blocks. Then the van pulled ahead of me and swung downtown. I tagged along, one lane to the left and a couple of car lengths behind. Suddenly the van took a fast right turn. I was blocked by a string of taxis from crossing lanes to make the turn. By the time I got over there, the van was out of sight.

I cruised slowly along Kilroy Street. Townhouses on both sides, with three feet of front lawn and sturdy iron fences to keep the freaks and the bums off the grass. Some were separated from their neighbours by the width of a narrow driveway, others were hunched shoulder-to-shoulder with scant walkways between. Some of them had garage doors flush with the sidewalk, without handles, probably remote controlled. In the time it had taken me to cross the traffic flow, the van could have radio triggered a garage door open, driven in and closed it before I showed up.

I took note of the street numbers and went on to the end of the block. No traffic here at all. A few people on the streets: sleepless old men walking their dogs, restless young kids looking for a fuck or a fight. I was bushed. I drove over to Wendy's place, left the Astro on the street and climbed seven flights of stairs to rap on the door. One of her roomies, Trish, a goodlooking brunette with big lips and small tits, opened the door the width of a chainlatch.

"Hi." Her eyes were at halfmast, weighted down by sleep or the golden glitter on her lids. She wore a safety pin in her nose. Trish was an aficionado of punkdom. "Who're you?"

"Keith. Where's Wendy?"

"Oh. Keith." She opened the door. "Come on in. Wendy's out with somebody. I don't think she's coming back tonight."

"Fine by me. I only want a place to crash."

"Get kicked out of your place?" She closed and locked the door. She was wearing very tight white leather pants with dirty knees and ragged cuffs below which showed her bare feet and red toenails. Her black T-shirt was artfully torn open in a dozen places.

"No. The cops are hanging around to pounce on me."

"Who could blame them?" She hooked her thumbs in her belt loops, pushed her shoulders back and her hips forward.

"Don't get any ideas," I said. "I came here for a rest." I pulled my jacket off and hung it in the hall closet, then, remembering the guns I was carrying for ballast, moved it to the closet in Wendy's room. Trish followed me to the door. I closed the venetian blinds, took off my shirt and draped it over the chair at Wendy's desk. From behind I heard the sound of a zipper.

"Want to see something neat?"

I turned around. Trish peeled her pants halfway down her thighs and finger-combed her pubic hair. It was trimmed to the shape of a heart and dyed blood-red. "Nice," I said.

"Want to play Cupid and stick an arrow in it?"

"Not tonight. Cupid's fagged out."

"Pretty please, with coke on it?"

"Couldn't you find someone on the streets to bring home with you?"

"He passed out an hour ago. I was just going out to the Riviera to hustle when you showed up. Come on man, let's get down. Wendy's told me all about you." She pushed her pants the rest of the way down her legs and kicked them away from her.

"Do you really have snow, or was that jive talk?"

She skipped out of the room, clad only in her black T-shirt, and came back in a minute with an aluminum film cannister. "We'd better lie down for this, 'cause it's going to lift the top of your head off."

We lay side-by-side on Wendy's bed. Trish opened the cannister and scooped her thumbnail into the fine white powder. She held it under my nose. I snorted through one nostril, she reloaded and I took a hit in the other half of my head. Blastoff. Coke acceleration slammed me back into the pillows. I sailed up into the ozone like Rocket Man.

Trish was up there with me in a minute. I shucked my pants. We rolled into each other's arms. I touched her, found her hot and wet. Her legs sprang open and I slipped into position. We started balling like there was no tomorrow. We were still at it when Wendy came home.

"You dirty sonofabitch," she screamed, swatting me on the ass with her purse. "And you've got the gall to screw the slut in my bed. Get out. Get the hell out, the fucking pair of you."

"Wendy..."

"I don't want to talk to you or ever see you again." She tried to bop me one in the nose. I grabbed her wrists and tussled with her while Trish scooted her ass out of there and locked herself in her own room. Wendy tried to knee me in the balls. I tossed her down on her bed. For a moment I had the idea of jumping on her and finishing what I'd begun with Trish, but she had a murderous look in her eye that effectively castrated my passion. I got dressed.

"I'll call you tomorrow," I said.

"Don't fucking bother. We're finished. Kaput. Fuck off."

I got my jacket from her closet, let myself out of the apartment and went down to the car. Half an hour ago I'd been ready to go to sleep. Now, with a headful of snow, sleep seemed very remote. I got in the car and drove around. I was still nervous about going home in case the cops were hanging around. I drove over to Lothario's but I'd missed Tracey by about ten minutes. I had a couple of beers there anyway to calm my jangled nerves. Then I drove back downtown to my office and spent the night on an air mattress I kept for such emergencies.

8

In the morning I went straight to the City Records building and spent fifteen minutes learning how to punch the computer cards that would produce the information I wanted. When I thought I had the hang of it, I went to work and punched out cards for Uranium, Natalie Ferris, the Riordons, Billy Crabner, Ron LeVeen and Jordan Ferris.

The information supplied consisted of full name and social security number, date and place of birth (timed to the minute in some cases), last known address and occupation, as well as a coded listing of relatives whose vital statistics one could dredge up by punching a corresponding retrieval card, if one were interested in constructing a family tree.

Uranium and Crabner were straightforward enough. I copied their birth data and noted that their previous addresses corresponded to the ones I already had. When I came to Ron LeVeen, it turned out that he had a brother. That missing pigeon was still on my mind, so I punched a retrieval card and took a look at Dale LeVeen. He was a stage designer and he lived in my part of town. I jotted down the address.

The twists began with Natalie Ferris. She wasn't listed. At least, the one I wanted wasn't. There was a Natalie Ferris, but she was seventy years old. Definitely the wrong lady. And then the Riordons. Bud was listed as a chauffeur and Viv, a nurse. That was fine, and their birth dates looked about right, but they had no daughter. I thought that perhaps I'd made a mistake in punching the card, thereby omitting the relative code listings, so I went ahead, intending to check with the librarian to see if I hadn't slipped up somewhere. But when I came to Jordan Ferris, whom I'd believed to be a bachelor, things took a turn towards the unexpected. If I was reading the printout properly, it seemed that Jordan Ferris had been married twice, and had fathered a daughter in each marriage. I followed through on the retrieval cards. The first marriage had ended in divorce, with the ex-wife reclaiming her maiden name, taking custody of the daughter and removing herself to California. The daughter, whose birth date looked right to me for the lady I had in mind, was one Natalie Cumming. Jordan's second wife had died, obviously in child-birth according to the date, and the second daughter's name was Muriel. Her birthdate checked out with the Muriel I was looking for.

So Muriel wasn't the Riordons' daughter after all. Jordan Ferris was her father.

Now some of the puzzle pieces began to fall into place. I knew Jordan Ferris was running for mayor in the upcoming election and his major policy promise was an all-out war on the organized crime establishment that was bleeding the city and forcing it ever closer to bankruptcy. It made sense that some enterprising ganglanders might kidnap his daughter and threaten her life to force Jordan Ferris out of the mayorality race. That could well be the political complication Aquarius had seen in her chart. But if Muriel was Jordan's daughter, why were the Riordons pretending she was theirs? And if the ganglanders knew who they'd snatched, why bother squeezing petty cash from Mrs. Riordon when the real stakes were so much bigger: the enormous underworld rake-off from just about every money-making business in the city?

My brain was starting to overheat with questions that had no ready answers. I gathered the fruits of my labour and climbed out of the basement where the City Records computer was installed. In the lobby I saw *Department of Health* on the Floor Directory and was reminded of something I'd been meaning to check out. I went upstairs to the Health office and, passing myself off as an investigator with the Unemployment Insurance Bureau, enquired as to whether Billy Crabner, formerly of Scranton Street, was still receiving Disability checks.

"No sir," the clerk said after he'd checked the files. "We got a phone call from him a few weeks ago, saying he'd had a successful operation on his legs and he was no longer disabled."

"Any change-of-address?"

"Nope."

I said my thanks and hit the street. I found a phone booth and dialled the number Miss Ferris-Cumming had left me, but a gravel-voiced old boy at the Hutton Hotel informed me that he'd been instructed not to put any calls through before noon, and that I should try again at that time.

That left me with about two hours to kill, so I buzzed off to the University to see Aquarius. The secretary said he'd been called out on a referral but that he'd be back in an hour if I wanted to wait. I stuffed my City Records gleanings into a manilla envelope, scribbled a short note asking Aquarius to look over the data and be prepared to give me a general rundown on the bit players and a specific analysis of Jordan Ferris, and left the lot with the secretary to pass on to the professor when he returned.

I left the car in the University parking tower and took the subway to Rue Christophe, one of the streets that had undergone a name-change recently with the influx of a large Gallic population to the swinging-est neighborhood in the downtown area. I climbed out of the subway and crossed Sheridan Square. A neon Marlboro cowboy postured on the huge electronic billboard above the square. He struck a match on his tight-denimed ass, lit his cigarette and blew a smoke ring before going through the cycle all over again. Take a walk down Rue Christophe and you could see a hundred imitators doing the same thing.

I took a walk down Rue Christophe. It wasn't really warm out but there were scores of guys cruising in tight jeans and sleeveless T-shirts, their hair trimmed close, little bunches of keys jingling from their belts. I passed a young Chinese dude walking hand-in-hand with a much older man who wore a white Stetson and a leather holster with a dildo in it, the bandolier loaded with foil-wrapped suppositories. It was that kind of neighborhood.

I walked past Sly's, a notorious gay hangout. Through the doorway came the diddleybop sounds of disco. It was eleven in the morning but there were guys inside dancing under black lights, drinking crème de menthe and shrilling with laughter that coyly bordered on hysteria.

Dale LeVeen lived in one of the apartments above Sly's. I climbed six flights of stairs and looked for the numbers on the doors. Numbers seemed to be going out of style. The apartment doors were individually distinguished by minor works of art, ranging from floral prints through paint-by-number Beardsley reproductions right on up to blown-up photographs of the occupants' genitalia. If Marcel Duchamp were alive today and found this, he'd cart the whole place off to the Met and exhibit it as the *pièce de resistance* of Found Art.

Mr. LeVeen was a more conventional fellow. He'd simply put his name in Gothic script on a piece of white cardboard and taped it to the door. I rang his bell. I heard a 'just a moment' from inside and then the door opened the inevitable width of a chain latch and a young bearded man looked at me. "Mr. London? I didn't expect to see you so early. I won't have the set finished until later this afternoon."

"I'll be busy then," I said. "Let's talk about it now."

He opened the door and let me in. He had long hair, a neatly trimmed beard and the beginnings of a beer belly tucked inside a checkered shirt. It was a cosy little apartment: tiny kitchen with barely enough room to squeeze between the table and the fridge to get to a bathroom the size of a phone booth; pots of leafy green friends on the windowsills; Chinese bells hanging in the breezeway between kitchen and living room. In there: a corner couch, faded Indian carpet that smelled of hashish, stereo outfit on plank-and-brick shelf, albums scattered around, hookah on the coffee table, pack of Drum tobacco and a half-bottle of Ouzo on the floor. Beyond that was a bedroom-workroom with mattress and bedding on the floor and a draftsman's table by the window.

"It's coming along pretty well," he said, "but I'll have to go buy some more tin foil. Come look at it and tell me if you think the control console's in the right place." He beckoned me into the bedroom-workroom. On the floor was a business-like clutter of masking tape, colored construction paper and cardboard, tin foil, bits of balsa wood, scissors, ruler, pencils and geometry set. In the middle of it all was a model stage setting that I guessed was supposed to represent the interior of a space ship. "Now I was thinking," he said as he crouched beside the construction, "that I should place the control console here, so that when Captain Fallik brings the Plutonian Princess aboard for the final fuck scene, the audience will have an unobstructed view of the free-floating bed, while at the same time, they'll see the TV monitor that reveals the approach of the Klaxon warship for the climactic battle. What do you think?"

"You're a genius," I said.

"I was up all night with it," he said proudly.

"It shows."

"You don't think it'll run us over the budget, using that TV monitor? I mean, we could have one of the Corporals come in to announce the Klaxon ship, but it might spoil the intimacy of the Captain's scene with the Princess."

"You're quite right. You should be doing my job."

"Nikki told me to just go ahead and play with it," he said, moving the control console around the tiny set. "He was confident I could anticipate what you wanted."

I looked around the room. If he were so fucking intuitive, why didn't he hand over that key? I looked out his bedroom window. On the ledge was a wooden platform with a pair of dowel-rod perches and a scattered handful of birdseed. Spatterings of pigeon shit on the window ledge reassured me that I had the right man.

"To tell you the truth," I said, "I came here early to pick up a key Ron sent over. Did you get it?"

LeVeen looked at me as if seeing me for the first time. "How do you know my brother?"

"We've been balling the same chick. He was supposed to drop by and give me the key yesterday but he called and said he had to leave town suddenly on business. He said he'd send the key over to you with the pigeon and tell you what it was all about."

"Yeah?" LeVeen regarded me with suspicion. "Hermes flew in yesterday evening with a key on his leg, but there was no note. That's what we usually use him for—to send messages—it's a hobby with Ron and me. I phoned him at the time but there was no answer. Maybe he'd gone already. But it's funny he didn't phone first or send a note with Hermes. What's the key for?"

"Safety deposit box. He's been holding some important papers."

"A script?"

"Yeah. Can you give me the key? I've got to run."

"Ron wouldn't bother putting a script in a safety deposit box. His stuff is good, but not that good."

"Okay, okay. I probably shouldn't be talking about this, but seeing as you're Ron's brother... Ron's been secretly taping conferences at CBX. They're planning a couple of new series for the next season..."

"And you guys are going to pitch the word to Trans-World Studios? Is that it? Rip off their ideas and beat CBX to the punch with a new series?"

"Something like that."

"Wow. Big business espionage, huh?"

"For chrissake, don't tell anybody."

"Don't worry about me, Ariel." LeVeen stuck his hand in his pocket and pulled out a key. "Anything in this for me?"

"We'll talk about it when Ron gets back." Now I knew whom he'd mistaken me for. Ariel London was an avant-garde playwright.

"Fair enough." He dropped the key in one of my

hands and vigorously pumped the other. "It's been a pleasure talking to you, sir. Will you be at the theatre tomorrow?"

"Sure. It's my play isn't it?" I dropped the key in my pocket and got out of there before he started telling me how much he admired my work. If there's one thing I hate, it's flattery.

I was on my way back to the subway when I saw a butterfly alight on a potted plant outside a cafe. It was so extraordinary to see one in the city that the sight of it set off a chain of correspondences in my mind. Butterfly, giant bees, Muriel's insect portraits and thence to Mr. Moskovitz. Ever since Bud had mentioned that the art dealer was cosy with Mrs. Riordon, I'd had vague intentions of getting around to see the man. He was the only one in Muriel's circle that I hadn't interviewed and, if one could believe Bud, the art dealer had a vested interest in the girl.

I recalled that Moskovitz's gallery was on Greenwich Ave. Seeing as how I was in the neighborhood and had some time to kill, I might as well check him out. I hustled down Seventh, grooving on street freaks. A band of Hare Krishna devotees, orange-robed and head-shaven, were jamming on a streetcorner with flutes, bells, tambourines and a bagpipe. The sound was a bit unusual, even for them, and I was tempted to stand around and listen, but I had business on my mind and the bagpipe was sufficiently loud that I heard it for the next couple of blocks anyway.

I found the Realistik Gallery on Greenwich. It didn't look like much from the outside, just a storefront window with a couple of Pringle paintings on display, a squirrel and a bunny. Inside, the walls were densely hung with representative works of all the minor contenders in the field of Realism. I didn't have much time to myself before a big man in a green suit crawled out of his glassed-in alcove at the rear of the gallery and approached me with the rolling gait of an overfed bear.

"Good day, sir. May I help you?" His dark eyes swept disapprovingly over my attire. He'd probably like to help me on my way, but he was cautious. Even millionaires dressed like bums these days.

"Mr. Moskovitz?"

"At your service." He inclined his head a millimeter in a parody of a bow. There was a patch of hair on his florid nose and a pair of jowls under his jaw that would have looked just right on a grandfather hog. He had a fistful of gold rings on either hand and enough stones set among them to span the spectrum of the rainbow. A few other yellow trinkets held his shirt cuffs together and kept his tie fixed to his silk shirt. Mentally I added Art Dealer to the long list of jobs that paid better than mine did. But he had red-rimmed eyes and a nervous tic in his fat mouth that suggested life wasn't as smooth as he might have wished it.

"I'm looking for something unusual."

"We don't handle abstracts." He said the last word, with a twist of his mouth, as if he were speaking of raw sewage.

"I can see that," I said. "I'm looking for something representational, but something different from the usual subject matter of the Realists."

"We have a few Snowvilles here that are a bit out of the ordinary." He directed my attention to a large elliptical canvas of a butchered moose hanging from the rafters of a barn.

"Something more colorful," I suggested.

"You can't match the Magic Realists for brilliance. Take this Pringle." He gestured towards a canvas in which a dazzling speckled trout leaped from a cataract of frothing water.

"That's nice," I said, "but all these barns and vegetables and animals are a bit mundane for my taste. I'm looking for something that exhibits the artist's ability to view the world from different eyes."

"Just exactly what did you have in mind?"

"Oh, something around a thousand dollars' worth of eccentricity. The weirder it is, the better I like it. But it looks like you've got nothing along those lines." I'd taken a good look around by then and seen nothing of Muriel's. There wasn't a bug in sight. "I think I'll go visit some other galleries. Everything here is so..." I searched for something appropriately condemning while Moskovitz wrung his jewelled hands in despair. "...so...so traditional."

"Wait." Moskovitz grabbed my arm before I'd half-completed my turn towards the door. "I believe I might have just the thing for you."

"I don't see it here." I tugged my sleeve loose from his hairy paw.

"Upstairs," he said. "Upstairs I have a canvas or two which would surely interest you."

"How come they're upstairs? Not good enough to hang with the rest?"

"They've not yet been framed. Come." He plucked my sleeve again. I shrugged my shoulders and followed him. We took a stairway at the rear of the gallery. Upstairs was a bathroom and a large room lighted by a barred window and recessed ceiling lamps. A bench stood along one wall, upon which were arrayed various implements of the picture-framer's trade: hammer and shears, stapler and tacks, wire and paste. Beyond the bench a number of empty frames leaned against the wall and on the other side of the room, a dozen or more canvases leaning together. Moskovitz pulled the facing one, a giant apple, aside and revealed to me the one behind it.

A metallic black praying mantis clutched the corpus of a brown headless cousin. From a lifeline just out of reach, a tiny green inchworm formed an inverted question mark.

"Yesss," I said.

"You like it?"

"Very much." And I'd seen it before too, in Muriel's studio. "How much?"

"The figure you mentioned earlier might suffice."

"Got anything similar with a lower price tag?"

Moskovitz' lip curled, obviously disappointed with me. But now that he'd come this far, there was no turning back. He revealed one canvas after another, searching for my approval and subsequent dollars. He had most of the paintings I'd seen in Muriel's studio.

"Surely there is one among those you would like."

"No doubt about it," I said. "Will you take a check?"

"I prefer cash."

"Doesn't everybody? But who in their right mind would carry a thousand around with him in this town?" I pulled a checkbook from my pocket. "I'll take the praying mantis for one thousand. Is it a sale?"

"It's a sacrifice," he said, knotting his brow in economic consternation, but by then I had the check filled out and was waving it dry under his nose.

"But it's money in the bank," I said.

"Alright." He took the check. "Do you have identification?"

I showed him my array of credentials, everything except my snooper license. Thus reassured, he packaged the 2x5-foot canvas in heavy brown paper wrapped with twine, and even carried it downstairs for me as far as the door.

"It's been a pleasure," I said, taking the package from him. "Thanks for your trouble."

"Not at all," he said.

I strolled off to the nearest subway stop with my original work of evidence under my arm. The check I'd given Moskovitz was going to bounce like an India rubber ball but I wasn't worried. I thought I had it all figured out. He couldn't holler about the check for fear of drawing attention to the fact that he was dealing in stolen paintings. Then I had an uneasy feeling. If he knew the paintings were stolen, why'd he sell one so readily to a stranger who walked in off the street? Maybe he planned on making a sudden departure from the local scene. Then again, he might yet be unaware of Muriel's disappearance, and be quite innocent of Bud's little piece of subterfuge. In the latter case, he might well have the bunko squad beating on my door before the end of the day, or whenever he realized I'd passed him a bum check. That was all I needed: more cops on my trail.

In front of the subway entrance, another bearded-and-robed denizen of the astral plane was prostrate on his back in a painful-looking yogic posture. There were flowers strewn around him and, in the direct path of passersby, a large tin can with a paper note attached that read *Alms for Nicotine Nirvana*. I dropped a few pennies as I went by. The yogi didn't blink. He had a Camel in his mouth and a beatific smile on his face.

I took the subway back to the University. Dr. Aquarius was in his office, a neat patchwork of charts arrayed across his desk. I stood my package beside the door and took a seat.

"You're just in time for coffee." He poured us each a cup from a percolator and we got down to business. Referring to the chart for the Bowman-Watroboski fiasco, he pointed out the planetary configurations that indicated violent death. That might have been a fine piece of afterthought, but he also found similar indicators in Ron LeVeen's natal chart. I didn't bother to mention that he was dead too. Obviously the body hadn't been discovered yet and there was no need to alarm Aquarius by telling him I'd let another murder go unannounced to the police.

Miss Ferris-Cumming was a Sagittarian with a cluster of planets in the ninth house, Mercury at the midheaven, indicating that she had high aspirations related to the publishing industry. She came from a broken home, tended to vacillate and sometimes pushed things to extremes. She was more concerned with assigning work than doing it herself.

Crabner was a Cancer with a mother fixation, underworld connections and a strong romantic streak. He tended to find himself in situations over which he had no control. Uranium had a grouping of influences in the twelfth house, suggesting mysticism and confinement in institutions. He was obviously homosexual, Aquarius said, pointing out Venus afflicted by Saturn, Uranus and Neptune. Another victim of circumstance who showed poor prospects of recovering from his accident, the professor said. Bud Riordon was a horny Scorpio greedy for other people's money while Mrs. Riordon was a frigid Virgo with a devotion to service and hygiene that bordered on self-righteousness; sexual complications between the two were implicit, Aquarius said.

"Right now I'm most interested in Jordan Ferris. How's he look?" I hadn't told Aquarius that Jordan was Muriel's father.

"He has a stellium of planets in Capricorn in the tenth house. Excellent placing for a politician; indication of very high ambitions. But three of the planets are squared Uranus, creating a strong potential for bizarre compulsions and accidents. Particularly, Mars conjunct Saturn signifies danger when the squared Uranian factor is activated. Sun opposite Pluto shows the conflict between his basic purpose and that of the underworld. This week in particular is an especially difficult time for him, transiting Mars forming a square to its natal position, likewise, transiting Uranus forming a tension-filled opposition to its birth position. Both his person and his political career are endangered."

"I don't know how to thank you enough, Professor. Can I take this stuff with me? I have to run for an appointment at noon."

"Just give me a minute to photocopy these for my files. It'll remain confidential." He gathered up the charts and went down the hall to the secretary's office. When he came back he gave me the originals in a file folder and said, "By the way, I was thinking about that girl with the insect fixation. You know, there was a man in the Biology department that got himself rather a bad reputation on account of his obsession with insects."

"Do tell. Is he still around?"

"No, he got chucked out of the University because of the bizarre nature of his experiments. He attempted to graft a pair of insect pincers onto the forearm of a young man who'd lost his hand in an industrial accident."

"Wouldn't they be too small to be useful?"

"Apparently not the pincers from the Amazonian Crusher Beetle, if I remember the name correctly. Supposedly, they've got claws as big as a lobster's."

"And did the experiment succeed?"

"No, I don't think it did, but only because Dr.

Malkud was refused access to some of the Physics department's equipment. The Director of Research Studies thought the whole project quite disgusting and made such a stink about it that Dr. Malkud was asked to leave. I think he'd also done some radiation work on certain insects. I remember hearing some of his colleagues talking about a housefly bigger than a June Bug. At one time, they used to call Malkud the Einstein of Entomology but he's definitely *persona non grata* around here now."

I flashed back to those giant bumblebees I'd seen on Big Bass Lake. I knew I was onto something big now. "And what became of Dr. Malkud?"

"Oh, he's still around town, I believe. Apparently he's gone absolutely buggy since he was fired, but I couldn't tell you what he's been up to. Maybe somebody in the Biology department has kept in touch with him."

"Where do I find it?"

"The adjacent building to this one on your way to the parking tower. Try Dr. Mitsubishi."

Buzz lay on his back on the Doctor's operating table. Doctor said it was impossible, but Buzz felt the neutrons streaming through his body. The gun fired for only a couple of seconds, then stopped. Buzz felt a momentary sense of relief but he knew that strange things would continue to work inside him.

"How do you feel?" Doctor ran a stethoscope over Buzz's thorax. He shone a penlight into his multiple-lensed eyes. He drew off a small blood sample.

"Hungry."

"That's a good sign. Eat whenever you want. It's important to maintain your strength."

"I'm sick of chicken."

"We'll get some rabbits for you next week. Nice fat bunnies that bounce like a ball. Hippity-hop-hop." Doctor bunny-hopped his hand up Buzz's leg.

"That tickles." Buzz knocked Doctor's hand away.

"You don't mind when Molly does it. I've watched. You let her do everything. You like it."

"That's different."

"You have no gratitude," Doctor muttered. *"Where would you be if I hadn't taken you in? Still locked in that iron lung, taking food through one tube and shitting out the other. What kind of life was that? Now you're powerful and free and you forget your benefactor."*

"I'm sorry, Doctor." Buzz moved his pincers away so as not to interfere with his benefactor's pleasure. Better not make Doctor angry. One too many seconds under the neutron gun and who knew what might happen inside?

"Pah. It doesn't matter. I have more important things to worry about." Doctor detached Buzz's electrodes. "Do you maintain strict control over the bees? Will they do as you command?"

Buzz sat up and lowered his feet to the floor. "They understand me perfectly. Yesterday I drove down to the waterfront and pointed out a lone man working on a barge. No one saw them swarm onto him. The man was dead before he hit the water."

"Excellent. We only need execute this one job perfectly and we will gain money and power beyond our dreams."

Buzz tried a few shaky steps and returned dizzily to his seat. "Can I have my sugar injection now?"

In his own country Dr. Mitsubishi would probably have been looked up to as a freak of nature. Around the University he was just another Oriental with post-doctoral degrees up the yin-yang, albeit a Japanese that stood out from the rest by virtue of his height, six foot two. He was nicely filled out as well, somewhere above the two hundred fifty mark. If he'd been as athletic as he'd been academic, he might have made the Sumo wrestling team.

I watched him from the door of Fish Lab One, to which the Biology department secretary had directed me. Dr. Mitsubishi wore crepe-soled white shoes, brown slacks and the mandatory white lab coat. A bald spot the size of a child's hand shone coppertoned at the back of his head. He stood beside a fish tank dropping pieces of meat to a pair of dull yellow fish with black stripes. The fish moved as fast as a boxer's hands, lunging from one side of the tank to the other, snatching the morsels as soon as they hit the water.

"Dr. Mitsubishi?'

He turned with a frown. His eyes were black beads beneath puffy lids. "Close the door. You're causing a draft. It's bad for the tropical fish."

"My name's Waldram, Federal Parks Control." I showed him one of my many phony calling cards, culled from office desks, conference tables and motel rooms everywhere I went. "I'm enquiring after one of your former associates."

Dr. Mitsubishi took my card between forefinger and thumb, squinted at it and handed it back with a bloody print on either side. He dipped his hand into the plastic bag he carried, tossed a few more pieces of chopped liver to the fish and said over his shoulder, "Which one?"

"Dr. Malkud."

"What is the nature of your business with him?"

"Well, I don't know if you've been to any of our parks on the Eastern seaboard, but in the past couple of years the mosquito population has got way out of hand. They're making life hell for the tourists." I knew this was basically true, having read it in the papers, but I had to be careful not to get into technical waters because Mitsubishi would soon detect my ignorance. "So what we've been considering is the importation of large numbers of dragonflies, whose principal food is mosquitoes and their larvae, to curb the pest population. Knowing that Dr. Malkud had undertaken extensive insect research in the past, I hoped to discuss with him the implementation of our project."

"Why come to me?" Mitsubishi picked out a large piece of bloody liver, put it into his mouth and chewed it thoughtfully.

"I didn't know where to find him. I thought perhaps you'd kept in touch with him since he left the University."

"Hah." Mitsubishi shook the last of the liver into the

fish tank, threw the empty bag in a garbage can and sucked his fingers clean. "You can get Malkud's address from the department secretary. As for myself, I would as soon keep in touch with Malkud as I would put my hand in this tank." He flicked the water with a finger and both fish broke the surface with mouths gaping for his retreating hand.

"I understand Dr. Malkud's tenure with the University was allowed to expire. Does that mean his work was less than professional?"

"The man's technique was superior but he was hopelessly insane."

"How do you mean?"

"His researches in radiation therapy led him to believe in the possibility of grafting insect elements onto human bodies. Radioactive growth induction would bring the insect parts up to scale and then crossfire radiation techniques would permit the union of disparate elements. He envisioned a super-race of transmutations: athletes with grasshopper legs to catapult them hundreds of feet; people with moth-like antennae for super-sensitive hearing or compound eyes for 360-degree vision. And that was only the beginning. He intended to refine cloning techniques, the creation of unlimited quantities of identical creatures from a single formula egg. He might have created a world of monsters if he had been allowed to continue."

"Why did the University let him go?"

"It is not something I am permitted to discuss."

"I must know, Dr. Mitsubishi. There is a lot of federal funding available for this project. If there's something about Malkud that suggests he's unstable or unreliable, I'll have to look elsewhere for help, perhaps here among the staff in your department. Tell me why the Director of Research Studies fired him. Was it just professional jealousy or something bigger?"

"This must be kept in strictest confidence."

"I understand."

"*That* is more than I can say," Dr. Mitsubishi sighed. He looked around and found himself a stool to sit on. "Doubtless you've already heard about Malkud's accelerated growth experiments on houseflies. Using the same techniques, he could certainly produce a number of over-size dragonflies which, given their normally voracious appetites, would probably eliminate your mosquito problem in one summer. But what is known to only a few among us here at the department, Malkud had also experimented with accelerated growth techniques on a ladybug. Eventually the creature grew to the size of a turtle, more than two feet in length and weighing almost thirty pounds."

"That must have been a remarkable scientific feat. But how does that lead to the occasion of his dismissal?"

"One afternoon the Director went to Malkud's lab to show a visitor this remarkable achievement. The visitor was Miss Abigail Whittaker." Mitsubishi looked at me significantly.

"Nobody I know."

"An ancient fossil of a woman, but an alumnus of the University who has donated millions to the Science Faculty. This building is named after her."

"I see. And she didn't approve of giant ladybugs?"

"On the contrary. She had a gardenful of the small varieties and looked forward with high anticipation to meeting Lucy."

"Lucy Ladybug?"

"Malkud's pet name for the creature."

"But something went wrong."

"*That* is an understatement. When the Director and Miss Whittaker walked into the laboratory, they surprised Dr. Malkud. He was in the ladybug cage, naked upon a heap of dirt and weeds, copulating with Lucy."

"And Miss Whittaker was not amused?"

"Miss Whittaker suffered a cerebral hemorrhage. Her first words upon recovering were 'Get rid of that madman!' If she knew we had even so much as his address still hanging around here, she'd probably raze the building."

"I see. Well, thank you, Doctor. I'd better be going." I offered him my hand but he just looked at it. Perhaps he didn't want to get too close to a potential associate of

Dr. Malkud. Everybody was worried about tenure these days. I turned on my heel and headed for the door.

"Good luck with the mosquitoes," Dr. Mitsubishi called after me.

I got Malkud's address, 2030 Kilroy Street, from the department secretary and used a payphone in the Whittaker Center lobby to call the Hutton Hotel. Miss Ferris-Cumming was prepared to receive me; I told her I'd be right over.

The Hutton was a hundred-year-old hotel in midtown. The Duke of Bristol had stayed here to avoid rubbing elbows with the *nouveau riche* rabble so often encountered at the Waldorf-Astoria. His presence lingered still in the large canvas portrait in the lobby: the Duke, resplendent in his Vimy Ridge officer's tunic, eyes still puffy from an attack of mustard gas, glared across the lobby to the desk. Leaning against his leg was a surly bulldog with a little sailor's cap fixed jauntily over one ear. On either side of the Duke's portrait hung a flag: the Union Jack and the Bristol coat of arms, three rampant bulldogs in a field of geese. The bellhops were old men dressed up like English butlers. A suit of armor stood guard at the entrance to the oak-panelled elevator. It was that kind of hotel. It didn't seem to be Miss Ferris-Cumming's sort of hotel, but then I didn't know her very well.

My guide, a recent graduate from the British Butler Academy decked out in black pressed pants, spats, grey vest and a starched white shirt with sleeve garters, showed me to the suite of my appointment. Miss Ferris-Cumming was in the living room, a silver service tray with teapot and accoutrements on the polished coffee table. She looked up from buttering an English muffin as Jeeves announced me.

"Please have a seat, Mr. Savage." She gave me a smile and took a bite from her muffin. "Would you like tea?"

"No, thanks anyway." I sat down and shook out a cigarette. Jeeves pulled an ashtray out of his sleeve, set it before me on the table and faded into the background. I lit up and blew smoke at the ceiling. Miss Ferris-Cumming was wearing a green silk kimono with little white peacocks strutting around on the fabric. She was lightly made up around the eyes and her blond hair was fixed in a neat bun at the top of her head. "How was the West Coast?" I asked.

"Laid back." She polished off her muffin and poured a cup of tea. "Have you found Muriel?"

"Muriel who?"

"My sister."

"You mean, Muriel Cumming?"

She flushed. "I can guess you've been busy with more than just finding Muriel. I call that snooping out of bounds."

"If I had known we were going to play games, I'd have had you explain the rules."

"If I'd known you were going to be a smartass, I wouldn't have hired you."

"Fine. I'll drop the case right now. You can hire someone else to pick up the pieces."

"What do you want? More money, I suppose."

"That'll do for starters. But I'd like some information too."

"How much?"

"Another five hundred bucks and your side of the story."

"How close are you to Muriel?"

"I'm getting warm."

"I want to know everything."

"So do I. And you're going to tell it first."

"I should tell you to go fuck yourself."

"But you've got a deadline to meet."

"You really have been working overtime. How much do you know about me?"

"Enough to know a lie when I hear one. So don't tell me any."

"Where do I begin?"

"Family history."

"Jordan Ferris made his money from gasoline. He started with one gas pump and built it up to an empire of refineries. Back in the early years of his success, he married my mother, who had been his personal secretary. Two years after I was born, it became obvious to my mother that Jordan was bent on transforming his secretarial pool into his private harem. She bailed out with a generous settlement, taking custody of me, and moved to the West Coast where she eventually remarried."

"So your legal name is . . . ?"

"Natalie Cumming. My father made it clear to my mother that he would be pleased if he never saw either of us back East again. He married a rich society lady. Her health was poor and she was on drugs much of the time. She died giving birth to Muriel."

"If your parents weren't keeping in touch, how did you know about Jordan's affairs?"

"The grapevine. My mother has friends among Jordan's associates."

"And Muriel's disappearance?"

"From Mrs. Riordon."

"I don't follow."

"I'm a reporter for the *Continental Confidant*. Are you familiar with the publication?"

"A scandal rag." I knew the sort of thing they thrived on. SEX LIVES OF THE STARS. MOTHER EATS ONLY CHILD. VAMPIRES IN THE SUBWAYS. Any story would do, no matter how tenuous the connections to fact, so long as it titillated the public interest. They had a distribution in the millions and paid their writers high salaries for offbeat stories, the more bizarre, the better. "What've you got planned for Muriel?"

"My editor heard about her from a local art dealer. The details were sketchy: limbless girl living in seclusion makes a name for herself as a paint-by-mouth artist. A human interest story. It was put on the board for future assignment. When it caught my attention, I had no idea that it was Muriel. Acting on a hunch, I came East to check it out. I visited the Realistik Gallery and saw her paintings. Moskovitz couldn't tell me anything but he gave me the phone number to call Mrs. Riordon. I must have caught her at a bad time. She was practically in a state of hysteria. Then suddenly her name rang a bell with me: I'd heard it in connection with Jordan Ferris from my mother's friends. I told Mrs. Riordon who I was, Muriel's half-sister, and I wanted to see her. I gave her a sob story about a family reunion and she got worked up to the point where she blurted out that Muriel had disappeared. I pried Uranium's name out of her but then she clammed up, as if she felt she'd said too much already."

"Why didn't you follow up on Uranium?"

"My editor recalled me to the West Coast to be put on a bigger story. Didn't you see this week's paper? The Governor's suicide?"

"Guess I missed it."

"Big smelly scandal. We'll be writing follow-up stories on it for months. So with that kind of headliner, I had to drop everything here and get back out to the Coast, regardless of how intrigued I might be with this revelation regarding my sister's secret identity and disappearance. So I hired you to locate her in my absence. Now I'm back. Where's Muriel?"

"Where's my money?"

"You're something else, mister." She left the room and came back in a few minutes with a check made out to me for five hundred dollars, signed again by the unknown Stanfield Coughlan. I asked her who this guy was. "My editor. Now spill. Have you found Muriel?"

"Not yet, but the trail is getting hot and increasingly complicated." I filled her in on my interview with Uranium, the Bowman-Watroboski mess, the weird scene with the Riordons, the inter-connections with Moskovitz, Dixie, Crabner, LeVeen and possibly, Dr. Malkud. She seemed to take it for granted that murders might obstruct my search for the missing artist. I omitted to tell her of the considerable help I'd received from Aquarius.

"I'd like to get this wrapped up as soon as possible. How soon do you think you'll get in touch with her?"

"Maybe today, if I get a break."

"Will you be able to deliver her to me?"

"That depends on whether she's been really

kidnapped or has just gone into hiding. Even if she's free to leave, what makes you think she'll want to talk to you?"

"She's my sister."

"Half-sister. And why should she bother? There's a story in it for you, but what's she got to gain?"

"You just get us together and we'll work it out between ourselves. I hired you as a snooper, not a family counsellor."

"I'm just curious. What kind of story have you planned to write?"

"That depends on how our interview goes. Probably a standard profile-of-the-artist story."

"Nothing like MUTANT MILLIONAIRESS ESCAPES FAMILY PRISON THROUGH ART?"

"Really, Mr. Savage, that is the furthest thing from my mind."

"Perhaps, then, a political angle?"

She picked her oyster shell off the coffee table, flicked it open and withdrew a strawberry-colored joint. "What makes you think that?"

"Don't mind if I do." I helped myself to one of her joints and flicked a match alight with my thumbnail. After a smoky lungful I blew it out and answered her question. "A story on Muriel right about now would be a clever way to capitalize on Jordan's position in city politics."

"Anything goes in this business."

"Including blackmail?"

"What are you implying?"

"A story that revealed Muriel's virtual imprisonment in her own home could hurt your father's chances of winning the mayorality race. He'd probably pay you well to keep it out of the *Confidant*."

"I never thought of that."

"I'll bet you didn't. You've got nothing but love and respect for the man that double-timed on your mother, and hustled the pair of you out the back door when success came knocking at the front. Right? You just want to use Muriel to get at your father."

"That's not true. I could write that story without Muriel. With quotes, pictures and everything. We do it all the time."

"I don't doubt you do, but that doesn't mean it's commendable. Your father's trying to drive organized crime out of this city. Whose side are you on anyway?"

"I don't see a moral issue here. All I see is a story."

"Well, it looks like a dirty story to me."

"It doesn't have to be. You bring Muriel to me and we'll see what happens. I appreciate what Jordan's trying to do. If she co-operates with me, I'll write a positive story."

"And if she doesn't?"

"I'll write whatever sells."

"Meaning, a scandal."

"Only if I can't do something better with it. I've got a story to deliver but I've also got a conscience to live with. After all, they're my family. Now are you going to help?"

"I took your check, didn't I?" I butted my joint in the ashtray and headed for the door. "By the way, if you don't mind my asking, what's a modern young lady like yourself doing in a suffocatingly conservative old dump like this?"

"The Holiday Inn was full. There's a Disco Convention in town." Miss Ferris took a roach clip from her oyster shell case and extracted the last few tokes from her joint. "Besides, our usually reliable sources have informed me that the Earl of Rugger is presently maintaining a suite in the Hutton."

"The notorious Earl of Rugger?"

"Yes. The same 'Bugger of Rugger', as he's been called by less circumspect papers than our own, who has an inordinate fondness for young boys in the spanking prime of life."

"Spanking?"

"Would you like to listen in on a session?" She lifted a cushion at the end of the sofa and withdrew a pair of earphones. "He's in the suite next door." She put one earphone to her head and arched her brows in mock astonishment.

"I'll pass. Check with you later this evening, tell you what's happening." I beat it down to the street. I'd heard it all today. A scandal sheet reporter with a conscience. Next thing, murderers would be turning themselves in for rehabilitation and snoopers like myself would be pursuing truth out of the goodness in our hearts. I hopped in the Astro and scooted off to cash my check at the nearest bank. Like everything else these days, the pursuit of truth was an expensive proposition.

9

I drove over to Kilroy Street and parked the car a few doors away from 2030. I sat there thinking a few minutes, trying to decide how I was going to introduce myself and present my problem. 'Excuse me, but I'm from the Missing Artists Bureau. Do you have in your possession a limbless girl who paints insects and answers to the name of Muriel?' Whatever it was, I'd have to come up with something better than that.

I shuffled through my collection of calling cards to see what I might use for cover. Mr. Waldram's card was soiled with bloody fingerprints so Federal Parks Control was out. I had a few cards from representatives of scientific equipment suppliers but I was leery of using them. I hoped to get an interview with Dr. Malkud but I couldn't take the chance of having him uncover me with a couple of intelligent questions on scientific apparatus I had no knowledge of. Then I came across A.P. Bergmann, Assistant Personnel Director to McGill University. He looked like a good man. Chances are Malkud wouldn't be familiar with that university and I could invent freely if questioned about salary, benefits, research facilities and whatever else an unemployed scientist might enquire about.

I got my goatee out of the glove compartment and put it on, along with a pair of horn-rimmed glasses. I checked myself in the mirror. Decidedly academic. I pulled my attaché case out of the back seat and walked back along the sidewalk to 2030. Malkud's place was a three-story brick structure with a tarnished copper roof and venetian blinds pulled down in every window. A small brass plaque beside the doorbell read *Bionic*

Limbs Clinic. I rang the bell and walked into a rather dreary little hallway lit only by meagre sunlight filtering through a half-moon of stained yellow glass above the door.

The ceiling was high enough that the cobwebs in the corners couldn't easily be swept away with a broom, and the walls looked a bit mildewed, although a glass caseful of mounted butterflies added a little color to the place. Straight ahead, a stairway with a warped balustrade ascended to the second floor, and immediately on my right was a small office from which a secretary behind an old wooden desk asked, "Do you have an appointment, sir?"

I stepped into the room where there was a sort of half-light coming in between the slats of the venetian blind. It didn't do anything for the girl behind the desk. Her skin was a mottled grey-green and her hair, trimmed short around a pair of feather-like ears, was a mass of thick bristles like those on a soiled scrub brush. She had an oblong face and yellow unblinking eyes. Her dress fit close around her neck but fell loose and shapeless from a pair of blunt mounds on her chest. Her arms were very slim and her hands had only three fingers with single joints. I couldn't see her legs beneath the desk and I'm sure I didn't want to. She looked like something that had crawled out from under a rotten stump.

"No, I don't have an appointment, but perhaps Dr. Malkud would give me a few minutes." I flashed my card. "My university is looking for a scientist of high qualifications to head our prospective Center for Entomological Research."

"Dr. Malkud is currently engaged..."

"Send the gentleman in," the intercom on the desk said in a harsh whisper.

"That way." The secretary stiffly inclined her head towards the door on my left.

I stepped through and closed the door behind me. On either side of me were display cases of insects: beetles and ants and flies and mites and things too small to identify. I walked further into the L-shaped room. In the corner was an alcove of bookcases on two walls and a leather upholstered chair with a footstool. Above it was suspended a plastic globe four feet in diameter and inside it, like the yolk in a monstrous egg, was a glowing orange lightbulb. As I came closer, I saw that a pair of dun-colored objects the size of softballs were fixed to the interior of the plastic shell. A big red spider crawled out of one of them and bounced around inside the globe. Soon others crawled out of their nests until a dozen of the hairy little creeps were jiving around like popcorn kernels in a hot pan. They were all the same kind of spider as the one that had jumped out of the sci-fi book and put the bite on Joel Uranium.

"Please take a seat, sir." From the inner wing of the L-shaped room a small man behind a large desk beckoned to me.

"Dr. Malkud, I presume?" I skimmed my card across his desk and he snatched it up with a quick and hairy hand. I took a seat in a straight-backed chair and lit a cigarette.

It would have been a waste of sarcasm to call Malkud a handsome man. He had a swarthy face with a handful of coarse black hair plastered wetly across a balding head. Silvery tufts of hair sprouted from his small and leathery batlike ears. There was an obscene pucker and twist at one side of his mouth, as if someone had clamped a pair of red-hot pliers on one cheek and yanked it around a bit. He wore a clean white shirt with a dark blue tie and a tailored black suit that did him some justice, although no tailor was so skillful as to hide a pair of lopsided shoulders, one of them almost up to his ear, the other, six inches lower. Fifty or sixty years ago, some clumsy midwife had made a mess of things and this was the result.

"Mr. Bergmann from McGill." Malkud fixed me with a pair of jetblack eyes squeezed tightly between puffy eyelids. "That's in Montreal, no?"

I nodded. "Land of the free, home of the brave."

"You must know Dr. Eli Windsor. An old colleague of mine. Head of the Biophysics department?"

"Never heard of him."

"Good. Neither have I." Malkud laid my card on his desktop and tapped it with a squat finger adorned with a heavy gold ring in the form of a scarab. "What is your proposition?"

"We're looking for a man to direct advanced researches in Entomology. I understand you have considerable experience in the field."

"This is true, but unfortunately I am not available. I am presently engaged in my own researches."

"We have been endowed with two million dollars to expand our facilities. These funds would be put at your disposal to further whatever researches you deemed practical."

"An attractive offer, but I already have adequate means at my disposal, thank you." Malkud fingered my card some more and then slid it back across the desktop at me. "Now please tell me, for I am curious to know, how you came to approach me with this offer."

"I've spoken recently with Dr. Mitsubishi at the City University. He suggested your name."

"I consider that highly unlikely. He is a fool but he would never recommend me." Malkud tugged at one of his bat ears. "Come now, you may confide in me. What is your real purpose in coming here?"

Alright you bastard, I thought, if you want to have it laid on the line, I can be as brazen as the next man. "I'm looking for a girl named Muriel Ferris."

Malkud's hand twitched upon his earlobe but his face remained impassive. "A girl, hmm? We have girls, yes, but I do not know this Muriel Ferris. What is her specialty?"

"She paints."

"Then I am afraid you have the wrong place, my friend." Malkud's free hand moved beneath his desk. "We have girls who are available for certain... ah... entertainments in the arts of love, but not..."

I wasn't listening to him any more. I was suddenly gripped by an irrational but overpowering fear. On the wall behind Malkud was a smoky mirror etched with a mandalic design and I had the most uncomfortable sensation that someone was watching me through it.

Someone or something so terrible that I barely dared lift my eyes to meet its unseen gaze. I was so shook up that the hairs in my false goatee were bristling with alarm.

"I'm afraid I've made a mistake." I jumped out of that chair the way a reprieved convict departs the one that had been assigned to electrocute him. "Sorry to have taken up your time."

"Perhaps you'd like to see some of our other girls..." Malkud was saying but by then I had the adjoining door open and was halfway through the secretary's office.

I bolted down the steps of 2030 Kilroy and dashed along the sidewalk towards my parked car. I heard a sudden rumble of metal runners on a rail and as I glanced over my shoulder I saw the garage door in the street wall of Malkud's house slither open. I didn't waste time standing around. I climbed into the Astro and pulled away fast. In the rearview mirror I saw the snout of a dark blue van poke out of the garage door but by that time I was squealing around the corner on two wheels and heading back uptown as fast as my little wagon would take me.

I went directly to the National Trust Corporation and arranged to speak with the Securities Manager, a baby-faced young man with long blond hair curling around his shirt collar. Mr. Nigel took me into his cubicle where I produced a card identifying me as Samson Rinehart, of Durkheim and Rinehart, Attorneys-at-Law. I told him I'd been asked to recover certain documents from the security box of Miss Muriel Ferris, presently in England and implicitly unavailable for certification. I produced the NTC key I'd recovered from Dale LeVeen. Mr. Nigel was, to my relief, unsuspecting. He took me to the basement and the securities vault where we found the numbered box corresponding to the key I held. He used his prep key; I used Muriel's. He showed me to, and left me in, a big closet where I locked the door and spilled the contents of the box on the table.

There were ten thousand dollars in crisp hundreds, a portfolio of investments securities and a cassette tape. I put the tape in my pocket, took a quick look at the portfolio before returning it and the money to the box and the box back into the vault.

As I crossed the street from the bank, I saw the dark blue van parked half a block away. As I drove away, it followed. I ran a zig-zag path going uptown and it stuck with me on every turn. Except for the one I pulled on a one-way street, and had to mount the sidewalk, scaring the shit out of fifty pedestrians, to get back onto the downtown flow on Seventh. My escapade left two irate cops raging at the intersection. My tail man didn't choose to run the same route.

I ditched my car in my favorite parking yard and slipped up to the office. I checked the Memoryphone for messages. There was a call from Sergeant Mundt, telling me I was wanted for questioning in connection with the Bowman-Watroboski affair and if I were smart, I'd turn myself in. I wished I could oblige him by turning myself into Invisible Man. For the time being, I'd have to settle for locking the door. I plugged in my cassette player and inserted the tape. I was all set to push the Play button when I heard someone coming up the stairs. I held my breath and kept silent. I didn't want to see any clients.

A key grated in the lock and the door banged open. Sergeants York and Mundt strolled in, guns, malicious smiles and all. York closed the door behind them. He was the polite one. Mundt reached across the desk, grabbed me by the throat and threw me against the wall. He followed up with a pile-driving fist into the gut. He spun me around as I grabbed the walls for support. He frisked me and took the guns and pushed me down into my chair.

"You're up to your eyeballs in shit, snooper," York told me.

"Beretta," said Mundt, hefting the little gun I'd taken from Dixie. "Same make that killed LeVeen."

"Stupid fucker's still wearing the same disguise too." York sat on the corner of my desk and gave me the evil dexie eye. "We've got a witness that saw you leaving LeVeen's apartment in this get-up. When we got a call from National Trust that a turkey in the same costume impersonated one of their clients, we knew we had something cooking."

I peeled off my false goatee and used it to sop up the blood that was leaking out of my nostrils. "I want to call my lawyer."

Mundt fanned out the deck of calling cards he'd fleeced from my jacket pocket. "Who'd you like, Durkheim and Rinehart? I'm sure they'd love to represent you after you've been misrepresenting them."

York noticed the power light on the cassette player. He popped the cassette free and looked at it. "Is this what you took from the security box?" he asked me.

"Must be," Mundt said. "He's got nothing else on him. Let's hear what's on it."

York put it back in the player and ran the tape. Slow-tempo jazz issued from the speaker: walking bass and a blues-structured piano. The singer had a fine voice but her lyrics were silly. She had the 'Ladybug Blues! York made a face. Mundt cautioned him with a wave of his hand to be patient.

We heard a door open and close. The girl stopped singing but the paino kept on walking the blues.

"Bud, what are you doing up here?"

"Hiya kid, don't stop singing. I just came up to listen."

"You've been drinking."

"Sure have. Want a snort?"

"Go away. I'm busy."

"Busy, huh? You're just lying around in your underwear."

"Don't touch me."

"I won't hurt you, baby. Just wanna make you feel good."

"Then take your hands off me. I'll scream."

"Scream your head off. Viv's not around."

The girl screamed so loudly that distortion came through the tape player.

"I love it, baby, love a screamer. Let me take off your T-shirt, baby, I want to suck on your tits. Oh yes, go ahead and holler all you want. Mmm hmm, you've got a lovely set, baby. Now let's see what the rest of you looks like."

The girl screamed and screamed.

"Ah now, isn't that nice? And it tastes good too. Now you're all wet and horny, aren't you? Just wait 'til I get my pants off."

The scream became a cry of pain.

"Oh yes, baby, you're tight tight tight but Uncle Bud's coming in just the same. Oh yeah, oh yeah, oh baby baby baby."

Then there was just the moaning of the girl and in the background, the jazz-blues piano plunking away as before. After a few minutes,

"Okay, baby, got to run. Viv's coming home soon. Here, lemme tuck you in. You're not going to tell on Uncle Bud, are you? No, I don't think so, 'cause Uncle Bud'll kill you if you do. Goodnight, baby. Sweet dreams."

A door opened and closed. The music continued. The girl cried. Then the tape ran out.

"Cute little scenario," Mundt said. "What's it all about, snooper?"

"I wish I knew."

Mundt slid off the edge of the desk and grabbed me by the throat. He had a hand that could have throttled a gorilla. As the blood pounded in my ears, he jammed the silencer butt of my Viper under my eye. "If you think you're going to clam up on us, snooper, you've got a hard lesson to learn. We just fooled around with you last time we were together. Now start talking, or we're going to put you through a routine that'll make the Inquisition look like a loan interview at your friendly neighborhood bank."

"Hssst," York said. "There's somebody outside."

"See who it is," Mundt growled over his shoulder as he ground the Viper into my bulging eyeball.

York pulled his gun and held it behind his back as he opened the door. Outside in the hallway stood a tall skinny guy in a pair of coveralls and wrap-around sunglasses. His long arms were bent at the elbows and his hands were pressed together in front of his chest as if in prayer. He looked beyond York to where Mundt and I were clinched in the corner.

"Looking for something?" York said.

Nothing happened for a moment and then everything happened at once. The man in the doorway snapped his arms straight out, seized York by the shoulders and jerked him forward with the swiftness and precision of a machine. York's gun fired a bullet into the floor. The stranger's face split open in a line across his chin and two bony appendages the size of butcher knives came out of his mouth and severed York's neck as effortlessly as a pair of garden shears snip a rose blossom from its stem. The arms snapped back out again. York's body, a fountain of blood pulsing from the neck, staggered back against one wall and slid to the floor. His head rolled under the desk and hit my feet.

The thing in the coveralls and shades stepped inside the room. Mundt spun around, the Viper going *spat-spat-spat* as his other hand grabbed for the Magnum in his shoulder holster. The thing and I jumped at the same time. Lucky for me that Mundt was in between us. I threw my arms in front of my face and dived through the window. The Magnum roared on top of a terrible scream. Amidst a shower of broken glass I landed in a heap of garbage cans below my window. I heard another scream, or maybe it was still the same one. I didn't stick around to listen to it. I pulled my foot out of a garbage can and ran for the car.

Buzz was in the basement lab feeding the bees when he heard the alarm. He squeezed the last of the nectar from the bag of flower pulp and left it dripping into their cage.

Upstairs was a small bathroom. Buzz went in without turning on the lights and closed the door. He opened the medicine cabinet and looked through the trick mirror into Doctor's office. He saw the back of Doctor's head, a spiral of hair around the red birthmark. On the other side of the desk was a man with glasses and hair that didn't look right on his face. He looked like the same one he'd nearly hit accidentally with the van on Scranton. Had the man taken the license number and come to complain? Buzz reached out with his mind and touched the edges of the man's thoughts.

The man felt it. He jumped from his chair and hurried from his room. Doctor looked in the mirror and said "Get him." Buzz didn't have to read his mind to know what he meant.

Buzz went to the door. The man was running to his car. Buzz went to the garage and started the van. As he came out onto the street, the other car disappeared. Buzz switched on the resonator unit. When he caught sight of the car going uptown, he took the resonator gun from its bracket under the dash, set the range and shot the car with the infra-sonic weapon. Now the car windows would vibrate for the next half hour and even if Buzz lost sight of the car, the omni locator would lead him to it again.

The bird led him on a run around the city. It made a smart move and so Bud let it think it got away. Maybe now it would go back to its nest. He'd follow and steal its egghead, bury it in the earth with the rest. Buzz liked to think of those seeds lying in the ground, sleeping all the long cold winter. And in the spring, what strange and wonderful flowers would seek the sun.

He found the car later. Same neighborhood as the snooper's office he and Crabby had visited one night. Buzz went there and found three men. He got two heads but the one he really wanted got away.

The vibration signal died before he could find the car again. Doctor was not going to be happy.

I drove straight back to my place, put the car in the garage and holed up with Grumpy and Werewolf. I was apprehensive about going up to my apartment. I knew I'd get that boxed-in feeling. After what had happened at the office, I had to keep escape hatches in mind. And a jump out a sixth story window was a wholly different proposition from a hop out of a second.

"You still got them coppers on your tail, Mr. Savage?" Grumpy pasted half a dozen papers together and rolled a joint of Columbian as big as a banana. He leaned back in his chair, put his feet on Werewolf and stuck the monstro joint in his grizzled face. An arm's length away, his shotgun leaned against the wall.

"I'm not sure just who, but somebody's after me." I sat on the cot in the corner, with Grumpy and Werewolf between me and the door. He was just an old man with an old dog, but now I felt secure for the first time since I'd left Malkud's place. I took the joint when he passed it over and got buzzed on the first hit.

"Life's like that," Grumpy said. "When I was young the women were after me; when I had a straight job and bought all kinds of shit I didn't need, the bill collectors; now that I've dropped out with my stash, it's the freaks and junkies. Hassle, hassle. It's enough to drive a man buggy."

"Take it easy, Grumps. Have another toke." The man was unpredictable. Out of the blue he'd start raving away like a wild man.

"Goddamn right." Grumpy waved the joint around like a demented conductor with his baton. "The women gave me the clap, the bill collectors gave me a bad credit rating and the freaks give me bad vibes. Fuck 'em all." He puffed up a storm, coughed and spat in a beer can. He jabbed me in the shoulder with a stubby finger. "And you know what?"

"What?"

"This lazy fucker." He drummed his heels on Werewolf's back. "This second-hand facsimile of man's best friend never gets hassled. Nobody dares say *boo* to him or he'd tear their legs off. By the whisperin' jesus, I wish I had a pair of choppers like he's got instead of these old plates." Grumpy tongued his stainless steel teeth halfway out of his mouth and made them clatter like a castanet. He bent over and pried up Werewolf's lip to reveal a yellow fang over two inches long. Werewolf sighed and opened a sleepy eye to see what was going on. "Now if I only had a pair of rippers like that," Grumpy said, "I'd be out every night putting the bite on all the freaks and punks and drip-dry assholes that hang around Beatnickel. They'd have to send a garbage truck around the next morning to pick up the bodies I'd left behind me. *Graowwwrrr*." Grumpy made clawing motions at imagined victims. "Hey, where you going?"

I was beginning to feel less secure with Grumpy. I took a quick run up to my apartment, got my other Viper out of the tool chest and a beer out of the fridge. I made a sandwich and ate it standing in the kitchen with my hand on the gun, listening for footsteps in the hall or scrabbling claws on the fire escape. After double-checking the locks on the door and windows, I figured I was secure enough to make a phone call.

Dixie's number was in Ron LeVeen's little black book but she wasn't home to answer the phone. Or if she was home, she couldn't answer it. I hoped it was the former. There were too many deaders cluttering this case already. I phoned out to Cloverlea and got Mrs. Ri rdon on the line.

"Mr. Savage, where've you been? I've been trying to reach your office all day."

"Why didn't you leave a message?"

"I had no intention of giving you the time to fabricate a defence. Mr. Savage, I demand that you return Muriel's paintings immediately or I'll call the police."

"What the hell are you talking about, the one I bought from your pal Moskovitz?"

"I'm talking about the dozen paintings that you removed from Muriel's studio last night."

"I was nowhere near Cloverlea last night. I'm afraid the removal of Muriel's paintings was your husband's work."

"Bud told me to expect some fabricated nonsense from you. You've certainly violated your position of responsibility, Mr. Savage. But to go so far as to threaten my husband's life is really too serious."

"You're not making any sense, Mrs. Riordon. Why don't you just put Bud on the phone and let me talk to him?"

"He's not here. He left more than an hour ago."

"Where'd he go?"

"He's leaving town for safety's sake. He was afraid you'd try to kill him."

"Now why would I want to kill Bud?"

"Because he caught you red-handed when you were in the process of stealing Muriel's paintings last night while I was out."

"Is that what he told you?"

"I'm certainly not making it up."

"You don't need to bother. Bud's used his own imagination enough already. He's the one that took Muriel's paintings. I've got alibis to prove I was elsewhere when the paintings were taken."

"Reliable witnesses, no doubt?"

I replayed the evening's events. Aquarius and his wife would back me up. But then there was Dixie later that same night. And she was Bud's little playmate. She'd back me up too. Right against a wall.

"This is silly, Mrs. Riordon. I didn't take the paintings. I found them. They're at Moskovitz' gallery. I saw them just before noon."

"Are you in the habit of drinking before lunch, Mr. Savage? I was at the Realistik Gallery this afternoon for a discussion with Mr. Moskovitz. I saw none of Muriel's paintings."

"They're not in the gallery. They're upstairs in the workroom."

"You are surely mistaken. I'm familiar with the premises. Muriel's paintings were not there."

I was getting annoyed with the way things were turning out. Now it looked like Bud, Dixie and Moskovitz were all in it together. Bud stole the paintings and delivered them to Moskovitz while Dixie and I fooled around on the carpet, leaving her the opportunity to disappear at a later date and leave me without an alibi for the time the paintings were stolen. And then to compound matters, I'd gone to the Gallery and bought one of Muriel's paintings, thinking I was smart to gain evidence that they'd been in Moskovitz' possession. Only he'd been smarter. He let me buy the best one of the bunch and now it was evidence against me if the cops were brought into it. The check was my receipt but it was a sure bet that Moskovitz wouldn't even try to cash it. By the time Mrs. Riordon paid her visit, the paintings had been moved. And now I was going to get screwed. I didn't like the idea.

"Fuck the paintings, Mrs. Riordon. Your husband is a murderer and I want to know where he's gone."

"You're insane."

"He killed a man yesterday in an attempt to get his hands on the key that you mailed to Billy Crabner's address. Ron LeVeen was Crabner's room-mate and now he's dead."

"How did you know about the key?"

"Never mind how I found out. I've got a nose for it and I'm finding a lot of unpleasantness lately. As you well know, the key was for Muriel's National Trust safety deposit box. Maybe you didn't know about the tape recording that was kept in it. Maybe it's just as well you didn't. I'm not sure you could face up to the fact that your husband is a sick man. Or haven't you any idea of what happened between him and Muriel? Mrs. Riordon, are you still there?"

Her choked sobs came over the phone as if from a great distance. I was glad I was doing this via phone. I hated to see women cry.

"Muriel had given me a cassette last month to be put in her safety deposit box. She said the tape contained some very special songs she'd written. I didn't see the sense of putting them in the bank but she insisted. Then the day after she left here, she phoned me and told me she was alright. But she told me to mail the safety deposit key to Crabner's address."

"She phoned and said she was alright? So you knew all along that she hadn't been kidnapped."

"I wasn't sure. I knew her friend Crabner wanted her to go and live with him but we both knew that her father would never permit it."

"You mean, Jordan."

"Yes. Bud and I are supposed to be the parents Mr. Ferris is ashamed to be, but he still has the power over the household. Yet we're responsible for Muriel's welfare."

"Muriel wanted to get out of the house, so she arranged a fake kidnapping that would relieve you of responsibility?"

"She talked about it. But I didn't know she would really do that. She has a lot of crazy ideas."

"You must have known something happened between her and Bud."

"I found blood in her bed and guessed the rest. I knew what Bud was like when he drank. Coming as it did after Crabner's persuasion to move out, I wasn't surprised to find her gone."

"Then why'd you hire Bowman?"

"I couldn't afford to do nothing. When Mr. Ferris returns he'll want to know all the whys and wherefores. I'd be fired if it looked like I had any complicity in her leaving. So I found an obviously inexperienced private investigator in Mr. Bowman and put him on the job, presuming he wouldn't find Muriel before she had time to get in touch with her father upon his return and sort things out with him."

"What about the ransom note and the ten thousand you paid in response?"

"I got that note after Muriel phoned to say she was okay. It made me wonder if she really was alright. So I took the money from a joint account we hold together. Now I think that was just her way of arranging payment for the people who helped her get away."

"Speaking of people who are getting away, where's Bud going?"

"I don't know. I saw an airline ticket but...."

"Okay, I'll take care of that. I've got to go now, Mrs. Riordon."

"What about Muriel? She's alright, isn't she?"

"I'm not sure. I think she's mixed up with some bad people. I'm going to try and see her tonight."

"Bring her back home if she's not happy there. She'll be okay here now that Bud's gone. I'll take care of her."

"I'll see what I can do."

I hung up and then used the phone book to look up the number of the local precinct station. When I got the desk sergeant on the line, I told him to record what I was going to say. He asked why and I said it was about a murder and I was going to give him the details fast and only once. He grunted okay and I started talking with one eye on the second hand of my watch. With a new tracer the police have developed in conjunction with the phone company, they can track an incoming call to its source in three minutes.

I gave the sergeant and his tape recorder the names and descriptions of Bud and Dixie and made up a story of blackmail and two-timing that had resulted in Ron LeVeen's death. I suggested Bud and Dixie could be found at one of the airports if the police moved fast. I hung up and looked at my watch. Two and a half minutes.

I replayed in my mind what I'd said over the phone, hoping I hadn't given them anything that might lead them to me. I'd wanted to tell them about a pair of headless cops in a certain downtown office, but I couldn't risk their putting out an APB for a suspected cop-killer with my name and description. I had enough trouble already without a thousand vengeance-seeking dicks homing in on me. With any kind of luck, I might be able to break the case open tonight. It was bad enough that I had to blow the whistle on Bud and Dixie, who might bring up my name, but that was the chance I had to take to make sure they didn't get away scot free.

I parted the curtain in my bed-sitting room and looked outside. It was dark. In the lighted windows across the airshaft I could see people going about their evening routines: making supper on two-burner stoves, taking baths in cracked porcelain tubs, settling down in half-collapsed sofas to spend the night entranced by flickering ghost-like images of sex and violence on TV. From the rooftops came the yowl of mercury-poisoned cats and beyond that, out in the city of restless millions, came the mechanized growl of street traffic and the wail of police sirens. Somebody was on the run and somebody else was chasing him. It was a game as old as the hills and it was replayed every day on the streets, on TV and in the books we turned to when the rest of life failed to live up to whatever notions of excitement we thought it owed us.

Enough of this fucking introspection, I told myself. You're scared and you know it. I'd seen the killer of four men and lost my nerve. I flashed back to what I'd seen of the thing in the doorway just before it got York. Hands clasped in front of its chest as if in prayer. Then it came to me: a recollection of a film clip from highschool science lab—a praying mantis. Foreclaws folded the same way in front of the body, then the lightning jerk and snatch that pulled the victim within easy reach of the cutting mandibles. The thought of it gave me chills. A giant praying mantis? Too bizarre. Then I remembered the giant bees on Big Bass Lake and what Mitsubishi said of Malkud's radiation-induced growth treatments and the grafting of insect parts onto human frames.

Could the thing be half-man, half-insect? If so, how to stop it? I thought of all the bugs I'd swatted and half-crushed. They were tough as nails and tenaciously mobile even after serious dismemberment. I didn't like the idea of a maimed and crazed praying mantis-man tearing the walls down to get at me. What I needed was a couple of grenades or a flamethrower. Failing that, I'd have to improvise.

I went back down to the garage and held a conference with Grumpy. He was higher than Telstar and readily got into my hypothetical problem of how to handle the extermination of a horde of cockroaches the size of rats.

"I'd load my shotgun with buckshot and arsenic."

"Got any arsenic around here?"

"No, but there's a big can of DDT in the back shed left over from when the landlord cleaned out the roaches a couple of years back."

We checked it out. There were a couple of gallons left in the can. It was in liquid form and the label said it was highly flammable in addition to being poisonous. Grumpy had a large collection of empty wine bottles in a bin behind his office. We found a funnel and some rags. I put him to work pouring an inch of DDT into each bottle while I walked down to the service station on the next block and bought two gallons of gas and a quart of motor oil. Back at Grumpy's, I topped up the bottles with gas, stoppered them with rags and gave each a good shake to mix the gas and DDT. I opened the can of oil and soaked each of the rag-wicks. I put a dozen bottles in a wooden pop crate and set it in the back seat of the car.

"What are you going to do with that?" Grumpy wanted to know.

"I've got a friend with a really serious bug problem."

"You ought to take Werewolf along with you. He'll eat anything. You never did take him out for a run the other night and he could use an airing."

"I'll take you up on that. Maybe you'd lend me your shotgun for the evening too. I'll leave you with this." I showed him the Viper.

"Now what would I do with a little popgun like that? Scare the rats? No, you keep it, and take the pump too." Grumpy handed me the sawed-off Ithaca and a box of #2 shot. "I've got an old double-barrel that'll see me through tonight."

"Thanks, Grumps. Okay, Werewolf, let's go." The big dog climbed into the back seat and we drove over to Herschel Domain.

I used the lobby phone to call Aquarius, asking him to meet me downstairs and to bring his German shepherd with him. He came down with Tojo and we went outside. I told him what had happened since I'd seen him last and explained what I was going to do.

"Break into Malkud's place? That's insane. Why don't you get the police in on it? They could get a search warrant and recover Muriel without your endangering yourself."

"The police would throw me in jail and I have no positive proof, just a gut feeling, that Muriel's being held captive there."

"But what do you want Tojo for?"

"Protection. And if Muriel's hidden somewhere within the house, he might be able to sniff her out."

"I don't like it."

"Well, fuck you, professor. You talked to me before about a moral responsibility to uphold societal norms. You draw your little charts and outline your notions of good and evil, and say you want to contribute to a better world, but when it comes to the crunch and a girl's life is at stake, you pull in your horns and say you don't want to get involved. Thanks for caring and thanks for nothing." I turned and walked towards the car.

"Alright, Savage, you win. Take Tojo. Do you want me to come too?"

It was a decent gesture, but I couldn't accept it. I didn't need his fear reinforcing my own. All I needed was his dog and I could handle the rest on my own.

"You've done enough already. Thanks."

I opened the car door and whistled for Tojo. He was apprehensive about climbing into the back seat with Werewolf. I talked them both into an uneasy truce. They grumbled and growled a lot but they didn't fight. I closed the door on them and drove away.

10

It was nine o'clock when I got to Kilroy Street. A little early maybe for skulking around but there was nothing to say I should wait for the witching hour to engage in some skulduggery. There were a few lights on at 2030 as I cruised by. I went down almost to the end of the block and nudged the wagon up to the curb between a pair of big sedans.

I had a little rucksack under the front seat with some basic burglar's tools. I got it out and put the shotgun and a couple of DDT cocktails inside. I left the car unlocked and walked back up to 2030. With two big dogs in the car, I wasn't worried about anyone tampering with it. I tried Malkud's front door but it was locked. There was an alleyway at the side of the house and I went around there with the Viper in my hand and the safety off. The backyard had a plot of grass and flowers set in the middle of a concrete patio that butted up against the next-door-neighbour. Up on the third floor, a bit of slatted light came out through venetian blinds. A pair of garbage cans stood beside a locked back door.

I got my lockpicking tools out and went to work with a prayer that there would be no burglar alarm. In a minute I had the door open. I slipped inside and closed it behind me. I crouched low on the floor and snapped my penlight on. I was in an empty garage. At the far end was an electric door that faced the street. I shone my light along the adjacent wall and saw another door that led into the house. I tried it and found it unlocked. I stood on a landing facing two sets of stairs, one going up, the other, down. I went down a flight into the basement, opened another door and stepped into a laboratory that would have been a credit to any government-funded research institution.

I walked down the aisles of equipment, shining my light over half-recognized apparatus: oscilloscopes and electron microscopes, dosimeters and scintillometers and a lot of other goodies I couldn't put a name to. In one corner of the basement was a closed room with an observation window set in one wall. I shone my light inside and saw a compact little operating room with oxygen unit, x-ray machine, biological monitoring devices and racks of surgical equipment: everything the private surgeon could ask for.

Along one wall of the laboratory was a row of large refrigerators. I looked inside them. Blood plasma, toxins and cultures in one. Hundreds of frozen insects, each separately sealed in little plastic baggies, in another. Same thing in the next fridge, only the insects were fewer and considerably larger: beetles and ants as big as mice, butterflies and moths the size of sparrows, a pair of bumblebees as big as my fist. But the last refrigerator held the shockers: inside it were huge insect parts that had been blown up to human scale. Hard-shelled limbs with rough spurs on the elbows and claw-like appendages where hands or feet would have been on human limbs. Eyeballs the size of plums, each with thousands of tiny facets glinting beneath the penlight's beam. Dagger-like stingers were joined by tubes to sacs of what might have been toxic venom.

Enough is enough. I closed the fridge door and moved on. It didn't comfort me to think there might be creatures upstairs equipped with appendages like that. I flicked the light around the lab in a nervous gesture to make sure nothing was sneaking up on me. All I saw was the flicker of reflection on rows of test tubes and shelves of bottled chemicals. I fixed the light on two huge glass cisterns labelled C_2H_5OH. Ethyl alcohol. I could have used a drink about then, but I didn't see any mix lying around.

As I mounted the stairs back to ground level, I was wondering to myself where Malkud got the money to stock a lab with such an impressive array of equipment.

At a conservative estimate, I'd say he was sitting on a million bucks' worth of scientific gadgetry. Was the Bionic Limbs business so good that he didn't even need to keep a listing in the Yellow Pages? Or did he have a secret contract with the government or industry?

Malkud's and the secretary's offices took up one side of the ground floor, along with a tiny bathroom at the end of the hall. On the other side of the hall was a kitchen and adjoining dining room. I took the briefest of looks into each of these rooms, then ditched my rucksack in the hall closet and climbed the stairs to the second floor with the Viper in hand. I could hear voices. When I got to the head of the stairs I stopped to check the lay of the land. Light came from two facing doors at the far end of the hall where a window overlooked the street. At my end of the hall were another two doors, each to a bedroom. The foot of the stairs to the third floor was at the far end of the hall. I walked towards the front of the house on pussy feet.

From the room on the right came the sounds of a TV and a pair of women talking, one of whom sounded like Malkud's secretary. The other one wondered whether Mr. Kent was going to keep his appointment. Another female voice suggested that maybe he'd chickened out, that he wasn't quite so kinky as he'd pretended to be. A chorus of female giggles followed after that. I dug into the inner pocket of my jacket and pulled out one of those little dime-sized mirrors on a six-inch handle that dentists use to check their patients' uppers. I hunched down by the doorframe and poked the thing just around the corner until I could see the interior of the room reflected in the mirror.

The secretary was there alright, with another half dozen of her kind, all of them lounging around in dressing gowns and see-through negligees. One girl had a pair of thorny grasshopper legs that put her well over six feet. She stood against one wall doing high kicks out of boredom. Another creature with cape-length moth wings wrapped around her sat at a vanity table and applied makeup to a pair of fern-like antennae. Sitting on the sofa watching TV were more buggy beauties: a stick-beetle woman with glowing iridescent eyes, a lady with a wasp waist and body hair in alternating stripes of yellow and black, a fat water-beetle-woman with speckled breasts; and a slimy-looking thing with soft horns and about two dozen legs curled up in a chair all by its lonesome.

I yanked my mirror back and rubbed my tired eyes. I felt like puking. What had I stumbled onto? A regular little theatre of the absurd. These babes were sitting around like a bunch of whores awaiting assignments. But who in their right mind would want to make it with one of them? The very thought of bristly grasshopper legs wrapped around me was nauseous. I'd better find Muriel and get the hell out of here before I was discovered.

I sneaked my little mirror inside the other door and spied Malkud talking on the phone. At first I thought he was alone but then I saw he was stroking something in his lap. It was a red-and-black ladybug as big as a turkey and it was looking right at me. I jerked the mirror back and got to my feet. No sound of alarm. Malkud was still talking on the phone. I heard him mention my name and strained to hear the rest.

"... up to his apartment and leave a couple of spiders. Just in case he's gone to the police, you'd better get out of town tonight. You could drive to the other side of Cloverlea and spend the night in the van. That way you could be up at the camp first thing in the morning. I'll see you when you return tomorrow. Don't fail me."

Malkud hung up the phone. Then I heard him rise from his chair and shuffle towards the door. I had to move. I went up the carpeted stairway three steps at a time, banking on the TV and the girls' chatter to cover any noise I made. I'd just reached the top of the stairs and scooted around the landing out of sight when something dropped on me from above. He was all hairy arms and legs, with an extra pair of arms to wrap around my neck with a wrestler's grip while he snatched my gun away. I tried to break his stranglehold but he jerked one leg out from beneath me and we went for a tumble down the stairs.

I was yelling my head off while the girls stood bugeyed in one door and Malkud very solemn in the other. I told him he'd better hand over Muriel Ferris and let us go or the police would come. Malkud snapped his fingers. The thing on my back bit me on the nape of the neck and I went out like a light.

Buzz went back to the snooper's office. The headless cops had begun to smell. Buzz went through the snooper's desk and filing cabinet but couldn't find a home address for Keith Savage. Then he looked through the cops' pockets and found what he wanted in a small notebook.

He went to the address and parked the van. He sensed dog close by. He got the shivers. He had to reason with himself.

It was a long time ago. He was only two years old when his mother took him with her and many other people on a picnic. They ate their food and went for a walk in the woods. A man came with them and put his arm around mother. They kissed and laughed and left little Buzz alone with the empty picnic basket while they walked down a little valley and into the trees. While he was alone and afraid, two big dogs came running through the woods chasing a squirrel. The squirrel ran up a tree and chattered angrily at them. The dogs came sniffing around Buzz. They tore the picnic basket apart. Buzz started to cry. They growled and jumped on him. Buzz screamed for his mother. The dogs bit him and tore his fingers off. He kicked and yelled and tried to crawl away but the dogs caught his feet in their jaws and ripped him and pulled him and chewed on him until his mother and the man came running and yelling and drove the dogs away. Buzz hurt all over. And that was a long time ago. But now whenever he saw a dog he got scared all over again, no matter how strong he'd become. He was frightening to look at but he was frightened inside. And dogs knew it. They weren't fooled by masks. They might see a monstrous insectman but they'd know there was only a scared little boy inside. Scared little boy, afraid of dogs. Shut up, shut up. It was a long time ago.

He tried another line of reasoning. Think of no-dogs. He saw no dog, he smelled no dog, maybe there was no dog. One had passed here maybe and left a scent on a fire hydrant. Buzz convinced himself it was safe to get out of the van. Just to be safe, he took a pair of bees with him, one in each breast pocket of his coveralls. He carried the two red spiders in a glass jar.

He broke into the apartment and put the spiders inside the bed. He looked in the kitchen to see if there was anything sweet to eat. He found a bottle of maple syrup in the fridge and drank that. The bees didn't like it in his pockets. He hurried back down to the van and set them free in the back. They crawled into their cubbyholes and Buzz drove away.

He spent the night parked in a camping ground on the other side of Cloverlea. He put Wagner on the tape deck and listened to the stormy music as the silver moon curved up and over the earth. He opened a tin of honey. He and the bees had a picnic. They were irritable but the honey pacified them. They were Aryan bees, ferocious and restless, and they didn't like to be cooped up. They wanted to be on the wing, foraging and hunting. Tomorrow they would get their chance.

I awoke to find myself strapped into a bed. I was in a large room with heavily curtained windows. A single overhead light with a red filter cast an eerie glow over the room. At the far wall stood three easels with paintings and in the corner, a card table with a jar of brushes and tubes of oils. I heard a humming sound and twisted my head around on the pillow. A girl with dark hair and pretty features motored up to the bed in a wheelchair and looked at me with solemn eyes.

"Muriel?"

Her eyes widened. "How do you know my name?"

I went through the whole routine, how I'd been hired by her half-sister to arrange an interview for the *Continental Confidant*. Then the accident with Uranium and the spiders, the murders of Watroboski and Bowman. I told her how I'd played dodge with the cops and enlisted the help of Aquarius to put me on the trail of the missing tape and Dr. Malkud. I told her about the phony ransom demands, the theft of her paintings and my total confusion as to what was really happening.

"It all began when Billy and I became penpals through an ad in *The Speaker*. We exchanged letters and photos and tapes and got to know each other as well as could be expected through correspondence. I wanted to go to him or have him come see me but my father wouldn't hear of it. He'd prefer to keep me a secret. He can't reconcile himself to the fact that he'd fathered a deformed child. If it ever got out, he was afraid it'd ruin his image.

"I'd been painting for a year and Mrs. Riordon was delivering my work to Moskovitz and all the proceeds were going into accounts at NTC that my father knew nothing about. I arranged to have money sent to Billy so that he could have an operation to overcome his muscular dystropy and help him walk again. Around the same time, I had my chart done by mail and sent Uranium some money. I had lots of money and since my father wouldn't let me out of the house, I was determined to spend it on someone who deserved it.

"Meanwhile, Billy told me that none of the specialists he'd seen could do anything for him. But then he found out about this Dr. Malkud who was doing incredible things with mutants. Little did I know what Billy was getting into. I sent him more money to go to the clinic. Then the thing with Bud happened and by accident it got on tape. I should have destroyed it but I didn't. I had Viv put it in the safety deposit box thinking maybe I would use it to convince my father I had to get out of the house. I don't know, it was crazy. It happened again with Bud. Viv knew when my periods were and when she found blood in my bed at the wrong time of the month, she must have known what happened, but we were both too uptight to bring it into the open.

"Then I started getting morning sickness. I was pregnant and I knew I had to get out. I wanted an abortion. I told Billy everything. He was furious. He was already jealous of Uranium because I was sending him money. He wanted to have Bud killed. I talked him out of that and persuaded him to have me kidnapped. He and Buzz came to the house, Billy crawled up the chimney and took me out, and then Buzz carried us both out to the van in a phony air conditioner. They would have killed Bud at the same time but Buzz was afraid of the dogs and they never got another chance.

"They brought me here to he clinic but I hate it. Billy's so weird now that I can't believe he's the same one who used to write me all those sweet letters. He sent the spider to kill Uranium because of all the money he'd bummed from me. Later he figured out it hadn't been Joel at all, but this guy Watroboski at the Comix store who'd been intercepting Joel's mail and writing me sob stories for more and more money. So Billy sent Buzz off to take care of Watroboski and retrieve my letters so there'd be no trace of what happened. Only Bowman showed up at the wrong time and Buzz killed them both.

"Malkud gave me the abortion and promised to fit me with new limbs, but after I found out what's been going on here, I changed my mind. Maybe you saw those other girls. They're all victims of the Nuke Fluke, horribly deformed, but Malkud operated on them and turned them into even more bizarre creatures to hire out to the sex freaks. I could rattle off a list of names of closet weirdos who come here for their kicks: people in the government and big business, movie stars, sports personalities, any creep at all who's got a grand to shell out for the kinkiest fucks in town.

"Malkud's got the same plan for me but I say no way. He won't force me; he's trying to brainwash me into agreeing. I guess he figures I'd freak out from psychological shock and die on him if he just went ahead and operated. I think he's done something with the foetus he aborted. Billy knows but won't tell me. He thinks Malkud's a genius. The lab in the basement was wholly funded by the underworld organization. Billy thinks it's great that he and Buzz are going to be the mob's secret hit men, along with the swarm of giant bees that Malkud's developed."

"I heard Malkud talking on the phone to someone. Sounds like they've got something planned for tomorrow. Know anything about that?" I asked.

"No. They keep me cooped up here in this room so I'm not privy to their plans. All I know is that they're crazy. If my father gets elected, there's going to be an all-out war on organized crime."

"Maybe they'll use you as a hostage to coerce your father into dropping out."

"I doubt he would. His career means too much to him. He'd probably sacrifice me for the cause. It'd create sympathy. GANGLAND SLAYING OF DAUGHTER INTENSIFIES FERRIS' WAR ON CRIME."

"Maybe they've got something else planned for your father."

"Oh oh. Buzz left this evening with the bees. Billy told me this was going to be the big test."

"Where's your father's retreat?"

"Porcupine Mountain. It's about three hours' drive northwest of Cloverlea."

"What time is it now?"

She looked at my watch. "Four AM."

"Everybody in bed?"

"Maybe, but they're probably not sleeping. This place doesn't usually get active until after midnight. What've you got in mind?"

"I want to get out of here and take you with me. As soon as Buzz comes back, I'm dead meat."

"They might not kill you. I wouldn't be surprised if Malkud did a transmutation number on you and turned you into a plaything for the gay perverts. Probably cut out your voice-box, work you over to look buggy, give you radiation treatments to increase your cock size..."

"Ugh, I get the picture. I'd rather they killed me. But maybe we can get away. Any chance of unfastening these straps?"

"Sure. What'll I do, gnaw through that nylon harness?"

"Oh shit, I forgot. Sorry."

"Doesn't bother me. Any other ideas?"

"There must be something sharp around here. Knife? Scissors?"

"I've got a small razor stylus I use to scrape off excess paint."

"Get it, and lock that door while you're at it."

She motored across the room in her wheelchair and used her tongue to push in the lock-button in the doorknob. Then she went to the card table, picked the stylus up in her mouth and motored back to the bed. "Now what?"

"Cut through this waist strap."

She leaned against the bed and, gripping the stylus between her teeth, sawed the razor tip back and forth across the heavy nylon strap. I wished I could have wriggled an arm loose to help her but she was on her own. It was hard work. All the strain was in her neck because she had no arms to brace herself as she sawed at the two-inch strap. Sweat beaded on her flushed face and I smelled her perspiration. She wore one of those body suits that ballerinas wear and it was soon moist between her breasts and down the sides below the vestigial stumps of her shoulders.

When she got down to the last few strands, I strained my hips upward and parted the strap. Now my arms were free below the elbows. I took the stylus and cut away the strap across my midriff, then sat up and unbuckled the one across my knees. I swung my legs off the bed and took a few shaky steps. I was still pretty woozy from the injection I'd received in the back of the neck.

I raised the venetian blinds and pried the window open. Outside was a three-story drop to the concrete walkway between houses. I took the severed straps from the bed, joined them by reef knots and anchored one end to the radiator beneath the windowsill. That gave us about ten feet of lifeline and a fifteen foot drop, enough to shake a guy up but, I hoped, not enough to break a leg. I pulled the intact strap free from the bed and said to Muriel, "Let's go."

"Someone's coming," she hissed from her position at the door.

"Muriel." Somebody banged on the door. "Open up." A key was fitted into the lock.

"It's Billy," said Muriel as she scooted across the room to my side.

I didn't have time to do anything before the door swung open and Crabner came in. He was the hairiest little guy I'd ever seen. Less than four feet tall, he had the muscular look of a midget wrestler, with short bowed legs and long arms covered with thick black bristles. Sprouting from his midriff was another pair of shortened forearms with pincers instead of hands. His head was an unkempt mop of hair and from his coarsely bearded chin protruded a pair of sharp little barbs, probably what he'd bitten me with earlier.

"What's going on here, snooper?" Crabner looked from Muriel to me. "I thought I put you to sleep for the night."

"I'm insomniac," I said. "I think I'll go out for a walk." I still had one heavy strap in my hand. I backed up to the bed and snatched the razor stylus.

"Well, think again," Crabner said. "This time I'll shoot you up with a double dose and you won't wake up until next week."

"Why don't you try some of your own medicine? You could use some beauty sleep."

He rushed me with arms outstretched to grapple me. I slashed him in the chest with the razor stylus. He screeched with pain and hit my hand with a pincered forearm. I tried to yank the stylus back but it was snarled in his body hair. He jumped clear, pulled it from his chest and flung it out the door. He came at me again. Using the strap like a whip, I snapped him in the face with it. He dropped to the floor and charged my ankles. I leapfrogged over him and looped the strap around his neck. He kicked upwards and we went tumbling across the floor. I landed on my back with him above me as I tried to throttle him. He was clawing away at me with his pincers and I was trying to keep my distance from those venomous barbs. He started hollering his head off. Someone might show any minute.

Muriel wheeled up in her chair, a tube of paint gripped between her teeth. Crabner kicked at her chair, but not before her face contracted abruptly and a jet of red oil paint spewed from the tube. Her chair toppled over and she went head over tail under the bed. Crabner shrieked and convulsed so violently that I couldn't hold him. I jumped clear and backed up to the window to defend myself against the next attack.

But Crabner didn't know where I was. His face was one big glob of red paint. He rubbed his eyes and spat crimson. Sudden spasms shook him like a puppet whose master had the jitters. He ran in circles around the room, snapping his pincers and groping for us, then smacked headfirst into the wall. He recoiled from the impact, leaving a red splotch on the wallpaper, and fell on his ass. I scooped up Muriel, hugged her against my chest and bound us together with the nylon strap. I got one leg over the windowsill when Malkud charged in the door.

"You fool," he howled. "Stop them."

Gripped as he was in the frenzy of his convulsions, Crabner couldn't have known who it was. He bowled into Malkud's legs and the pair of them went tumbling to the floor. The last thing I saw as I lowered myself out the window was Crabner hunched over his patron, driving his poisonous barbs again and again in a blind fit into the screaming and, then, silent Dr. Malkud.

When I got to the end of the line, I let go and dropped heavily but unhurt to the walkway below. I ran down the street to the car, unstrapped us and put Muriel in the front seat. I opened the back door and grabbed several DDT cocktails. The two dogs jumped out and we went back up the street to 2030. The front door of the Limbo Clinic burst open and half a dozen people in various stages of undress came spilling down the steps and piled into a pair of Caddies parked out front. I recognized at least three faces I'd seen in newspapers or on TV. The Caddies took off with a squeal of tires and I went inside the clinic.

I got my rucksack from the hallway closet and slung it over my shoulder. I told the dogs to stay there at the foot of the stairs. Tojo stayed but Werewolf bounded up to the second floor. In a minute I heard a lot of inhuman screaming. I hurried down to the basement lab; threw open the fridge doors and toppled the contents onto the floor. I smashed the cisterns of ethyl alcohol; it spilled across the floor and filled the air with its cold taste. I went into the operating room and opened the valves on the oxygen tanks. It whistled out under high pressure as I trotted for the door. I closed it from the outside, lit the wick on one of the DDT cocktails, then jerked the door open and pitched the bomb into the lab. I made it up to the garage before the basement blew apart.

I picked myself up off the floor, lit another bomb and pitched it against the back door. Flame and noxious smoke billowed out to fill the garage. I scrambled up the wrecked stairs into the house. The hall floor was warped and smoke was coming up through split seams in the woodwork. I whistled for Werewolf and he came bounding down the stairs, his jowls messy with blood. I shoved the two dogs outside, smashed all the DDT cocktails but one at the foot of the stairs and stepped outside with the last bomb. Twenty or thirty people were gathered on the sidewalks, drawn by the sound of the explosion and the shrieks from within the house. I lit the wick of the last bomb and pitched it through the front door of the Limbo Clinic. An explosion of fire and smoke billowed out the smashed portal.

I heard sirens coming this way. I hustled the dogs back into the Astromobile, gunned the engine and left the neighborhood at reckless speed. It had been a good night's work but I wasn't finished yet.

"Potassium nitrate," Muriel said.

"Huh?" I shot a glance at her leaning against the passenger door. I reached over and snapped the lock button. After pulling her out of that bughouse, I didn't want to lose her on a fast turn.

"Potassium nitrate in the paint. That must have been what triggered the convulsions. I only meant to blind him long enough for us to get away. But he got a lot of it in his mouth."

"Don't lose any sleep over it. You probably saved our necks."

"Van Gogh tried to commit suicide by eating oil paints."

"Who's he, another of your weird friends?"

"A spiritual father." She stared vacantly at the nightlights of the city as we sped cross-town.

"That's what your father-in-the-flesh is going to become if I don't find him before Buzz does. Just exactly where would I find his mountain retreat?"

"Porcupine Mountain. I don't know any details about its location."

"Well, think. Didn't he ever mention what it was like? Is it near a river or lake? At the bottom of the mountain or the top? There must be hundreds of camps up there. I don't have the time to go knocking door-to-door."

"My father never said anything about it but, knowing him, it's probably as inaccessible as he could manage. Well off the beaten track and as high up the mountain as possible, so that he can look down on everyone else."

"Is it my imagination or do I detect a trace of bitterness?"

"More than a trace. If he'd shown me some love and understanding instead of being so selfish, things might not have happened the way they did."

"Okay, I don't want to get into a big issue over your relationship with your father. But maybe you wouldn't mind my dropping you off with your half-sister while I take care of some business?"

"That scandal-monger? No thanks. I don't know her from a streetwalker. Better take me back home to Viv. She's probably worried sick about me. And I miss her."

"Sorry, but that's not an alternative. The police might well have your place staked out waiting for me to show up."

"Then send me home in a taxi."

"Negative, kiddo. Buzz is camped out somewhere around Cloverlea. After springing you from Malkud's place, I won't take the chance of having that creep get his hands, or pincers, whatever they are, on you again. Looks like no matter how you slice it, the lady journalist is going to be your babysitter."

I pulled up in front of the Hutton Hotel, tucked Muriel under one arm and carried her into the lobby. After a bit of browbeating and a nominal fee of five bucks, the desk clerk agreed to disturb Miss Cumming 'at this ungodly hour.' Moments later, I carried Muriel into her relative's suite.

Natalie wore a gold-and-green quilted housecoat, fluffy white slippers and a face that glowed with sisterly compassion. "You poor darling," she said, opening her arms to take Muriel from me, "you look quite exhausted. Now the first thing we'll do is give you a cup of hot chocolate, and then a good soak in the tub before we put you to bed. I know you've been through a lot in the past few days."

Muriel's face crinkled around the eyes and then she was crying great tearjerking sobs while Natalie rocked the girl in her arms and stroked her hair saying, "You're alright now. I'll take good care of you."

I stood there empty-handed feeling like the third party on a honeymoon. I spied a bottle of Scotch on the sideboard and that took care of one hand while the other groped in a pocket and found a pack of crumpled cigarettes. I had a couple of quick snorts from the bottle, boor that I am, and drew meditatively on my cigarette while Natalie propped Muriel up in a nest of pillows on the sofa and went to work in the kitchenette producing hot chocolate and coffee.

"I want to know the whole story, from start to finish," Natalie said. "Where'd you find her?"

"I'll fill you in later. I'm not finished yet."

"What's happening?" She shoved a hot cup of coffee into my hand.

"Something really big." I gulped at the coffee, burned my mouth, cooled the cup with the last shot of Scotch and tried again with better success.

"You're still working for me," she said quickly. "When do I get the story?"

"With any kind of luck, later today, a story the like of which your paper has never dreamed."

"They dream up some pretty wild ones."

"This'll top the wildest."

"If it does, you'll get a bonus."

"I should hope so." I set the empty cup on the sideboard. "Got to run. Don't press Muriel for too much tonight. She's been through the mill."

"I can see that. Don't worry, I'll be cool."

"I'll get back to you later. Bye, Muriel." I waved but she didn't. She was slumped in the pillows and looked asleep. I scored a good luck kiss from Natalie and hit the road.

11

On the way out to Cloverlea, I stopped at a 24-hour service station for gas and picked up a map of the area that included Porcupine Mountain. I used the payphone to call the Ferris manor. Mrs. Riordon answered on the tenth ring.

"This is Savage. Sorry if I got you out of bed. Are the cops there?"

"I haven't been to bed since the police left at midnight. They picked up Bud and his girlfriend at the airport and then a couple of detectives brought the Mussolini back and questioned me. They were terribly keen on finding you. They said two of their men had been found butchered in your office. I told them everything I knew. I hope that was alright: I was just too exhausted to tell anything but the truth. They seemed satisfied with that but they instructed me to get in touch with them if I learned of your whereabouts. Have you found Muriel?"

"She's safe in town. I left her with a friend."

"What's the phone number?"

"I'll tell you when I arrive, providing there's no cops there."

"Fine. I'll be expecting you."

I hung up and went back out to the Astromobile. The dogs had been restless in the car so I'd let them out when I stopped. They sniffed around and pissed on my hubcaps. Now they both had their noses pressed to the window of the coffee shop eyeing a truck driver as he shovelled down a breakfast of eggs and sausage. I was kind of hungry myself but we didn't have time for that.

The sky in the east was opening up in pastel bands of

pink and blue as I whistled through the sleepy suburbs of Cloverlea. It was six in the morning and the dairy trucks were making their rounds. Birds were cheeping in the trees as I went up the driveway to the Ferris residence. Hansel and Gretel were out on the front lawn chasing squirrels. When I parked, they bounded up to the car and started barking. Tojo and Werewolf scrabbled at the windows to get out. I rolled the windows down just far enough for them to trade smells and get used to each other.

Mrs. Riordon, wrapped up in a heavy grey coat sweater, met me at the front door and ushered me to the kitchen where she had a fresh pot of coffee waiting. She seemed a little dopey and I guessed maybe she'd taken a tranquilizer. "How's Muriel?"

"She's fine. Just tired is all." I jotted Natalie Cumming's name and the Hutton Hotel phone number on a slip of paper. "You should get some sleep yourself and then call her after noon."

"Can't sleep. Got a migraine." She rubbed her temples and sipped from a cup of tea. "Is she really Muriel's sister?"

"I believe she is. Didn't Jordan ever mention her?"

"He's a man of many secrets. I didn't even know he was previously married."

"He's got too many secrets for his own good. I wish I knew where his mountain camp is." I spread the map out on the kitchen table. There was only the one main road from Cloverlea out to Porcupine Mountain, with a couple of small towns, Sheffield and Norton, along the way. I noticed that Norton had an airport. My best chance was to get out on that road before Buzz and intercept him on the way to the mountain.

"Going hunting?" Mrs. Riordon peered at me over the rim of her teacup. "Jordan usually gets a few grouse up there this time of year."

"I'm after bigger game." I folded the map and put it in my pocket. "Would you mind if I borrowed the dogs?"

"They're Jordan's dogs."

"I'm sure he wouldn't object." I finished my coffee. "I'd better get moving."

"Can I pack you a lunch?"

"No thanks. What kind of car does Jordan drive?"

"A red Mercedes."

"Does he drive it up on the mountain?"

"He did."

"Fine. If the police call, I'd appreciate it if you didn't tell them where I've gone. At least for a couple of hours. By noon you can tell them anything."

Outside, the dogs had settled down to some friendly canine chatter. I debated whether to take one of the Riordon cars. The Mussolini would be fast but there wouldn't be room for all the dogs. The station wagon would be large enough for them but probably not fast enough for me. I opened the doors of the Astro, put Tojo in the front seat and crowded the other three in the back. I drove off, found my way to the highway interchange and took Route 11 to Porcupine Mountain.

I passed everything on the road. The windows were rolled down and the dogs had their heads stuck out in the breeze. Kids stared goggle-eyed as we sailed past schoolbuses. I dragged the Astro down to the speed limit as we came into Sheffield. No sense in attracting attention. Buzz might whisk right by me and out of sight while I sat in a Highway Patrol car getting a ticket and a lecture. That's if he wasn't ahead of me already. I worried about that but there was nothing more I could do now. Norton was only another twenty miles along the line. Once past that, I'd pull over and wait for the dark blue van that had to come.

There was a funny smell in the car. Tojo acted like he was about to jump into the back seat. I looked in my rearview. Werewolf was hunched over Gretel. There was a lot of heavy breathing back there. I didn't have a bucket of water to throw on them so I just turned up the radio and blasted along on the piston-rocking rhythms of WNAZ.

Then I saw it. A quarter mile ahead, a dark blue van. I matted the accelerator and jacked the Astro up to a hundred. I saw now the mirrored windows at the rear of the van and the plexiglass bubble on the roof. It had to be Buzz. I closed in. There was no point putting off the confrontation. I could tail him right up into the woods but there was no telling he mightn't spot me and lose me somehow. I planned to run him off the road and kill him. It was a simple matter of self-preservation, with a little vengeance for Bowman thrown in.

With a steady hand on the wheel and my foot pressed to the floor, I pulled the shotgun out of the rucksack and pumped a shell into the chamber. It was going to be easy. He wouldn't be expecting me. I'd pull up alongside him, stick the shotgun out the window and blast him out of the driver's seat. It sounded good in theory but I hadn't counted on interference. I was a hundred yards behind him and closing when we roared past a Highway Patrol car parked on the traffic island of the divided highway.

The *'whup-whup-wheeeeoowwrr'* of a siren screamed behind me. I looked in the rearview and saw the flash of red-and-blue beacons and a cloud of smoke as the patrol car burned up the road to catch us. It might have had a dragster mill and rocket fuel because it was on my ass in ten seconds. The patrol car whipped up alongside of me and a grim-faced trooper jerked his thumb at me to pull off the road.

I made a furious face back at him and pointed to the blue van ahead. "Cop killer," I hollered into the hundred-mile-an-hour slipstream between our cars. The passenger patrolman looked startled, said something to his driver, then gave me the thumbs-up signal as their car shot ahead to catch up with the van.

Well, that takes care of Buzz, I thought, but what happened in the next few seconds gave me a whole new appreciation of the bugman's resourcefulness. The bubble dome atop the van popped open and two monster bumblebees catapulted out and made a kamikaze dive on the patrol car. I could have sworn they were carrying something in their legs. They smashed into the patrol car; twin explosions flung it in a somersault over the highway. Glass, garbage and junks of flesh flew through the air as I spun the wheel of the Astro. We careened across the road, smashing through twisted remnants of the patrol car, ploughed up and over a smoking boulder that had once been an engine.

The Astro spun off the shoulder, rolled over in the ditch and landed right side up, the windows smashed, the roof crushed down around my shoulders and the dogs howling in my ears.

I grabbed the shotgun and crawled out through my window. I had a bloody hand from broken glass but otherwise I was okay. The dogs were pretty shook up but they seemed fit to continue. But where and how?

I climbed up onto the shoulder of the highway. Buzz was out of sight. I tried to flag down passing cars but they wouldn't stop. What was the matter with them? Couldn't they see there'd been an accident? Pieces of cars and patrolmen were scattered fifty yards down the highway. I waved furiously to stop somebody but they just slalomed around the wreckage and kept moving. Then I realised nobody was going to stop for a guy with a shotgun in his hand.

I was about to return it to the side of the road when I heard a distinctive sound muttering off in the distance. I looked across the field next to the highway and saw a light plane gliding down to a landing. The Norton airport. I whistled for the dogs and we went bounding through a quarter mile of tall grass to the airfield. Half a dozen corrugated metal hangars were lined up at one end of the asphalt airstrip. A dozen light planes, single- and twin-engined, were lined up outside the hangars and beyond them, sitting by itself like an ugly duckling, was a helicopter.

I told the dogs to stay put and I went up to the door of the control shack where a sign said *Norton Flying Club*. A boisterous roar came from within as I approached the door. Sounded like a party in progress. But at eight in the morning? I didn't want to spoil the mood so I slipped the shotgun under the doorstep before I went inside.

I looked into a lounge with fake wood panelling walls plastered over with large aerial maps. Some tired-looking furniture slouched along the walls towards a fireplace at the end of the room where a big wooden propellor was mounted above a mantlepiece crowded with trophies. A few model airplanes of World War

Two vintage hung suspended by threads from the ceiling. At a lower altitude, eight or nine men with glasses of beer in their hands stood around yukking it up. In the center of this clubby group was a fresh-faced youngster wearing a shirt and tie and a grin as big as a dinner plate. His tie was raggedly snipped in two and his shirt was soaked with beer but he looked like he was having the time of his life.

"Who's the helicopter pilot?" I asked no one in particular.

"Doug'll take you up for a flip," said a short little bird with bushy eyebrows and a grease-smudged nose. "Won't you, Doug? Hell, two solos in one day. You'll set a club record."

The kid blushed and fingered the ragged half of his tie. Another man gave him a glass of beer, saying, "Now don't spill it on yourself like that last one," at which the crowd broke out in horse laughs.

"What's the going rate for helicopter rental?" I said, trying to generate some genuine interest in my case.

"Hundred bucks an hour, pilot included," said a guy in faded grey overalls. He had bright blue eyes and a pair of mirrored aviator's glasses propped atop his close-trimmed black hair. "What've you got in mind?"

"A trip to Porcupine Mountain. Can we leave right away?"

"Soon as I see your money."

I gave him a hundred. "You got anything against my bringing some dogs along?"

"Guess not, so long as they behave." He pocketed the money and wrote me a receipt. "Floyd Mackay's the name. Most guys call me Flicker."

"Right." I shook his hand. "Let's get going." We went outside.

"What's that for?" he said as I pulled the shotgun from under the doorstep.

"Mountain grouse."

"With a sawed-off pump?" We met the dogs on the way to the chopper. "And these are your retrievers?" The four dogs muttered a collective growl.

"Nervous?"

"Mister, I did two hitches in Nam jockeying Hueys

through monsoons and machinegun fire. Nothing makes me nervous anymore. Get your crew aboard and we'll bugger off."

It was a squeeze job but I got the four dogs into the chopper's back seat and threaded the seat belts through their collars to hold them in place. I climbed in front with Mackay and he started the engine. The rotor spun up to lift rpm, then Mackay twisted the throttle of the joystick and the chopper pulled itself into the air. A touch of rudder and the aircraft pivoted above the hangars and clattered off on a northwest tack across patchwork fields and orchards.

"Accident," Mackay hollered over the drumbeat of the engine and jabbed his finger downwards.

Out on Route 11, a fresh team of patrolmen detoured traffic around the wreckage while a trio of white-suited ambulance attendants tried to decide whether to use brooms or mops to clean up the carnage.

I made *tsk-tsk* sounds for the 'accident' victims. Buzz was running up quite a score. I hoped I could stop him before he made game point.

Mackay wanted to make straight for Porcupine Mountain, which we could see about seventy miles away, a purplish lump of rock and trees standing up out of the morning haze, but after shouting in his ear for a minute I made it understood that I wanted him to follow the road.

"What's the point?" he hollered back. "Why hire a chopper if not to fly straight there and cut your travel time?"

"Who's paying for this?"

He shrugged and did as I said. Fortuitously enough, he had a pair of binoculars in the cockpit so I used them to scan the highway that unravelled beneath us. Time passed and I saw no dark blue vans. I had an uncomfortable few moments wondering if Buzz hadn't changed vehicles. We moved up the lower slope of the mountain. The main road snaked over rugged terrain and across swift-flowing streams. Small rockbound lakes, surrounded by summer cottages and hunters' camps, glittered under the sun.

Halfway up the mountain I spotted the van whistling

along the tree-lined road. I focused the glasses on it and saw Buzz twist his face upwards to watch us as we went sailing by overhead. I started scanning the land uphill from us, looking for a metallic splash of red among the more subdued tones of changing autumn leaves. I found it in a couple of minutes, the red Mercedes about a half mile upslope from us. It was parked beside an A-frame cabin, screened from the main road by a grove of hardwood, but easily visible from our altitude. Smoke was rising from the cabin's chimney.

I asked Mackay to set us down as close as possible to the camp. He jockeyed the chopper in over it, flattening the tops of mountain ash and poplar beneath the propwash. The driveway was too closely overgrown to allow the helicopter a safe landing. Mackay angled the chopper upslope a hundred yards to where an outcropping of rock afforded a landing area among the trees. We were fifty feet above the ground when an explosion rocked us wildly.

"Tail rotor's gone," Mackay hollered as he struggled with the controls. I looked back and saw the mangled end of the tail boom where the stabilizing rotor had been blown away by another of Buzz' kamikaze bumblebees. Without rudder control, the chopper began to spin but we didn't get to spin long because the ground came up with dizzying speed. The chopper's bubble canopy exploded with the impact. I was pitched forward in my harness as the chopper nosed over. The big rotor smashed to a halt.

The doors sprung free. I unfastened my harness and scrambled outside. A big bumblebee came whirring in over the trees. I jerked the shotgun up and fired. The bumblebee blew apart with a roar that knocked me on my ass. "Get the dogs out," I hollered at Mackay as I pumped another shell into the chamber, ready for the next flying buzzbomb.

But there were no more, for the time being at least. Mackay climbed out of the cockpit and the dogs limped out behind them. Gretel was hurt. She coughed and shook her head, then lay down and whined. The crash must have injured her neck.

"Have you got a gun?" I asked Mackay.

"Not with me. I didn't know we were going into combat. What the hell's going on up here?"

"Come on, we'd better make a run for the camp." Down below in the trees I heard the sound of the van coming up the dirt driveway. Mackay and I went dodging through the bush, the three male dogs on our heels. We came out of the trees on the uphill side of the A-frame. I mounted the porch, tried the door and found it locked. I smashed the window, unlocked the door and stepped inside.

"Get out of my house." A tall heavyset man with grey hair and moustache stood up from his breakfast table. He wore a dark green sweater, a pair of khaki workpants and a face that was rapidly turning florid. "What do you mean by breaking in here?"

"No time to explain, Mr. Ferris. Somebody's here to kill you. Do you have any guns?" A quick glance around the room answered my question. Above the fireplace were an automatic shotgun and a bolt-action rifle. I pulled the shotgun off the rack and tossed it to Mackay. I grabbed a box of 12-gauge shells and spilled them out onto the kitchen table.

I looked out the window. Down below in the driveway, the dark blue van was parked so as to block the only exit. The air was full of bumblebees. I knocked a pane out of a window and started blasting. Mackay took another window and did likewise. Ejected shells spun across the room while outside the morning's peace was being ripped apart by the roar of detonated charges. After a dozen rounds apiece, we'd downed all the bomb-bearing bees, but even the remaining ones were deadly if they got inside and started stinging.

"Are you any good with that rifle?" I hollered over my shoulder at Ferris as I pumped up another shell and blew a droning bee to oblivion.

"So-so." He was white-faced now but he took the rifle down from the rack and snapped a clip into the magazine. "What do you want me to do?"

"The guy in that van is running this show. Try to pick him off. Failing that, put holes in his tires so he can't get away."

Ferris opened a window and started shooting. The

sharp crack of the rifle counterpointed the booms of the two shotguns. Star fractures appeared in the van's windshield. I saw Buzz jump out of his seat and dodge into the trees. Ferris drilled off a couple more shots and the van slumped to rest on the rims of its flat tires.

"Look out, behind you!" Mackay yelled.

I whirled and dropped to one knee. Half a dozen bees swarmed through the broken window of the porch door at our rear. I pumped shell after shell through the Ithaca. Wings, legs and guts spattered the walls and ceiling. Mackay and I ran out of shells simultaneously. He began to reload. Two more bees as big as softballs snarled in through the window. I grabbed a frying pan off the stove and knocked one to the floor. Werewolf pounced on it and snapped its head off. The other bee hit me in the arm. Before it could drive its stinger in, I punched it away. It hit the table and bounced once before I brought the frying pan down on it and spread it all over the tablecloth. By then, Mackay had reloaded and was knocking down the remaining few that straggled through the back door. I shoved a fistful of shells into the gun and got another bee on the wing. Then everything was quiet. We scanned outside, watched nervously around the broken windows for a sneak attack.

"Those bees give me the chills. Did we get all of them?"

"Nothing buzzing."

Inside and outside, little bits of shotgunned bees were littered inch-deep. The dogs began to eat the remains off the floor.

"Collar those guys. If they eat a stinger, they'll be sorry."

We took the dogs outside and checked the van. The rear interior had two walls of oversize honeycomb chambers but there were no bees left in them. In the front seat Mackay found an omni-directional locator, the visual display needle pointing at Ferris' red Mercedes.

The dogs were going crazy to run. We let them go and ran after them. We went up the wooded slope and past the rocky outcrop where the chopper crashed. A hundred yards uphill we saw the three dogs bounding through the scrub brush. Twice that distance up the mountain, a tall skinny figure climbed swiftly through a jumble of car-sized boulders.

"Think you can hit him?"

Ferris jerked the rifle to his shoulder and fired twice. We saw the bullets spatter low and wide; the whine of the ricochet floated down moments later. Mackay took the rifle from Ferris but before he could shoot, Buzz disappeared behind an outcropping. The dogs reached the same checkpoint only seconds behind him. We got our wind back and went doggedly after them.

When we got up there and around to the other side of the outcropping, we found a sheer cliff face of a hundred feet with a hill of granite rubble at the base. We mounted the rubble and looked up the cliff. Surely Buzz couldn't have scaled it that fast. And where were the dogs? We heard a hollow echo of barking and snarling.

"The cave," said Ferris, pointing to the base of the cliff. Half-covered with rubble, a dark cavern opened into the side of the mountain. "I've gone spelunking in there. It goes in about two hundred yards and there's no way out."

"Can you get a light?"

Ferris went back downhill to the camp. Mackay and I crouched at either side of the cave entrance with our shotguns at the ready. From way inside the cave we heard the sounds of a fight, the dogs yelping and snarling while an inhuman voice screamed and raged. Ferris came back up the hill with two flashlights and a roll of tape. Mackay and I mounted the lights under our shotgun barrels. We waited half an hour, whistling and calling for the dogs. It was silent inside the cave.

"Did you find Gretel?" I asked Ferris. "She got hurt when the chopper came down."

"She's back at the camp. Do you want me to get her?"

"I don't think we need her now." I imagined the three big males back at the end of the tunnel were having a feast. "Let's go in and pick up the pieces."

We turned on the lights and went inside. The cave was little more than a tunnel five feet across, dipping gently into the mountain's interior. Walking with heads stooped under the low ceiling, we followed the winding cavern down. Chill water dripped down on us as we went further into a suffocatingly dank atmosphere.

Fifty yards in, our lights found Tojo. He lay crumpled against one wall, his severed head lying a couple of feet from his body. The rock floor was slick with his blood. Aquarius wasn't going to be happy about this.

I shone my light further into the cave and saw something lying there. It was an arm with half a grey sleeve clinging to the shoulder stump. I picked it up. The arm was longer than my own, a mottled blue shell encasing a mass of bloody muscle. At the end of the arm was something like a giant lobster claw with sharp serrated ridges on the inner edge of its grip. A knot of dog's hair was caught in the joint of the pincer.

"My god," Ferris whispered, "what kind of monster ... ?"

Another hundred yards in, we found Hansel. His belly was slashed open and his guts lay in a tangled knot beside him. Like Tojo, he'd lost his head. We found it a few feet away, the powerful jaws still locked around the knee joint of a long leg. The limb had the same purplish exoskeleton as the other we'd seen and wasn't much thicker. The pantleg was torn off but a heavy-soled boot remained on the thing's foot. I didn't take the boot off to look at the foot. I wasn't *that* interested.

It didn't matter anyway because when we got to the end of the tunnel, we found the other leg with the boot torn off. The foot looked strangely human and frail, except that its three big toes were hard-shelled like the rest of the limbs. We shone our lights along the floor, wall to wall with blood. Here was a pair of wraparound sunglasses, unbroken, and there was a dog's tail. Here was the rest of a pair of bloody coveralls and there was a pile of viscera spilled on a mat of dogskin with a few bones showing white amid the red roughage. It'd be a closed coffin burial for Werewolf. I hoped Grumpy had fond memories of his old pal because that's all there was left of the dog.

We couldn't find Werewolf's head. Worse, we didn't find the other head either, to which was still attached a torso with one arm. What we did find was a crevice in the wall a foot wide. There was a bad smell but we couldn't see anything. I stuck my shotgun in as far as I could reach and pulled the trigger a couple of times. The pellets ricocheted and smashed my flashlight.

"Now what?"

"Let's get out of here." My flesh was crawling.

Buzz crawled into the hole on his hands and feet. Even with the sunglasses on, he could see his way, and when he took them off, he saw perfectly. But his heart pounded with fear. The dogs were coming in after him. He faced them and screamed at them to go back, back to another place and another time where they were only figures in a nightmare.

They attacked him and he fought them. They tore away one of his arms and the old pain came flooding back with the new, the little boy in his memory screaming for mother, the insect man crying in rage. He bit off a head and went scrabbling deeper into the cave. Down into the mountain where the dogs didn't belong. Go back to the forest, dogs, and leave me alone.

But they caught him by the leg and he fought with them again, killing one and losing his leg. The awful hurt exploded in him, rushed out to fill his every sense, the bitter metal taste in his stomach, the searing fire of the wound, the betrayal of his mind when he willed himself to run again and, falling, rediscovered the loss and pain of his leg. This was no picnic—this was real.

The last and biggest dog sprang upon him. They thrashed across the floor, ripping each other. He broke the dog's back and flung it off him as it tried to get his arm. If he lost it, he was dead. The dog, lurching on its skewed body, tackled him again and severed his leg. Buzz slashed its belly open before it got any further. They lay for a moment looking at each other and then

Buzz dragged himself away with his one remaining arm, clutching at outcroppings with his strong pincer and pulling his bloody thorax across the rock.

The dog dragged itself after him, pursuing him still with its tortured growls. They came to the end of the tunnel. The dog growled closer. Buzz told it to shut up. It wouldn't shut up so he crawled back across the floor to it and ripped it into small pieces. Everything but the head. He gripped it between his two long cutting mandibles and sucked on its brain juice.

He found a crack in the wall. He put his arm inside and pulled the rest behind. The crevice twisted and dipped down into a humid warmth. Buzz felt hollow inside, like he'd lost half his guts. He wondered if he was still alive or was this just his mind taking a slide into a deep and hidden nothingness?

He smelled water. He reached out his claw and touched it. Putting the dog's head behind him, he pulled himself to the pool and drank. He ate the dog's brain and rested. From above came a sound like a heavy door slamming shut.

We walked back down the hill to Ferris' camp. Gretel lay yawning on the sunny back porch. Mackay and I stooged around in the van and found a parcel of plastic explosives with impact detonators. Mackay had handled similar stuff in Nam. He put all the little buzzbombs together and made one big one. We took it back up the hill to the cave, set it in the crevice at the end of the tunnel. The makeshift timer Mackay put together with a pair of flashlight batteries and Jordan's alarm clock worked fine. We got back out with ten minutes to spare before the charge set off a rumble beneath our feet.

Several stiff drinks later, we got the van maneuvered off the driveway and helped Ferris pack his belongings into the trunk of the Mercedes. The politician preferred to let somebody else do the housecleaning. While loading the trunk, Mackay found the tiny transmitter by means of which Buzz had located the car. Ferris couldn't imagine how it got there. I could.

We took Gretel and drove down the mountain to Norton where we dropped Mackay at the airport.

"Sorry I dragged you into such a battle," I said in parting. "I hope your chopper was well insured."

"More than it's worth, considering the overhaul it needed anyway. Probably the best thing that's happened to me since I bought it. A little excitement never hurt a guy either. You know, for a couple of hours today I felt really alive."

"I know what you mean." I felt like I was up to my ears in adrenalin. It might be a day or two before I could loosen up and go to sleep.

"I'll let you guys go," Mackay said. "Mr. Ferris, pleasure meeting you. If you ever need a chopper man to ride shotgun on the campaign trail, give me a shout."

"Consider yourself hired," Ferris said. He took a bottle out of the dash and we had a last drink to that and then he moved over to let me drive. We left Mackay there and drove to Cloverlea.

On the way, I brought Ferris up to date on what had happened since he went to the mountains. After my spiel, he asked a number of pertinent questions, to which I had most of the answers. He was pretty perturbed to learn that the child of his first marriage had re-appeared on the scene to hound him across the headlines of the country's worst 'slander paper', as he called the *Continental Confidant,* and even more upset to learn that his two daughters might put their heads together and turn his political career upside-down. After that, the story of Malkud's operation was pretty pale stuff. Mutations, sex perverts and underworld assassins were bit players compared to his treacherous daughters, the like of which had not been heard since King Lear got the sharp end of the stick from Regan and Goneril.

After he'd raged on about that for a while, he settled down to finish his bottle in silence. I imagined he was already outlining his moves and statements with a view to recovering from a sticky situation. He came out of contemplation just as I wheeled the Mercedes up the driveway of 800 Birchcrest. "I realize, Savage, that you've gone out of your way to help me, risking your life when you could just as easily have backed down, and obviously, without any guarantee of recompense."

"It seemed like a good idea at the time."

"I pay men high salaries for good ideas. Do I make myself clear?"

"What did you have in mind?"

"You'd be in charge of my investigative and security forces."

"A glorified security cop. Thanks, but no thanks, Mr. Ferris. I like my independence too well to trade it for that."

"Well, you've got to let me do something for you." I parked the Mercedes and we got out. Gretel took a trot off to the nearest flower bed and dug up some geraniums. Ferris squared off in front of me. "Name it."

"Lend me your Mussolini so I can drive back into town. My car got trashed on the road to Porcupine Mountain."

"Lend it? I'll give you the goddamn thing." He checked to see that the keys were in it and signed over the registration. "I must have sent this car to the body shop a dozen times and they never captured the shade of yellow I wanted."

"There's an artistic notion if ever I heard one. Sounds like you might have more in common with Muriel than you know."

"*What was silent in the father speaks in the son.*" Ferris looked thoughtful for a moment and then he reached for my hand and we shook warmly. "Do you think she . . . ?"

"Both of them would . . . like to have a long talk with you."

"I've been a fool."

"You make mistakes so you can learn from them."

I left him chewing on that one and drove off in the Mussolini. It had a black leather interior as plush as the down on a teen queen's belly and an engine that must have been designed with *gran turismo* in mind. I had to hold tight rein on it to keep from doubling the posted speed limit. When I got back to town, I sailed off the expressway exit and came to a perfect four-point landing in Lothario's parking lot. I hoped my favorite cheerleader was on duty. I still had an over-abundance of nervous energy and I had big ideas on how to work it off.

She saw me from inside the hut, waved and came out with a smile and a sexy walk that should have been put to music. And how I'd love a jam session with her.

"What keeps you coming back here?" she said. "It can't be the service."

"Must be the hottest buns in town."

"I see you've changed your image." She ran a hand over the Mussolini's fender and I could have sworn I heard the motor purr. "Did you buy this to impress me?"

"Save your impressions until later. What time do you get off work?"

"Half an hour. What have you got in mind?"

"Dinner, drinks and bed, not necessarily in that order."

"Like anything while you're waiting?"

"A kiss and a beer, in that order."

Tracey brought her lovely mouth in to meet mine. One kiss from her and I lost control of my hands. She managed to break loose after a couple of minutes. I unsnapped my seatbelt before I gave myself a hernia.

"Stay cool, lover." She mouthed a kiss at me. "The anticipation will do you good."

12

Two days later, the *Continental Confidant* hit the stands with a big picture of Jordan Ferris holding Muriel in his arms, above which the headline proclaimed FATHER-DAUGHTER TEAM CRUSH UNDERWORLD OPERATION. That was stretching the facts a bit, but that's what scandal sheets were all about. The story went on to relate how Muriel had infiltrated an organized crime ring engaged in sexual perversion, extortion and political terrorism. It was implied by Jordan himself that he had masterminded the whole affair, although he admitted having been assisted considerably by a local investigator who wished to remain anonymous. That was true enough: I could live without vengeance-seeking mobsters knocking down my door at all hours of the night.

In the back pages of the same issue of the *Confidant* was a short filler entitled MOM PULLS PLUG ON HOMO SON. There was a picture of Mrs. Uranium and her brief story of how she'd turned off the oxygen to her comatose son so that "Joel could return to the astral plane where he belonged."

I phoned Ferris at his office to see how he'd made out in his efforts to pour oil on the troubled waters stirred up between myself and the police department in the past week.

"Lay low, my friend. The air is thick with flying shit. An out-of-town vacation may be in order."

"It can't be that bad," I complained.

"The police get upset when any of their boys get greased as a result of a citizen taking the law into his own hands. Even if he is a licensed investigator."

"*Especially* if he's a snooper, you mean. What about Bud and Dixie?"

"It's shaping up to be twenty years apiece but they've got a good lawyer who might get them off with half that. Moskovitz'll get a suspended sentence, I imagine."

He went on to give me bits and pieces of Bud's story. Race track debts had forced Bud into working for the mob as a runner of hot goods between mob fences and Moskovitz, who funnelled over a million dollars' worth of stolen art works, paintings, Ming vases, gold figurines and coins, rare stamps and Louis XIV furniture, back into the art market. The operation gave Moskovitz ulcers and Bud a little time to get his shit together. But his love affair with the ponies got him in trouble again. He planted electronic bugs in Jordan's car and home so that the mob could keep tabs on their 'friend'. He and Dixie worked a blackmail racket with her moneyed paramours. A telephone relay system in a dummy apartment had triggered the ransom demand I'd been witness to. Bud had also used it in a few cases of extortion set up by the mob.

"And what's new on Kilroy Street?"

"The Limbo Clinic? They're still turning up bodies. Either the attrition rate is high for mutant prostitutes or the doctor had a lot of operational failures before he came up with some working models. There's a half-hearted investigation underway to expose his clients. It'll get dumped pretty soon when the hush-money gets distributed by the concerned parties."

"Do I detect a note of cynicism?"

"Would you like to hear a chord? I've been in this business long enough to appreciate human frailty, especially when it comes to sex and money. Besides, I've got a couple of my own trusted investigators putting together a stack of dossiers on the people that count. I'll play my cards when the pot gets big enough."

"Getting any mileage out of the whole affair?"

"Next month this time you can call me at the Mayor's Office."

"And the girls?"

"One big happy family. Nat's going to handle my

PR. Muriel's gone to a Zurich clinic—best in the world—and she's going to come back beautiful."

"So you're riding high."

"Damn right." Jordan chuckled. "And it couldn't have happened to a nicer guy."

After spending those two days lying low with Tracey, I finally decided it was time for me to get out and face the music. I'd already done the dirty work over the phone but I knew my conscience wouldn't give me any rest until I'd offered my condolences in person.

The route from Tracey's apartment to mine led past the University so that put Aquarius first on the list. I found him in his office. He wasn't too happy to see me and he didn't pretend to be otherwise. Never one to be easily iced out, I expressed my appreciation anyway.

"I've really got to hand it to you for the way you read the stars, professor. You saw the political connection behind Muriel's disappearance and the underworld threat to Ferris. And without your analyses of all the other characters, I never could have sorted the mess out so quickly."

"Too bad I hadn't done a chart on you, Savage. I might have known better than to have entrusted Tojo with you."

"There'll be other dogs. And twenty percent of my thousand in fees will give you two hundred to find a really good pup."

"I don't want your goddamned money." Aquarius picked up a file folder and flung it at me. Mimeographed horoscopes fluttered down around me like autumn leaves. He pounded his fist on the desk, then lowered his head to his forearm and had a good cry.

I sat there and smoked a cigarette, paralyzed by the electricity in the room. After a while, it faded and I was able to say, "I'm really very sorry."

Aquarius lifted his head and looked at me with red-rimmed eyes. "You probably think I'm silly."

"Emotional, maybe. But I understand."

"I really wish you'd go now. And take that painting with you." He indicated the praying-mantis canvas I'd forgotten here when last I visited. "I don't need that to remind me of how Tojo died."

I carried the painting outside to the car and put it in the back seat of the Mussolini. I stopped at a liquor store and bought a fifth of rye before I continued on to my place. Grumpy was propped up in his chair with his feet on the table, watching TV while he rolled a joint. I rapped on the window of his office, held up the bottle of booze as evidence of a peace offering, and he waved me to come on in.

"Did you hear what happened to your little blonde girlfriend?"

"Wendy? What happened? Is she okay?"

"Yeah, she's alright. But when she let herself into your place the other night she found a dead cat burglar in your bedroom. Killed by two big motherfucking spiders that laid eggs in his nose after he went down. I had to go up there and shotgun them. Now I ask you, what kind of pet is that to let run around the house? Why can't you get a goldfish or a budgie like a normal jerk? Are you some kind of weirdo, Savage?"

"Don't play cop with me, Grumpy. I'm a tired man."

"Want a dexie?"

"No thanks, but how about a pair of glasses and we'll see if we can make a dent in this Canadian Club?"

"Nothing like an Irish wake to see an old pal off. I don't suppose you knew Werewolf was part Irish wolfhound." We clinked glasses and had quite a few stiff ones in memory of Grumpy's dog. "Tell me how it happened," he said.

I went through the whole story and recounted how the dogs had taken a major part in the last act. Grumpy pressed me for all the gory details. I gave him the facts as I had seen them. If anything, he was more exhilarated than horrified over Werewolf's end.

"He was a fighter to the end, god bless the old hound. I hope to go down swinging myself."

"I'm sure you will, Grumps." We hoisted a few more for the cause and smoked one of his super-bombers. By the time we finished that, we were both pretty well anaesthetized.

"But is that buggy bastard really dead?"

"Sure he's dead. We buried him under a mountain."

"They bury vampires too."

"But they don't come back if you drive a stake through their hearts.... or... cut off their heads."

"Or burn them," Grumpy said. "And you didn't do any of those things."

"But..."

"You'll never know for sure, will you?"

Thanks for nothing, Grumpy. His skepticism left me with more than a few sleepless nights.

Above, the surface of the mountain lake was a ceiling of translucent ice through which daylight barely penetrated down into the frigid winter waters. Fish, their lean streamlined bodies contracted against the cold, fed upon the underwater insects and vegetation that flourished along the shore.

A large trout, nosing down the sloped lake bottom in search of meatier prey, saw a flicker of light and turned to make a run at what might have been a pair of minnows. Not until it was within three feet of the twin lures did a branched stick jerk up from the bottom and snatch the trout with startling swiftness.

The thing with the glittering eyes drew the fish into its mouth and used its single claw to drag its way back through a crevice in the steep rocky slope of the lake. Light from above danced along the curved swell of the large air bubble imprisoned within its hollowed shell.

Up inside the rocky cavern, where air met water, the thing rested and ate its fish. A dull pleasant fire suffused through its body. From the healed wound at its shoulder, the tiny sprout of a claw began its long process of regrowth.

I woke up in a cold sweat. Something was strangling me. I flung Tracey's arm off my chest and sat up. A column of sun slanted from the skylight above the bed; motes of dust floated in the silence. I turned in the bed and looked at the painting on the wall above us. The praying mantis gnawed silently on its late lover. I collapsed back into the pillows.

"What's your trouble, darlin'?" Tracey's sleepy voice came from under the covers.

"That painting's going back to the living room where it belongs."

"You gave it to me; I put it over the bed. I think it's kinky."

"It's giving me nightmares."

"You've got an over-active imagination."

"Are you complaining?"

"Not when it's channeled into the right activities. Come here." She reached out to her bedside table and hit a switch. The inimitable bump and grind of reggae rock burbled out of the overhead speakers. She lit a slim number which we consumed in about four tokes before making our undercover rendezvous. I lost myself in her hair, the smell of her, the taste of her mouth, the squeeze of her legs around me.

Later in the day we crawled out of the sack and drove up to Cloverlea for a private dinner with Mayor Ferris and family. We all got nicely stuffed on the six-course meal and smashed on century-old wine. Natalie was there with a hip young attorney from Jordan's office; Muriel, with an older man, one of the Zurich team who'd given her limbs. Even seated as she was in the temporary wheelchair, we could see she was going to be stunning when she got on her feet. She pulled me down to head level and gave me a big smack on the mouth.

"That's a thank-you kiss from the whole Ferris family, snooper."

"Behave yourself, kid, or I'll be kidnapping you next."

Jordan appeared with a few more bottles of Moet & Chandon and we got down to some serious partying. Somewhere in the middle of the evening, he beckoned to me and said, "I've got something to show you."

We went to a room at the back of the house and he showed me Gretel lying on a small cot. She raised her head and gave us a low growl, then flopped her head back down and sighed. Between her sprawled legs, three pups jostled each other for position at her teats. I picked up the biggest of them.

"That one doesn't look like a Doberman at all." Ferris pointed out its long tail compared to the little stubs on the other two.

"He's a guy and they're girls too." I stroked the pup's nose and he chomped his gums onto my finger.

"But he's no pedigree," Ferris said. "The vet's going to put him to sleep."

"I'll take him off your hands."

"Be my guest."

"Here's some company for you, Grumpy." I walked into his office and dropped the pup in his lap.

"Well, I'll be goddamned," he cried, lifting the little mongrel up by the scruff of the neck. "It's Werewolf Junior." He tucked the pup inside his shirt and gave him a hug.

"Careful you don't squeeze him too hard."

Grumpy made a face and pulled the pup out of his shirt as a wet stain spread across his waist. "Just like his old man: full of the devil."